SOLDIER SAVED

THE TERALIN SWORD

D.K. HOLMBERG

ASH PUBLISHING

If you want to be notified when D.K. Holmberg's next novel is released and get free stories and occasional other promotions, please sign up for his mailing list by going here. Your email address will never be shared and you can unsubscribe at any time.

www.dkholmberg.com

MAP

THE LANDS OF LIIS
SOUTHLANDS
NORTHLANDS
GREAT VALLEY
THE UNKNOWN LAND
LAKE GORALT
SALVAT ISLAND

1

Endric made his way up the ramp leading to the second terrace within the city of Vasha. The bustle within the city was no different than it had been the last time he was here, which seemed so long ago, but much had changed. The city had a vibrancy, a sense of life, but an air of pomp to it that Endric had never been fully aware of before. His head throbbed from days spent riding, pushing the Antrilii horse as hard as he could as he made his way south. There had been a time when traveling as long as he had and for as hard as he had would have made him incredibly tired, saddle sore, and achy. Time spent in the Antrilii lands, time spent hiking through the mountains, attempting to stay alive, had hardened him in ways that even his Denraen training had not.

It had been nearly a year since he had been in Vasha. A year since he had slept in what had once been his bed. A year in which he had sought to understand how to balance the parts of him that were Antrilii with the parts of him that were Denraen. In that time, he had come to understand the Antrilii and had helped restore a certain unity among the clans, all while trying to understand himself. Were it not for a summons from Tresten, he might not have returned as soon.

Now he understood that he had to be both Denraen *and* Antrilii. He was not one or the other, and he never could be. Surprisingly, he felt that his father had failed in attempting to separate himself in such a way. There had once been a time when Endric would never have suspected his father to have any failings, but first with Andril, and then with the Antrilii, Endric had begun to understand that his father was not infallible.

And now he would see Dendril again. Was he ready for it?

He didn't know. After his time away, he had begun to question whether he *could* return, but if he didn't, he would be as much an oathbreaker as what the Antrilii had believed his father to be.

Returning wasn't as easy as he had anticipated that it would be. Not only was he different, but so was his perception of the city. In addition to the noise, the city had a distinctive odor to it. There was the bite of the cool northern wind, gusting in off the northern mountain chain. Vasha was not snowcapped like so many of the neighboring mountains were. The teralin found deep within the mountains ensured that.

The ore had a distinctive odor, one which added to the breeze that he detected, filling the air with it. Much of the northern chain smelled similarly. It made him miss and long for the smells of Farsea, that of the Antrilii lands, and the rolling grasses and the forests that led up and into the mountains. There was a certain peace in those scents. Would he ever know them again?

As he made his way along the ramp leading to the next level within the city, he hesitated. It was nice to be home, and he missed the city, but not nearly as much as he once would have expected. More than the city, he missed his friends. It had been a year since he had seen Senda. Would she understand the time that he'd been away? He suspected Pendin would, but maybe he'd be as angry as

Senda. What of his father? What reaction would Dendril have following his return?

His father had allowed him to travel north and had agreed that Endric needed time to understand his Antrilii connections, but it would have been a difficult time for the Denraen. Listain had died, leaving a leadership void. Someone would've had to have filled that void, though Endric had not been here to be a part of it. Would Senda have stepped up to fill in for her uncle? Listain had made it seem as if Endric had exposed Senda and her connection to him, but Endric wasn't certain that mattered. What mattered was the mind and the ability to determine the next course of action, taking all the different pieces of information and putting them together. That was something that Listain had done better than almost anyone. Possibly better than even Endric's father.

He took a deep breath before patting the side of the horse. The Antrilii steed was a sleek gray stallion, trained by the best horse masters of the Antrilii. He had been fast and sturdy, and yet he seemed to recognize Endric's desire to enter the city more slowly.

Not stealthily.

He doubted he could enter stealthily, even if he were to want to. The Denraen guarding the city gate would have already sent word ahead of him, moving far more swiftly than he could, especially as tradition held that he would lead his horse through the city rather than ride it. He expected his father to meet him or send an envoy, though Endric wasn't sure what he would say to Dendril when they faced each other again.

So far, there had been no envoy, and he was left to make it along the ramp leading to the second terrace within the city all alone.

Often, there would be Denraen moving along here, but he saw no sign of his brethren. Had they been sent on patrols? It would be rare for the city to be emptied of Denraen, but he'd seen only the soldiers at the gate, and not nearly as many others as he had expected. Who patrolled within the city?

When he reached the second level, he veered off, heading toward the entrance to the barracks. He considered heading to the third terrace and the palace to find Tresten before doing anything else but decided he should seek his father. Tresten and his request to join him could wait.

Finally, he noted a sense of activity. Denraen practiced on the barracks lawn, the green grassy field filled with soldiers marching in formation and the clatter of practice staves as men worked through their catahs, practicing sword technique. He saw no sign of anyone practicing with the long staff that Senda preferred, but that was not altogether uncommon.

He paused at the stables, finding an empty stall for the stallion and brushing him down briefly. He ensured that the horse had food and water and patted his side once more. The horse had been a constant companion over the last two months, time that he had spent traveling along the north, listening to the sound of the merahl as they called out on the path back to the city, before finally veering toward Vasha and making his way through the difficult mountain passes.

Having the merahl leave them had been the hardest transition. He had grown to appreciate the constant nature of their howls, feeling a connection to them. The cub who had followed him out of the mountains after the Chisln had grown to full size in Endric's time with the Antrilii, and parting with him had been almost as hard as leaving. But these lands were not for the merahl. They needed to stay in the north and hunt groeliin, and Endric needed to be back here in Vasha.

Didn't he?

He shook the thought from his head. That wasn't the way he should be thinking. What he needed to be doing was finding his father, sharing what he'd been through, and then… what? Resume command? Would anyone even follow him after all the time that he had been gone? Was there even a command remaining for him?

He sighed. This was his responsibility. His oath. He was Denraen.

After all the time he'd spent with the Antrilii, it was easy to forget that. Returning to Vasha made it completely clear.

Endric pulled his cloak tight around him and hurried from the stable, moving with a more determined step than before. When leading the horse, he could take a more leisurely approach and didn't expect anyone to stop him. Now that he was here, he needed to reach the officers' quarters and needed to report to his father.

More than that, Endric needed to know what might have changed in the time that he had been away. What new difficulty did the Denraen face? When he'd left before, the Deshmahne had begun to become a threat, but the Denraen had managed to push them back, moving them away from the northern continents. How long would that last? How long before someone else like Urik tried to invite them into their lands?

As he departed the barracks, he passed a few Denraen and nodded to them. None seemed to recognize him, or if they did, they said nothing. That was not altogether surprising. He wore Antrilii clothing, though none of the Antrilii war paint they preferred when hunting the groeliin. It had been months since he'd shaved, leaving a thick beard covering his face, hiding the scars the Denraen so prized. Endric had acquired a few more in his journey, but the beard would conceal some of them.

Why had no one stopped him? If they recognized him as Endric, son of Dendril, there would be no reason for them to stop him, though there would be reason to salute him, as he outranked most of these men. He doubted that his father had demoted him in his time away. If they didn't recognize him, why did they not attempt to confine him?

Perhaps he read too deeply into what he was experiencing.

Maybe the time with the Antrilii had made him question the Denraen more than he should. They were good soldiers. Skilled. They didn't deserve to have him question their motivation, especially not after he had abandoned his responsibility the way that he had.

Endric started toward the officers' hall and had reached the door when someone grabbed his arm in a firm grip.

That was better. Someone should have stopped him much sooner than this.

Endric spun and saw a familiar face that he would have expected to find eventually but was surprised to see so soon.

"Where are you..." Pendin trailed. He had an angular jaw and his miner ancestry left him with a solid build that years spent training with the sword had only intensified. Pendin would have been equally at home working the forge as he would the mines, or the sword. He was not only Endric's oldest friend, he was—or had been—his steward.

"It's good to see you as well, Pendin," Endric said.

Pendin blinked before pulling Endric into a tight embrace, squeezing the air out of his lungs with his muscular arms. He pushed back, shaking his head as he did. "Endric? I can't believe you finally returned."

"I always intended to return," he said, studying Pendin. There was something different to him, an edge or a darkness that hadn't been there before.

Pendin's brow furrowed in what Endric recognized as a troubled expression. "We thought you would have returned long before now," he said.

"I would have."

"Would have? That makes it sound like you couldn't."

Endric sighed. Were it only so simple. "I think I could have returned long before, but at the same time, I needed to stay."

"Needed to stay?"

"When I reached the Antrilii lands, I discovered something there that needed my attention."

Pendin watched him for a moment, and Endric recognized the concern on his face. "Well?" he asked.

"Well what?"

"Do you intend to tell me?"

Endric offered him a tight-lipped smile. "If only I could," he said.

He hated saying that to Pendin, telling his friend that there were things he could not share, but there were things about the Antrilii, and the creatures they hunted, that Endric couldn't reveal. Endric was descended from the Antrilii, which meant that he had a right to that knowledge. Pendin was not, and therefore could not know the same information. For him to know might place him in danger.

Pendin frowned but said nothing. "I imagine you want to see—"

"My father," Endric said.

Pendin tipped his head, glancing over his shoulder. "Not Senda?"

Endric sighed. In the time that he'd been away, he had thought of her frequently and had been looking forward to the time when they could be reunited. He missed the closeness that had formed between them in the months before he had headed north, and he missed her counsel, but now that he had returned to Vasha, he needed to report first and only then could he find her.

"I want to be around her when she realizes that you didn't go to her first."

"She'll understand." If nothing else, Senda was as committed to her responsibility within the Denraen as Endric was.

Pendin grunted. "I'm not so sure she will. I think she would rather have a chance to fill you in before you met with him."

"Fill me in on what?"

They were making their way through the hall, and Endric had

nearly reached the general's office when Pendin rested his hand on his arm again. "In the time that you've been gone, a few things have changed."

Endric frowned. There would have to have been change. He'd departed after Urik's capture, leaving after the Denraen had finally captured him, bringing an end to the danger he posed. Urik had discovered the secret to using teralin and had used it against the Denraen—and the Urmahne priests—in such a way that he'd essentially become the very thing that he had wanted to fight.

"What's changed, Pendin? I don't need for you to shield me from anything."

Pendin had opened his mouth to answer when he suddenly clamped it shut once more.

Endric looked behind him and saw his father striding down the hall.

Dendril was a large man and had a hint of wrinkling around the corners of his eyes, with a deep crease in his brow. He was dressed in the crisp gray uniform of the Denraen, and wore his sword Trill strapped to his waist. Prior to Endric's challenge, the sword had remained hanging on the wall in his office. Since that day—since the Deshmahne attack—Dendril had worn it.

"Sir," Endric said with a curt nod.

Dendril pressed his lips together and nodded. "You returned."

"I've gotten that response a few times now," Endric said.

"I expected you to have returned much before now. I thought that Nahrsin would share what he knew and then you would come back to us. It's been nearly a year."

"Nearly a year, but it was necessary. The time was well spent for me to understand the Antrilii, and to understand where I come from so that I can understand how to better help the Denraen."

"The Denraen are not about a single soldier. They are about serving peace."

"I know."

"And yet still you have remained away."

Endric met his father's eyes, matching the intensity that his father showed him. How much should he tell his father? There was no questioning the fact that he should have returned much sooner than he did, but he also had discovered more about his father, and about the way things had been left with the Antrilii, that Endric had been forced to deal with.

Was his father even aware?

Watching the man, he thought that he had been, but perhaps that was incorrect. Perhaps his father was not aware of the way that his absence had been perceived in the Antrilii lands.

Interesting if true.

Then again, how was Endric's absence perceived?

"The Antrilii required that I fill an obligation," Endric said. Let him be vague, so that his father was not embarrassed in front of Pendin.

Dendril's brow furrowed even deeper. "An obligation?"

Endric nodded once.

"What sort of obligation were you asked to fulfill?"

Could he not know?

That seemed difficult for Endric to believe, especially as connected as Dendril must have been. Dendril had been the one to summon Dentoun, and his uncle had saved him following his foolish challenge. There must have been some communication that remained, but perhaps not nearly as much as what Endric believed.

"The kind of obligation that required I travel the mountains alone, naked." He met his father's eyes unblinkingly. He could feel Pendin watching him and suspected that whatever else he might keep from his friends, there would be questions he would need to answer about this. That would be for later. For now, he would focus on Dendril's reaction and see what he might say about this.

Endric had anticipated Dendril being appreciative of what he'd been willing to do, the sacrifice that he had made. Because of that sacrifice, Dendril would be welcomed back to the Antrilii as something other than an oathbreaker. Could he not see that?

"You have no obligation that would require such a task," Dendril said.

"I am the son of Dendril, descendent of the Antrilii. That gave me an obligation."

Dendril grunted. "That gives you the right to learn, and the possibility of leaving. Nothing else. That should not be mistaken for an obligation to the Antrilii."

"You would have had me do otherwise?"

"I would have had you return sooner."

"I thought you accepted that I needed to understand the Antrilii."

"Understand, yes. What you did…"

"Made me Antrilii."

Dendril took a deep breath before letting it out in a long sigh. "I suppose it did."

Endric frowned again. Why would his father be so opposed to his being gone so long as he had? Endric had been only newly raised to his role, and there would have been many others within the Denraen who could serve in his stead. Listain's death would have been difficult, but not insurmountable, especially not with Senda having returned to the city.

"What happened while I was away?"

"It's not so much as to what happened as about what remained."

Endric frowned. His father made no sense.

"You prove that you can charge the teralin. There aren't many who can do that."

"Tresten can charge teralin," Endric said.

"Tresten has been away from the city for a while as well," Dendril said.

"What is this about?"

Dendril flicked his gaze to Pendin for a moment and then back to Endric. He stepped forward, grabbing the handle of his door, and pushed it open. "Step inside, Endric. We have much to talk about."

Endric glanced at Pendin, who nodded at him, encouraging Endric to follow.

What was it that Pendin knew that Endric did not? What was it that his father wasn't sharing with them?

Not only was it strange, but it was frustrating as well. Why did there have to be such mystery upon his return?

As he stepped inside the room, he realized that someone had been there before them.

And then he understood the reason for the mystery.

Urik stood near the far wall. He was dressed simply in all gray —not a Denraen uniform but close enough—and looked well. Certainly better than he deserved.

Endric's hand went to the hilt of his sword almost instinctively, ready to unsheathe it. The last time he'd faced this man, he had barely won. Endric had improved since then—the time with the Antrilii had taught him much—and he didn't intend for there to be a challenge.

Endric's mind began racing, trying to work through what he'd seen and what he'd heard. Pendin and his father had talked about what had changed, and his father had mentioned teralin, something the man standing in front of him had much experience with.

Endric forced his hand away from the hilt of his sword.

There was more taking place here than he understood. Urik was not a prisoner—or at least did not appear to be. This in spite of the fact that he had betrayed the Denraen and attempted to usurp his father's rule.

Urik smiled at him, one that seemed flat and devoid of emotion. "Endric. It's good that you return home."

2

The pint of ale sitting in front of Endric did nothing to improve his mood. The ale tasted flat and bland, two traits that made for a miserable mug. The only thing that made it better was the fact that he sat across from Senda and Pendin as he drank it.

"It's better in the officers' hall," Endric muttered.

Pendin grunted before chugging his mug and setting it down with more force than necessary. "Aye, better, but you needed to be away from there. I feared that you might do something—"

Senda watched him, saying nothing. Every so often, her gaze would drift to Pendin and she would purse her lips together as if she wanted to say something but never did. Her hair had grown longer in the time that he'd been away, and she tied it back with a leather thong. She wore tight-fitting green pants with a shirt that showed far more cleavage than he would've expected from her. Not that he minded. Though, from the leering glances she got from others in the tavern, he suspected few men minded.

"Might?" Senda asked. "More likely would do."

"The man deserves to die," Endric said.

"The man has information," she told him.

He looked over and she met his gaze unflinchingly. He breathed out heavily, realizing that perhaps Pendin was right and he should have sought out Senda before searching for his father. They might have better prepared him so that he wasn't so surprised.

"After everything that he did, after what happened to Listain, you would allow him to live?"

"It's not my choice. My commander has decided that he can serve the Denraen."

Dendril had been quite vague about what Urik could do to serve, and Endric wasn't sure that he even wanted to know. If he did, what would it change?

"What happened while I was gone?" Endric asked.

Pendin grabbed Endric's mug of ale and tipped it back, taking a long drink. He glanced around the tavern, a place called the Climbing Trellis, a tavern that he should have known better than to have agreed to come to. Not only was the ale terrible, but the waitress was a woman Endric once had known far better than Senda would like.

"He asks us about what happened while he was gone, and he's the one who was sent away from the Antrilii and into the mountains naked."

Senda grinned and looked over. "Naked?"

"It's not quite like you think."

"I think it means that you were naked."

Pendin motioned over a waitress, who set another mug in front of him. "The way Endric prefers to enter every battle," he said.

Endric shot him a hot glare, but Pendin either ignored him or managed to withstand the heat of it as he focused on the ale.

"It's not something I did by choice."

"So the Antrilii got you naked against your will?" Senda asked.

"I was hoping you would be willing to share a little bit about this," Pendin said. He took a drink and leaned forward on his elbows, watching Endric. It hadn't taken very long for them to fall back into the playful pattern they once had. Endric was appreciative of it. If nothing else, it meant that not all things had changed during his time away.

"It was about my father," he said.

"You had to get naked because of your father?" Senda asked. "I know the Antrilii have different customs, but that..."

Endric shook his head. "They view him as an oathbreaker."

He could share that much with them, even if he couldn't share what oath his father was believed to have broken. What did it matter that the Antrilii hunted groeliin? What mattered was that there was an oath, and his father—and by association, him—was felt to have violated it. He had needed to satisfy that oath and do what he could to reclaim their place within the Antrilii.

"They felt that he did not meet an obligation that he had committed to. Because of that, I was required to serve in his place."

The smile faded slightly from Senda's face. "Why did you have to go naked into the mountains?"

"Presumably to die."

"How would you die?"

Endric shrugged. "There are dangerous creatures that roam the mountains in the far north. They sent me without weapons and without clothing and expected me to either die or kill a pack of them." He hoped that was vague enough, but at the same time would provide detail that would allow Pendin to not think Endric was holding back. He didn't want his friend to know. As he looked at Senda, he suspected he would have to tell her more. There was a question in her eyes, one that would not be satisfied by vague answers.

"Since you're here, it seems that you managed to kill as many of these creatures as you were supposed to?" Pendin asked.

Endric shrugged again. "I made a club out of a tree branch and used that to kill a laca, and then used its fur to keep me warm. After that, it was easy."

Pendin watched him and seemed to be waiting for more—as if Endric were telling him a joke, and when he didn't, he laughed anyway. "That's it?"

"Isn't that enough?" Endric asked.

"Probably enough, but I still don't understand why you decided you were willing to risk yourself like that," Pendin said. "You went for answers and you were put to a test."

Endric stared at the now-empty mug sitting in front of him. After being gone as long as he had been, he should have wanted to drink it, but he wanted nothing more than to rest. He'd come back to Vasha to continue his role as en'raen—promotion to Raen would be unlikely considering how little time he'd actually spent *leading*—but he'd found only more questions.

"I went for answers, and I found them. They weren't the answers I thought I wanted—or needed—but they were answers anyway." The waitress returned and set another mug in front of him. He took a drink and when he set it down, he noted Senda watching him.

She had a sad expression on her face and he forced a smile, knowing there was nothing he could say that would change the time they'd spent apart. Maybe it had been too long apart. When they'd last been together, there had been the promise of something more—the promise that they would begin to grow the closeness between them. His choice had been to leave her, knowing that it risked what they were developing, but knowing as well that it was something he needed to do. He *had* to know more about the part of himself that was Antrilii. Without knowing that side of himself, he would never know what more he could be, if anything.

And his father intended for him to be general. Endric didn't know if that would happen, but understood that he could never be the Denraen general without knowing all that he could about his past and what it meant for his future.

"We don't have to talk about this now," Senda said softly.

"If not now, then when will we talk about it?" Endric asked.

"I can see that you're in no condition to do this. You've barely returned to the city—"

"That doesn't mean I'm not prepared to do what's necessary to understand Urik's betrayal—and my father's sudden willingness to work with him."

"Your father had no choice."

"None? I think there are plenty of choices. We've seen how many there are, and what happens when the wrong one is made."

"You don't understand, Endric. Your father didn't have any choice."

Endric fixed Senda with an intense stare. In the time that he'd been away, she had changed. She still had the playfulness to her that had always drawn him, but there was a serious edge there as well. That hadn't been there before. She carried tension around the corners of her eyes, and her mouth was pinched in a bit of a frown, as if she disliked the fact that he sat across from her.

Endric hadn't given much thought to what Senda had been doing over the last year. Without Listain, she likely had been placed in a greater role, one with more responsibility to the Denraen, one where her particular talents—the developing of assets much as Listain once had done—would have been essential. How much of Listain's network had been destroyed with his death? Would Senda have known enough about his network to have been able to maintain it, or had the Denraen lost even more than he had realized with the spymaster's death?

Senda seemed as if she wanted to tell him something, though whatever it was never escaped her lips. There were many secrets that she kept to herself, and he'd never been upset by it in the past, but he'd never had an opportunity to feel as if he were deserving of more information. When he'd been little more than a simple soldier, it wasn't his role to know more about the Denraen. When he'd been raised to the level of en'raen, he'd been kept separate from Listain's knowledge as well, though that was more about the fact that he wasn't ready for what the spymaster knew, and his father had wanted to prevent him from endangering the Denraen.

Now, Endric felt as if he needed to know what they were keeping from him, and he needed to understand details.

"What is it that I don't understand? I thought I was coming back so that I could help guide the Denraen. I hadn't realized that I would be coming back to face the traitor who had betrayed us."

"If your father had any other choice, I don't think he would have allowed this," Senda said.

"You keep saying that. Why wouldn't he have any other choice? There are others who could help with the teralin. I've seen it myself. What about Novan?" Brohmin had been in the north with Endric before disappearing somewhere to the east, but the historian should have been available. He wasn't entirely certain what role the historian played in everything that had occurred, but there was no doubting the fact that he had significant skill, and likely a connection to the teralin, even though he'd been tainted by the dark teralin the same way that Brohmin had been.

"Because he needs to charge the teralin. He recognizes the need so that the Deshmahne can't acquire any more of the teralin found within the mountain."

"Why not Tresten?" The Mage had been responsible for charging most of the teralin when Endric had last been here. If anyone were to continue working with it, it would be him. Maybe that was why Tresten had sent the summons.

Senda and Pendin shared a glance. "You don't know?" Senda asked.

"Know what? I haven't been back in the city long enough to know anything."

"Tresten."

"What about Tresten?"

"He's gone, Endric."

"When will he return?" He hadn't heard of too many of the Magi leaving Vasha, but if any would, he wasn't surprised to learn that Tresten would be among them. There was something unusual about Tresten, a uniqueness that few of the Magi possessed. He was thankful that he could consider Tresten something of a friend. Could his departure be the reason that he'd sent a request for Endric to return?

"He's not returning," Senda said.

"Not returning?"

As he looked at Senda, and saw the way her eyes had taken on something of a haunted expression, he realized what it was that he was missing. It wasn't only that Tresten wasn't returning. Tresten was gone. And likely for good.

"What happened?"

She shook her head. "We don't know."

"You don't know, or you won't tell me?"

She blinked, and he couldn't tell whether that meant that she was keeping something from him or whether it meant that she didn't know anything. With Listain's absence, it was possible that she didn't know anything. The spymaster had been the one to maintain most of the assets outside of the city, though Senda had once been one of those assets. She also had cultivated her own assets.

"I don't know," Senda said, lowering her voice.

"Was it natural?" Tresten had been old when Endric had known him, and even the Magi eventually succumbed to time and age. It wouldn't be altogether unsurprising for him to have passed simply by nature of his advanced age. Something told him that wasn't exactly the case.

"He… he fell," Senda said. She hesitated before answering, and he couldn't tell whether the hesitation implied uncertainty about what she told him, or whether it represented concern about sharing at all.

"Fell? The Magi don't simply fall."

She shrugged. "Tresten did." She held her hands up and met his gaze. "I can't get clean answers. He was in the palace and something happened to him, though word does not make it outside of the palace very easily. It never has. The Magi are tightlipped, more so since the Deshmahne attack, and even more since Listain has been gone."

"Listain still had connections within the palace?" That actually surprised Endric. Listain was well-connected, but he would not have expected the man to have maintained that network among the Magi.

"He had his sources. Not all within the palace are Magi."

Endric grunted. Leave it to Listain to utilize the servants even within the palace. It required a special skill to think in that manner, and Senda certainly shared it.

"You don't think it was entirely natural."

She took a deep breath, and if he hadn't have known her as well as he did, he wouldn't have realized how carefully she chose her words. "I have no reason to believe it was anything but a natural occurrence. People fall all the time." She held his gaze and did not blink.

Endric glanced over at Pendin, but his friend remained buried in his ale.

He was missing something, and he hated that. If nothing else, Listain—and for that matter, Urik—had taught him to think through things so that he could be better prepared. He felt unprepared now. Tresten *had* summoned him. That was why he was here.

Senda wouldn't share with him what she knew. Either she had been told not to, or she didn't view him as high-ranking enough to share. Which meant that he had only one option.

After as long as he had been gone, would his father tell him anything further?

3

The inside of the officers' hall had not changed in the last year. Food remained available at all times, piled on tables for easy consumption, and there was a tapped keg of ale in one of the corners. Mugs were stacked next to it. It was one perk of serving as a ranking officer, and one that Endric had not taken full advantage of prior to his departure. Pendin, on the other hand, had often enjoyed the officers' ale.

When Endric entered, he had expected to see the room empty. A solitary figure sat near the hearth, his head bowed as he scanned the pages of a book, a steaming mug sitting on the table next to him.

Endric tensed as he entered.

"You don't have to stand in the doorway," Urik said.

Endric suppressed an annoyed sigh and entered the room, closing the door behind him with more force than was necessary.

Urik glanced up from his book. His eyes had taken on a weathered expression and his face continued to share that neutral, average look to it that had made him so dangerous and so easy to overlook. "You weren't pleased to see me when you returned."

Endric resisted the urge to let his hand slip to the hilt of his sword. Hopefully, Urik had spent the last few months locked in a cell, his skills languishing, though Endric no longer knew if that were the case. How long had he been freed? That was the question he hadn't asked Senda—or Pendin, for that matter.

"I would have been pleased to see you in your cell," Endric said. He made his way to the back table and grabbed a chunk of bread as well as a stack of smoked sausage before leaning against the wall.

Urik sniffed. "Yes, I imagine you would have been quite pleased to see me confined in the cell."

"You may have convinced my father that you are no longer a threat, but you will not convince me."

Urik tipped his head to the side. "I've convinced the only person I must convince."

Endric gritted his teeth. There was nothing he could do to override his father. Dendril commanded the Denraen, and if he said that Urik was to be trusted, then there was nothing Endric could do that would change that. That didn't mean he had to like it. That also didn't mean he wouldn't make it difficult for Urik. The man had betrayed the Denraen, which had set up Andril's death.

"Your father will not return for some time," Urik said.

"Now you know my father's schedule?" Endric asked.

Urik looked down at his book once more and shrugged. "He listens to my counsel. That is all."

Endric took a bite of his bread to keep from saying anything. At least it was only counsel, not anything more. It would be much worse were Dendril to have welcomed Urik back into the Denraen.

But, wasn't that exactly what he'd done? Hadn't he welcomed him back simply by allowing him access to the officers' hall?

Endric ate in silence, watching Urik as he did. He kept his focus on the book, unmindful of the fact that Endric glared at him, shooting daggers from his eyes. Were Endric to unsheathe, he could end Urik in little more than a simple sword thrust.

That would accomplish nothing other than bringing out Dendril's ire. Would it even satisfy Endric's desire for vengeance?

In between bites, Endric decided to ask Urik a question. "What do you know of Tresten's death?"

Urik glanced up, his expression unreadable. That had always been a trait of the man, and he rarely revealed what he was thinking. "A tragic accident. He was a respected Mage, one of the Council of Elders."

"You think it only an accident?"

A hint of a smile spread across Urik's mouth. "I've known the Magi many years," Urik said. "Age gets to the best of them eventually."

The comment mirrored Endric's own thoughts, but there seemed a strange intensity to the way that Urik said that.

"It is convenient that he fell."

Urik arched a brow. "Convenient? I would say his death would be considered most inconvenient."

"Not for the Denraen. I imagine the Denraen consider his death inconvenient. But for you."

If Endric had hoped for some reaction on Urik's face, he was disappointed. The man made no sign that Endric could read into, no evidence of anything that would betray him. It would be an interesting challenge trying to obtain information from him. Had Endric changed enough that he could do so?

"I suppose it could be viewed in such a way," Urik said.

Endric shrugged. "And now that I've returned, it seems my presence is quite inconvenient."

"How so?"

"If my father allowed you to leave your cell because of your knowledge of charging teralin, he will no longer need you now that I'm here."

"Ah," Urik said. "Your ability to charge the teralin. That is quite surprising. There aren't many who have that particular ability."

"How is it that you managed to learn it?" Endric asked.

"I've learned a great many things in my time."

"Such as how to betray everyone you care about?"

Urik's face remained unchanged, but he gripped his hands together, keeping them resting on top of his book. His knuckles whitened slightly. "I've done everything that I have for those I care about," he said.

"Your children? Is that why you did all of this? If that why you betrayed the Denraen and the guild? Do you think they would understand the sacrifices you've made, and the people you've hurt, for simple revenge?"

He shook his head. "There was nothing simple about revenge. I saw what needed to happen. I saw the depths the Deshmahne would go, the extent they would push, in order to fulfill what they considered to be their destiny. Do not lecture me about misunderstanding them when you only became aware of them after your brother passed."

"Was sacrificed." When Urik said nothing, Endric went on. "I wouldn't have known about the Deshmahne until you sacrificed Andril. That's what you mean."

"All of us must pay a price," Urik said, looking back at his book.

"A price for what? For your vengeance?"

Urik glanced up briefly. "For peace. Is that not what you serve? Does that not fit within the ideals of the Denraen? I may not have been the soldier you thought I was, but I never abandoned the ideals of the Denraen, much as I have not abandoned the ideals of the guild. The Denraen use force to establish peace. The guild seeks knowledge. You think I cannot be both?"

What would Novan think about such a response? The historian

was touchy about all things relating to the guild, and Endric doubted that he would have much sympathy for Urik, especially with how he had used the knowledge of the guild in ways that Endric still didn't understand, other than knowing it went counter to what Novan considered appropriate.

"Both? It seems to me that your betrayal has made you neither."

Urik took a deep breath and let out a sigh. "If that's the price I have to pay, so be it."

Endric shook his head, suppressing a frustrated laugh as he took another bite, this time shoveling in one of the smoked sausages. The meat was savory and not gamey, not at all like most that he'd eaten over the last few months. "Such a martyr," Endric said.

Urik looked up but said nothing.

They remained in silence for long moments before the door to the officers' hall finally opened. Dendril stepped in and noted Endric standing against the wall with Urik remaining seated, and grunted. "Out," he said.

Urik glanced up with a smile, meeting Endric's eyes.

"No. You. Out. I would talk to my son in privacy."

"I could remain and offer my guidance," Urik said.

Dendril grunted. "I don't need your guidance to speak to my son or to one of my officers. Do not think that your position places you above them."

The smile faded from Urik's face. At least Endric understood where the man stood. Urik believed that he still had Dendril's ear, and maybe he did. But he also wasn't nearly as ingrained as Endric had feared. There was that much to be thankful for.

Urik gathered his belongings and made a show of departing, casting a long glance at Endric before he left. When the door closed, Dendril motioned to the chairs stationed by the hearth and waited for Endric to take one. When he did, Dendril threw himself into the other, sitting down with a loud sigh.

"This does not have to be so difficult," Dendril said.

"Difficult? You made it difficult by allowing him access to the Denraen."

"Access? He has nothing but the freedom to move around this terrace. There is no other freedom that he has been granted."

Somehow that did not reassure Endric. Urik would know how to access the network of tunnels beneath the city. He'd already shown that he had discovered Listain's network, and if he knew how to access the teralin mines, he could get many other places within the city.

"Why?" Endric asked.

Dendril glanced at the door. "I admit it wasn't my first choice. Or my second. When options become limited, a soldier must make the least dangerous one." He turned his attention back to Endric. "Using Urik allowed me to ensure others remain safe. When you retake your command, you will understand."

Would he understand? Would he ever know what it was like to ally himself with the man who had betrayed everything the Denraen stood for in his quest to either get revenge, or to destroy the Deshmahne?

How could he understand that?

"Has he provided you any actionable information?" Endric asked.

Dendril grunted. "He's provided what I expected that he would. Little more than that."

"You didn't expect him to."

"I let him believe that I did. It made him relax, which opened him up to mistakes."

Endric allowed himself to smile. He thought his father had been swayed by the need to use Urik's knowledge, and perhaps he had to a certain extent, but not nearly as much as Endric had feared. His father was far too capable for that. Endric should have known, even before letting his anger get the best of him.

It seemed another lesson, and one that Endric did not need, not at this stage. He should be past needing these small lessons from his father.

"What happened with Tresten?"

"You heard."

"Of course, I heard. Did you think that I wouldn't?" He debated telling his father about Tresten's summons but decided to wait.

Dendril sighed. "I knew that you would, eventually. I hadn't expected that to come out quite so soon…" He frowned, studying Endric. "Senda told you, didn't she?"

"She did. Was she not supposed to?"

Dendril grunted. "I did not give her explicit instructions not to. I hadn't thought that she would find you quite so soon."

That seemed an odd comment. Why would his father offer direct commands to Senda anyway? "You knew about our relationship before. You are the one who encouraged it."

His father held his gaze for a moment too long.

"What is it that you're not telling me? What is it that she wasn't telling me?" Endric asked. Hadn't Pendin told him to seek out Senda?

"It matters little."

Endric wasn't certain that was entirely true. From the look on his father's face, it seemed that perhaps it mattered more than he was letting on, though Endric also doubted that he would convince his father to share.

"You haven't answered. What happened with Tresten?"

"He fell."

Endric grunted. "I continue to hear that. What I haven't heard is a reasonable answer as to how he fell."

"And we will not. The Magi keep quite tight-lipped about what happens within their palace walls. Were Listain alive, we might have heard something, but without him…" Dendril shrugged. "Senda attempts to regain those connections, but she will never make an effective spymaster, not nearly as effective as Listain."

"Because she's a woman?" Endric asked.

"Because she was outed far too soon." Dendril took a swig of ale and wiped his arm across his mouth. He sighed, shaking his head. "Listain was outed, eventually, but he had time to develop his network before that took place. Senda… she has not had the necessary time."

"Just because she's known doesn't mean that she can't still develop those connections. Others could report to her."

"You sound like her."

Why would Senda have to argue on her own behalf? Worse, why would his father not have listened? "You don't think that she can be effective?"

"When my own informants are more effective than hers, I know exactly how effective she can be."

Endric took a deep breath. "I hope you will give her time." This wasn't the conversation he expected to have with his father, and it wasn't the one that he thought he would need to have, but he had observed how sharp Senda's mind was, and perhaps Dendril had not had such an opportunity.

"As there are no other alternatives, what choice do I have?"

"Not allowing Urik into the officers' hall."

Dendril snorted. "If that's going to offend you, you could always refrain from coming here."

They fell into a tense silence. "Tresten wouldn't simply fall," Endric said.

He couldn't let go of it. He didn't know the Mage well, but knew him well enough to know that he simply wouldn't have slipped. There had to be another answer, though what would it be? Maybe the answer simply was that Tresten *had* slipped, but he owed it to the Mage to ensure that was all it was.

"Tresten wouldn't simply fall," Dendril agreed.

It seemed as much an admission as any that Endric was going to get from his father.

Both men sat drinking, remaining silent as they did.

After a while, Dendril set his mug down. "How was Melinda?"

Endric sniffed. "She's the one you ask about?"

"I imagine that if you spent any time in Farsea, you would have been around Melinda. She can be difficult in the best of times."

"Why not warn me of what I would find there?"

"To them, I was no longer Antrilii. I'm not certain that I can even make that claim with what you have done, but perhaps more than I could have a year ago."

Endric thought he understood. To the Antrilii, betraying their people to outsiders was not allowed. Had Dendril shared what he knew of the Antrilii, he would have broken another oath, one that might forever taint him.

When Dentoun had found Endric, Dendril had not betrayed the Antrilii to get Endric to help. The Antrilii had revealed themselves to Endric, which was allowed. And Endric had gone north, searching for more answers about them on his own, guided at first by Brohmin, and then—after they had been attacked by the groeliin—he had managed to make it to Farsea by himself.

"The Yahinv have been reunited."

Dendril frowned. "They were not united before?"

"There was disagreement amongst them as to what to do with the groeliin."

"There should be no disagreement. They consider it an oath to the gods that they have made to continue their hunting of them."

Endric smiled. "I am quite familiar with their oath, Father."

Dendril studied him a moment. "I suppose that you are, now. How did you survive?"

Endric closed his eyes, letting out a soft breath. The story was a long one, and one that his father deserved to hear. He shared as much as he could, trying not to relive the horrors of stalking through the northern mountains naked and afraid, only a club for support at first. When he'd finally reunited with the Antrilii, when he finally found a weapon, he thought that he would be saved, but that had only been another beginning.

Dendril listened, nodding every so often, twisting a dark band of metal that ringed his finger, the marker of the Conclave. Endric knew two others who were members of the Conclave, though not what such a position meant—or entailed.

"You discovered more than the Antrilii have learned in hundreds of years."

"Even with what I discovered, I don't think they will use it," Endric said.

Dendril grunted. "How can they? Doing so places too many of them in danger. There is a balance, one the Yahinv have understood. The Antrilii must maintain their numbers in order to face the ongoing threat of the groeliin. Risk sacrificing too many and the Antrilii will collapse."

"Nahrsin doesn't see it that way."

Dendril smiled slightly. "Nahrsin has always been more like his father. He is a good man. You will need to keep working with him."

Endric frowned. "You would have me return to the Antrilii lands?"

"That's not what I suggested. I'm suggesting that you will one day replace me." When Endric opened his mouth to object, Dendril held his hands out, placating him. "I'm not saying that it will happen anytime soon. I intend to continue leading the Denraen as long as I am capable, and as long as they are willing to have me, but at some point, there is no man who will be better equipped to lead them than you."

Endric sat in silence. It was a life of service. It was a life his brother had wanted, not one that Endric had ever thought he would claim for himself. After everything he'd seen, he no longer thought he could refuse it. He understood that he could be both

Denraen and Antrilii. His time in the north had demonstrated that. But he still didn't know how he could be general. It required a different set of decisions, and perhaps a different type of knowledge than what he possessed. Perhaps it required a different commitment than Endric had.

Watching his father, he wondered if he understood the difficulty that Endric had.

Likely he did.

"First, you'll have to defeat me," Dendril said.

Endric grinned. "I defeated Urik."

Neither of them needed to be reminded that Urik had very nearly defeated Dendril. Had he done so, he could have claimed command of the Denraen. That was a tradition as old as the Denraen. It had been the maneuver that Endric had not expected, and in all of his time sparring with his father, he would never have expected that Urik would have the ability to challenge his father, but his father would have fallen were Endric not to have interceded.

"You did. The Denraen owe you a debt of gratitude. That is why I allowed you to go north." He fell silent for a moment. "There will come a time, Endric, when you will be asked to do more than you have. You will be asked to give more than you have."

"I hope that time will not come too soon."

Dendril grunted. "Unfortunately, that time is now."

Endric frowned at his father.

"You have served as en'raen. From the reports I received from Listain before his passing, you served well. Now I need for you to serve differently."

"How would you have me serve?" he asked.

He didn't expect his father to send him away from the city. That wouldn't serve the Denraen, and there didn't seem anything more for him to do to help lead. Would his father promote him to Raen? That was a possibility, though it was one that Endric didn't feel he was particularly prepared—or equipped—for. Listain had always served as his father's Raen, a position that he'd held longer than most. Endric didn't know whether his father had chosen another to replace him, but hoped that he had so that Endric wouldn't need to.

"Something else draws my attention away," he started, looking down at his ring again. What was Dendril not telling him about the Conclave? "I would ask you to watch over Urik."

Endric blinked. "Urik? That's not a wise idea."

"Perhaps not, but you're the only one who can. I need information from him, and I don't think he will share with me."

"Then why would he share with me?"

"Because he still views you the way that many of the soldiers do."

Endric watched him, wanting to object, but what was there for his objection? When he'd left Vasha before, he had gone as a man who had barely earned his commission. Endric had made sacrifices since then and had risked himself, but few of the Denraen would have known that.

Even Urik probably wouldn't have known that.

It was a fact his father intended to take advantage of.

Endric would have been impressed were it not for the fact that he was the one being used in such a way.

He let out a long, frustrated sigh. What choice did he have, other than to do as his father—his commander—asked of him?

"What would you have me do?"

4

Endric stood within the barracks, staring up at buildings that had once been his home. They still were, he supposed, though not in the way that they had been when he was younger. Then, he had been more interested in meeting the barest requirements of what it meant to be Denraen as long as it meant that he could fight. Now… he understood what it meant to be Denraen, and he understood what was asked of him, even if he wasn't always the best at meeting those requirements.

The barracks yard was filled with soldiers. Most worked with the sword, practiced their formations, or drilled in other ways, but some were groupings of soldiers heading out for patrol. Endric watched those with the most interest. That had been him once upon a time.

"You're just standing there."

Endric jumped and saw Senda watching him. Was that a mournful look in her eyes? His father had alluded to something that she hadn't shared with him, and Endric wasn't entirely certain what that was, though he worried that it had to do with all the time they'd spent apart. Had she moved on?

He had not. She had remained within his thoughts; the one steady desire he had through everything had been his interest in getting back to her. But, he had been gone so long that perhaps she had no choice but to move on. It was something they would have to talk about, though now didn't seem the time—or the place—to do so.

"I met with Dendril," Endric said.

"It seems as if your experience with him hasn't changed in the time away."

He smiled. "It's changed. If nothing else, he no longer sees me as Andril's replacement." His father had never *really* seen him in that way. To Dendril, Endric had been a disappointment first and something else second.

"He asked you to keep an eye on Urik," Senda said.

Endric chuckled. Why was he surprised that she had already known? She really *was* brilliant, easily Listain's equal and possibly even better. "You knew?"

"I suspected that was what he would ask of you. There is only so much that Urik will share with Dendril. I think your father was too close to him. It places Urik on edge and keeps him cautious."

"And I will not?"

She smiled and spread her hands out. "You know the way Urik perceived you. Likely he thinks that you only got lucky beating him the first time."

Endric started. "I did only get lucky when I beat him the first time."

She watched him, saying nothing for a moment. "Did he ask anything else of you?"

"He didn't ask me to serve as his Raen, if that's what you're asking."

She tipped her head. "No. That position has already been filled."

Endric blinked. That took him aback. "Who is it? Fennah?" She had survived the Raver attack and had lived to escort many Denraen back to the city. Were it not for her leadership, even more would have suffered and died.

"Not Fennah."

"Then who?"

"Me."

Endric stared at her, not knowing what to say. How had Senda replaced Listain as Raen? "You weren't even an officer!"

She laughed bitterly. "That's your first response?"

Many other responses had come to mind, but that was the one that stood out. Typically, promotions happened from within. Endric was better suited to receive a promotion to that position, though he wasn't even sure if it was one that he would accept. For Senda to have been promoted to Raen would be unheard of, but was it altogether surprising? His father valued competence, and in spite of what he had alluded to, he very much prized Senda's mind. That was a sentiment that Endric shared.

"I guess I would have expected you to have told me before now."

"There wasn't the time."

"Not the time? You mean when we were sitting in a tavern, just Pendin, myself, and you. That wasn't the time for you to share with me your promotion?"

"No."

Endric grunted. His conversation with his father took on a different meaning now. He thought he began to understand why his father had been so odd about his comments surrounding Senda. It wasn't that he didn't want Endric to have the connection to Senda, it was that she had already taken on a greater responsibility within the Denraen.

He began to smile.

"What?" she asked.

He shrugged. "I suppose now I have to salute you, though you never saluted me when I outranked you."

"Did you outrank me?"

"I was en'raen."

"Yes."

"And you were..." He cocked his head, studying her. Had his father *not* promoted so blindly? "What rank had you held with Listain?"

Senda laughed. "It's funny that it's taken you this long to wonder."

"Why should I have wondered before? I knew that you worked with him, but I didn't realize you carried any rank in doing so."

"Did you not carry rank with each position you held?"

"Of course I did."

"How would my position be any different?"

"You were sent out of the city on assignments."

"I seem to recall you getting sent away the same way," she said.

"Mine was so that I could learn what it meant for me to serve as en'raen."

"Yes."

Endric watched her, realizing that he had been a fool. "How long did we share the same rank?"

"Does it matter?"

"How long?"

Senda sighed and glanced around the practice yard, her eyes darting around constantly, seeming to take in dozens of things that Endric could not see. When her gaze returned to him, she stared at him for a long moment before answering. "I had already been promoted to Listain's en'raen when you received your promotion."

"Why did you keep that from me?"

"I didn't keep it from you."

"Had you told me and I just don't remember?"

"Considering how much you drank back then, it's possible that I had."

"Fair enough. But you didn't tell me for a reason. I spent quite a bit of time trying to understand my place within the Denraen. You could have helped with that."

"No. I could not. Had I done anything different, my position would have been compromised."

"Your position? Why would it matter if it were compromised? Why would it matter if others knew that you served as en'raen?"

"You're not asking the right question."

"No? And what question should I be asking?"

"Why would Listain need to have his own chain of command?"

Endric hadn't given that any thought. Why would he have need for that? But then, it made sense for him to have his own chain of command. If Senda were to issue an order, it had to have the validity of the Denraen behind it. If she was off on an assignment, she couldn't take the time to return to Vasha, or send word to Vasha, in order to ensure that everything was communicated in the way that it needed to be.

"Why are you telling me this now?"

"I wouldn't except that your father told me that I needed to. He suspected you would have too many questions otherwise. It's tradition that none of the other en'raen know that the Keeper of Secrets has their own en'raen. The only ones to know are the Keeper, the Raen, and the general."

Endric didn't even know what to say. He was overwhelmed by the fact that so much had been kept from him, even when he had taken on a role where he should have had more authority. Even then, he had been restricted with what he knew and with what they were willing to share with him.

"What of the other en'raen? What did they think of your promotion?"

Her eyes narrowed. "They all know how I served Listain.

Dendril was quite clear that we needed continuity with information. No one has objected."

They made their way toward the entrance to the barracks when Senda paused. She glanced back, her gaze taking in the Denraen soldiers practicing with the sword, and Endric followed the direction of her gaze.

"You look like you still want to practice."

Senda shrugged. "Perhaps I do. I don't get the opportunity that often anymore. Too many people are intimidated by me to practice."

"Intimidated by your work with the staff or intimidated by your rank?"

"Does it have to be one or the other? Most of the time, it's a little bit of both. Your father has worked with me a little, but..."

Endric smiled. He could imagine Senda and his father sparring, both using the staff as they fought. Senda was skilled with the staff, and might be the most skilled among the Denraen. His father had a high degree of skill as well, and had spent quite a bit of time practicing with different weapons, including the staff. It was a sparring session he would have enjoyed observing.

Endric had spent some time training with the staff as well, though did not have nearly Senda's level of competence. "If you'd like to spar..."

Endric watched Senda, not expecting her to take him up on the offer. She had never spent much time sparring with him other than the time that he'd been out of the city on his mission with Listain. Then they had sparred, though she had easily defeated him. He'd improved since then, though suspected that she would have as well, especially if she'd been sparring with his father on a regular basis.

"Sure," she said.

She started away from him, heading toward the flat section of the barracks lawn where most of the Denraen spent their time sparring. Endric followed, smiling to himself, and grabbed one of the slender staffs lining the wall. Senda spun hers a few times, making a practiced movement before setting it into the ground and leaning casually on it.

Endric twisted the staff in his hands with a little less familiarity. Was it strange that this reminded him of his time in the mountains when he'd had only a broken branch with which to protect himself?

"If you need me to go easy on you, I can."

Endric grunted. "How will I learn anything if you go easy on me?"

"The great Endric now admits that he can learn something from a woman?"

Endric laughed, looking around the practice yard. A few of the Denraen had paused and now watched them both, probably as curious about what he would do with Senda as he was. There was a time when he might have been embarrassed about the fact that he would likely be quickly beaten, but he no longer felt that way. Now it truly was about learning and developing his skill so that he could be a better fighter.

"I'm happy for you to teach me many things," he said. "I seem to recall you being willing to teach me before."

Senda lifted her staff and spun it in a quick circle. Wind whistled off it. "I believe you are the one with experience," she said.

"Unfortunately."

"I never minded."

With that, she darted forward, snapping the staff toward him with a flickering motion.

Endric brought his staff up, blocking her first sequence of movements. She was quick, but she seemed as if she made a point of not striking quite as quickly as he knew her capable of. He flowed through a sequence of defenses before taking an opportunity to attack. The catahs used with the staff were similar to those with the sword, at least similar enough that he recognized many of the forms or their variants. They were different enough that he had to think through them, which caused him to act more slowly than he otherwise did, and certainly more slowly than he did when fighting with the sword.

Senda blocked him easily and turned in another attack.

This was one that he recognized, and going through the movements, countering the attack, loosened him up, allowing him to react more easily.

When he had defended the catah, he flowed from the defense into another attack, this time another one that was similar to his sword work but different enough that it seemed almost a new attack.

There were catahs that he'd learn from the Antrilii, movements that their sword Masters had possessed that few of the Denraen knew. His father likely knew them, and Endric intended to teach the rest of the Denraen—at least those who were willing to work with him—those techniques, incorporating them into the Denraen repertoire.

Senda's face tightened in concentration.

Her attack intensified, spinning in a tight, controlled movement, each one a flurry of speed, whistling as she struck at him. Endric blocked, defending as best as he could, finding that she increased the intensity of her attacks. Had he passed some sort of threshold for her? She seemed to be attacking with renewed gusto, throwing herself through each series of movements before falling back into another defense.

He couldn't tell whether she still intended to demonstrate various catahs or if this was simply about sparring now.

He fought back, doing everything he could to keep her staff from striking his arms, his legs, or his back. He deflected most of the blows, though a few caught him and altered his movements just enough that he was forced to attempt a different approach. He had a longer reach than she did, and greater strength, but she had speed and familiarity.

He had to use her speed against her and his strength to his advantage.

If they used the sword, he suspected he would have stopped her long before. He had few peers with that weapon, especially those who weren't enhanced in some way, such as the Deshmahne as they used their dark teralin swords. Years spent practicing had made him incredibly gifted. Time spent facing groeliin had made him even more deadly. There was a certain skill that was acquired when facing creatures that attacked with claws and fangs, the kind of attack that no man could replicate.

With the staff, movements were different. There was more spinning and twisting, and it required the same fluidity as with the sword, but there was also the need for using the leverage of the staff.

Senda caught him on the arm, and he almost lost his grip on the staff.

He grunted, twisting, spinning back, and brought his staff around.

He managed to do it faster than expected, and he could practically envision the way the staff would collide with Senda's head.

He threw himself to the ground, rolling rather than striking her in the head with the staff. As he did, her staff collided with his leg, stinging painfully. She had control of the movement even then, not connecting with as much force as he knew possible, the same sort of control that his father possessed. Endric swept the staff around and caught her on the back of the leg, dropping her to the ground next to him.

Senda grunted and had started to get up when he threw himself on top of her.

She glared at him. "This isn't sparring."

"Not anymore."

He looked down at her, noting her dark blue eyes and wanting to touch her hair, smoothing it away from her cheeks. It had been far too long since he had touched her skin, far too long since he'd touched anyone's skin.

Senda shifted beneath him.

There was so much he wanted to say to her, but now wasn't the time.

He licked his lips, swallowing back the words, and rolled off her. Endric took a deep breath, setting the staff down next to him, looking around the practice yard. Men had paused in their own sparring, some even paused in working with their regiment movements, all to watch him and Senda practicing. Now that they were done, most returned to their work, leaving him and Senda sitting on the grass alone.

Neither of them spoke for a few moments.

"You've gotten more skilled," Senda said.

"I've faced things that have required that I did."

"Naked."

Endric laughed. "Naked," he agreed.

Senda stood and reached a hand out, helping him to his feet. They replaced their staffs along the wall and she turned to him. "It's good to have you back in Vasha, Endric."

He studied her, wondering if she really felt that way or if too much had changed in the time they had been apart.

Senda was now the Keeper of Secrets. He doubted he would know.

5

The entrance to the mines had long ago been locked, the gate closed and barred with heavy chains. Those chains—and that lock—had not been enough to keep him out the last time. Endric hoped they would not be enough to keep him out this time, either.

He glanced behind him. On this level of the city, there was a different sort of activity. Brown-robed scholars made their way into the university, though few bothered to glance in his direction. Most were fixated on reaching the university, showing their mark so that they could gain entry. It was busy passing in and out of the university, much busier than he had ever understood. In the distance, he could hear the steady clack of staffs and suspected that scholars within the university were practicing much as he and Senda had practiced the day before.

The air on this level had a hint of the teralin bitterness, but it also carried the scents of the city. The smells of breads from bakeries and the savory meat smoked in the nearby taverns drifted to his nose. They were nearly enough to pull his attention away, drawing him back from the gate leading under the city, but he pulled himself back to his task and studied the chains.

What was he doing here?

His father had placed no expectations upon him. Since his return, he was en'raen in title only, but had not taken on any command. What was there for him to command? He was to watch Urik, but even that task seemed trivial. There was little for him to do to guard Urik. He had to interrogate him eventually, but he had to find a way to do that without Urik being aware of what Endric was after. He had to think through his approach before trying it.

And he'd come here alone.

After all the time he'd spent in the north, he felt comfortable by himself. Perhaps he shouldn't. Perhaps he should have asked Pendin or Senda to have come with him, but if he had asked either, it would have placed them in danger of his father's anger. He had done that often enough in the past to know that he was not interested in forcing them to suffer on his behalf. If anyone was to suffer, it would be him alone.

Endric glanced over at the university. Would Elizabeth still be there?

His desire to find her—and question her—was part of the reason that he hadn't shared with Pendin where he was going. It was best not to anger his friend—and telling him that he came to speak to his estranged mother would do exactly that.

Something told him that he needed to speak to her. She had connections that he suspected extended to the Conclave, the same connections that Brohmin and Novan shared. Possibly his father, though he suspected there was a strained relationship. And then there was the fact that Elizabeth might know something about what had happened with Tresten.

Endric couldn't shake the sense that discovering that secret was important. Somehow, he needed to know whether Tresten truly had fallen or whether something more nefarious had occurred, as unlikely as it was that one of the Magi might have suffered such a fate.

He jammed his knife into the lock binding the chains together, forcing it open. It popped open with a loud *crack*.

He worked quickly, moving the chains, unwinding them from the gate holding the mine closed. Once they were off, he opened the gate and crawled quickly into the mine, securing the chains once more.

Endric hurried through the mineshaft, ignoring the heat as much as he could. Teralin had a certain signature, one that was both hot as well as possessing an energy that pressed upon him. In his time away from the city, he'd grown more sensitized to the teralin connection. It was one that had a greater role than most knew. The Magi had once claimed that teralin was required to reach the gods, and though Tresten had changed that for them, convincing them that communication with the gods could happen without the presence of the metal, Endric's own experiences had shown him that there was something mystical to the metal.

The groeliin used it. He wasn't entirely certain how, only that it had been a part of their breeding grounds and that it had been necessary for new groeliin. They used the negatively charged teralin, drawing energy from it as they fed. It was a secret that the Antrilii had not known, and one that Endric still didn't know the significance of.

Not only did the groeliin use it, but the merahl did also. That, as much as the groeliin, told him that there was something mystical to the metal.

The mineshaft led straight. Had he not been here before, he might have been more uncomfortable, but he remembered from the time spent traveling through here with Pendin that it opened up farther along into tunnels where lanterns had once been set.

Endric practically ran along the length of the tunnel, not wanting to be trapped in the darkness any longer than necessary.

Every so often, he would glance back, looking to the mouth of the mineshaft, noting the daylight as it grew dimmer and dimmer, closing him in.

And then darkness surrounded him entirely.

He reached the end of this part of the tunnel and paused. When he'd been here last, there had been lanterns and a way for him to see through the darkness. There were none here now. Had the mines finally been abandoned entirely?

Tresten would have ensured that the mines were secure. He understood the dangers of teralin and the dangers that having the neutral metal placed upon the city. If they weren't anyone capable of charging the teralin, there would be no dangers, but since the Deshmahne had demonstrated their knowledge—and Urik had proven his willingness to continue working with others to reveal the use of teralin—the metal itself had become a weapon that could be used against Vasha.

The unmined teralin was still neutral.

He could feel it pressing on him. There was a strange, almost sizzling quality to it. The energy of teralin was a physical thing, one that he had grown not only attuned to, but that he could use. Somehow, he could draw upon that energy, and it made him stronger.

It was a secret he had not told anyone yet.

That was another reason he'd entered the mine.

He needed to understand whether his connection to teralin placed him in danger of drawing upon it in a way that he was not meant to. The Deshmahne were able to use the negatively charged teralin and did so to a devastating effect. What did it mean that he pulled upon the positively charged teralin? How was it changing him?

Endric had to believe that it was changing him, regardless of whether he wanted to admit it or not. How could it not? And in what ways?

He stood in the darkness, debating which way he needed to travel. He probably should return, leave the mines, and come back with a lantern so that he could find his way more easily. If he did, would he even take the time to return? Would his father's assignment of him—the requirement that he contain Urik—force him to remain so busy that he didn't have time to return?

Stubbornness won out and Endric plunged deeper into the darkness, heading along a sloping path.

He remembered taking this way before. The memory of it was vivid and he tried to recall what the tunnels looked like when lit by the lantern, ignoring the darkness around him as well as the sense of the teralin that pressed in on him. It wasn't an unpleasant sensation. Rather, it was familiar, somewhat seductive.

He continued to follow the path, running his hand along the wall. Heat surged from the stone, buried teralin making the walls hot.

He passed a few smaller openings leading off the main mineshaft. He recalled what Pendin had told him before and recalled how these were smaller tunnels, secondary shafts. They were not where he needed to go.

He thought that he knew how to find the entrance to the university, if only he could discover the larger mineshaft that led toward it.

After wandering for a while—far longer than he thought that he should have been—Endric stopped.

Had he missed it?

He didn't think that he had. It should have been an easier turnoff, but he'd found no sign of another larger mineshaft. He recalled one leading toward the university and a door that would lead toward stairs and out of the mines entirely.

Maybe there was another way for him to determine where he needed to go.

Given that he could detect teralin, could he use that in some way to navigate through here?

Endric remained motionless, focusing on his breathing. The sense of teralin pressed all around him. As he focused, he tried to pay attention to whether he could detect the positively charged teralin. It wasn't only that he needed teralin, it was that he needed a kind of teralin that had already been influenced. He could follow that to his way out of the mines.

It flashed within his mind.

It was subtle at first, but grew stronger. There was something about it that seemed a beacon, a pulsing brightness. It drew him, and he chose not to resist. It pulled him forward, along the central mineshaft, and he removed his hand from the wall, no longer dragging along the neutral teralin. Doing that influenced him, preventing him from detecting what he needed.

Every so often, he found himself pausing, focusing on the teralin again before continuing onward. The sense of it gradually increased, guiding him, letting him know that he was heading in the right direction.

At one point, he turned, taking a path that led him off the main mineshaft.

Was that right?

It had to be, didn't it? Where else was he to go, if not after the sense of the positively charged teralin?

The tunnel narrowed. This was different than when he'd been with Pendin.

He considered turning back. He probably should. Heading here, with no way of navigating the tunnel, he could wander indefinitely. It would be ironic for him to have survived all that he had only to die within the mines beneath Vasha.

But he felt pulled. Endric didn't resist that sensation, knowing that if he were pulled by teralin, he would find something that had been positively charged. Maybe it was something that Tresten had charged, something that would help them understand what had happened to the Mage.

The tunnel narrowed again.

Now the walls practically brushed his shoulders. There was still neutral teralin within the walls. Heat coming off it reminded him of baking beneath the hot sun when his father had defeated him, leaving him nearly to die.

He debated turning back again. Each time something changed about the tunnel, he spent a moment debating whether he should be turning back, but now he had come far enough that he wasn't sure he would find his way out very easily.

He pressed onward.

Time spent in the tunnels passed strangely. He didn't know how long he was here. It could have been hours, though he didn't think he'd been here a terribly long time. After a while, the walls began to widen once more, no longer brushing against him, tearing at his cloak. He stopped for a moment, listening for the sense of the positively charged teralin that had driven him here in the first place, and noted that it was still there. It was closer now. Close enough that he knew that it should be nearby.

Another couple steps, and a cavern opened before him.

A faint, glowing white light seemed to filter through the darkness. Endric couldn't be sure that he even saw it, but he'd been stranded in the dark for so long that it had to be real. It began as a lessening of the darkness, a graying of what had once been a pure blackness, an utter darkness that had surrounded him. As it changed, the darkness lessening, he looked around, wondering what the source of light was. Did daylight penetrate this deep?

That seemed unlikely. Stranger still was the fact that the light seemed to come from all around him. That wasn't daylight seeping in.

He noticed another change, one that he wasn't aware of until he began to focus on it, and now that he did, he recognized why he had been drawn here, and he recognized why there was the faint—and increasingly steady—light all around him.

It was teralin.

Not just teralin, but the positively charged teralin that had drawn him.

This was it? This is what he'd detected, and what had pulled him through the darkness?

There had to be something else. There had to be something more. But, he didn't think there was.

Endric felt a brighter pulsing of teralin in his mind, one that seemed to draw him forward even more. It was not this chamber that drew him. There was something else out there that he had not yet found.

The room stretched before him, and he had a sense that he'd been here before.

It took a moment to realize why he would have such a feeling. He *had* been here before, coming through this way when he'd first wandered through the tunnels alone, searching for a way out, following the Deshmahne attack.

There had been something else here before. He recalled other sources of teralin, though they weren't here now. Had Tresten moved them?

Was this where the teralin throne had been?

He still didn't know the purpose of that throne, but knew Listain had been trapped to it, chained, for longer than the spymaster had ever shared.

That was a question for Urik, if he could get the man to answer.

He passed through a doorway and reached another chamber, this one narrower than the last. The heat coming out of here was intense, more than anything he'd been exposed to before. As far as he knew, the polarity of the teralin didn't make a difference to how warm it was, but maybe it did.

He continued forward, drawn by something there.

Stairs.

Endric climbed them, hurrying along, wondering whether he would ever find a way out.

The heat continued to intensify.

At the top of the stairs, he found a doorway. Endric pushed it open and stumbled through.

Light spilled around him.

This time, it did not seem to come from the walls, nothing like the faint glowing that he'd detected in the other chamber. This was natural light—daylight.

There was an opening, and he pulled himself through it.

As he did, he realized where he was, though he felt a moment of shock. This was the ruins on the third terrace of the city. He had not known that it connected to the tunnels, though he hadn't ever spent time wandering the tunnels this far to know. Had the miners known?

They must have. And this must've been how the Deshmahne had reached this level.

Endric sighed as he stared up at the Magi palace. All the time he'd spent seemed wasted. He had made it so far through the mines but still hadn't found Elizabeth to see what she might know.

Hopefully he could sneak back down without his father detecting him. He didn't need the questions that would come were he caught here.

6

"I'm surprised that you were given this assignment," Urik said.

Endric glared at him. He did nothing to hide the hatred that burned in his eyes. What purpose would there be shielding it from Urik? The man knew what he had done to the Denraen—and what he'd done to Endric's brother—and knew that Endric would not be pleased to spend any time with him.

Endric glanced around the room. At least it wasn't a well-appointed room. There was a simple desk stacked with books, and a bed. There was nothing else. He was disappointed to see that Urik was granted access to books. It was his scholarship and knowledge that had proven the most dangerous.

"Trust me, it's not an assignment that I want."

"From what I hear, you don't want any assignments."

"What does that mean?"

Urik glanced up from the book he was reading and set it on top of the desk. He barely turned his attention toward Endric. "Only that you were more than willing to leave the Denraen following the attack. You were more interested in heading north, learning about the Antrilii, then you were about remaining with the Denraen. And after they had lost so much…"

Endric controlled his breathing, resisting the urge to punch Urik in the nose. "The Denraen lost what they did because of you."

Urik shrugged. "I was under the influence of dark teralin," he said. He kept his face neutral, but there was almost a hint of a smile to his words. "Even Novan understands how dark teralin can influence others."

Endric hadn't been sure whether Urik knew that Novan had been influenced by the teralin. The admission should not have surprised him, but still it did. "And now?" Endric asked.

"Now? Certainly, you've learned that Mage Tresten helped heal me from that influence."

Endric hadn't, but wasn't surprised that it had been Tresten who had been required to help Urik. Tresten was more knowledgeable about the metal than any of the other Magi, at least the other Magi that Endric had met.

"You don't take any accountability for your actions?"

Urik chuckled. "I find it interesting that Endric of all people would speak to me of accountability."

"I have taken accountability for my actions."

"Have you? You abandoned the Denraen. You abandoned your people, leaving behind the oath that you made so that you could understand… What, exactly?"

Endric resisted the urge to smile. Urik thought that he understood, and it pleased Endric that the man did not. He was fishing for information. Endric had to give him something, if only to coax him into sharing more.

"Little is known about the Antrilii," Endric said. "I thought that I could go north, that I could discover something."

"You mean you want to find more about who you are descended from."

Endric tried to keep his face neutral. Had Dendril shared with

Urik their connection to the Antrilii? Maybe he had, though if he had, it likely would have come at a time before or Urik had betrayed them.

"Don't you want to know more about your ancestors?" he asked Urik.

"I'm afraid I don't have anything nearly as exciting as a connection to the Antrilii."

Endric took a seat on the bed, sitting rigidly, keeping himself ready. He didn't think Urik would attempt anything, but if he did, Endric would use whatever force was necessary to prevent him from reaching him.

"Maybe not anything like the Antrilii, but you've lived an interesting life."

Urik's eyes narrowed slightly. "Interesting? Is that what you would call it?"

Endric shrugged. "You've been a member of the historian guild, a member of the Denraen, and you have managed to gain access to the Urmahne priests. You wouldn't call that interesting?"

Urik smiled. When he did, his face changed, going from neutral to something darker. "And yet, none of that would have happened were it not for the Deshmahne."

"Do you give them credit or the blame?"

"Both."

"What happened?"

"It no longer matters," Urik said.

"I think it does. What happened has influenced countless others. What you've been through—what you lost—has caused you to harm many others. How again would that not matter?"

Urik stared at him, holding his gaze for a long moment before shaking his head. "Is this your way of questioning me?"

Endric leaned back, remaining seated on the bed. "Does it have to be an interrogation?"

"Your father sent you to question me, didn't he?"

"My father sent me to keep tabs on you. Nothing more than that."

Urik shook his head. "Do you think he trusts you so little to lead?"

"Is that what you believe?" Endric asked.

Urik shrugged. "We're more alike than you realize."

"And how is that?"

"We've both betrayed the Denraen."

"I haven't betrayed the Denraen."

Urik smiled again. This time, there was an unmistakable hint of malice. "You may not call it a betrayal, but abandoning the Denraen for your own needs is no different than what I did. You broke your oaths."

Endric stared at him until Urik smiled and lifted his book up again, turning his attention to the pages. Endric continued to watch him, not knowing what to say—if there was anything to say.

Could he have betrayed the Denraen the same way that Urik had? Was *he* now an oathbreaker?

He hadn't considered it a betrayal, but then again, maybe Urik hadn't considered what he had done a betrayal either. Urik did what he thought was necessary so that he could force the Denraen to confront the Deshmahne.

What had been Endric's reason for heading north?

He had wanted to know about himself. Was that reason enough for him to have abandoned his post, to have given up his commission—even if temporarily—so that he could find himself?

Dendril had allowed him to go as a sort of reward for stopping Urik, but maybe that wasn't the point. Maybe the point was that Endric should not have needed to go.

Had he not, the understanding of the groeliin that he'd gained, the knowledge of teralin and the groeliin's connection to it, would never have been discovered.

Was that not valuable as well?

"What happened with you?" Endric asked softly.

Urik glanced up a moment before returning his attention to his book. "We've already gone through this."

"You were a good Denraen soldier."

Urik set the book down again and looked up. "The Denraen served ideals that I believed in."

"Then why the betrayal?" He raised his hand as Urik started to open his mouth. "I understand what you're going to say about me heading north to understand the Antrilii, and I agree that they're similar." Saying that was difficult, especially to Urik, but he needed Urik to confide in him. "But you had a different kind of betrayal. Yours was one of concealment."

Urik clasped his hands together on top of his lap. His face wore a flat expression, unreadable, as plain as the man who wore it. "Had your father listened to my counsel, the betrayal would not have been necessary."

"You attempted to convince him of the need to attack the Deshmahne?"

"From the moment I was chosen, my first days within the Deshmahne, I tried to convince those above me of the danger in ignoring their presence. None wanted to listen. When I gained my commission, when I reached a level of rank where I could actually influence others, I thought that would make a difference. It was the reason I pushed so hard, why I trained as hard as I did."

Endric could imagine the difficulty that Urik would have faced. If he really believed that what he did had been justified, then he might have tried to progress through the proper Denraen channels. And Endric couldn't deny that Urik had risen through the ranks through his skill. No Denraen was promoted unless they were worthy.

Until him.

"What was your experience with the Deshmahne?"

Urik stared at his hands. "I had a family once."

"I know."

"As the Deshmahne gained strength in the south, they paid little mind to those they hurt. They had their demonstrations of power. They used that to help with conversions. My son... He was a casualty of one such demonstration." Urik fell silent, still staring at his hands.

Endric felt a moment of guilt at forcing Urik to speak of what had happened. It would be no different than forcing his father to speak about what had happened with Andril. Endric wouldn't ever imagine doing that to his father, not wanting to have him relive the experience of seeing his dead son's head sitting in a canvas sack on his desk. Endric didn't want to relive it. What had happened was horrible, the kind of devastation that some people never recovered from.

It was the kind of devastation that could motivate a man to betray those he cared about.

"Were you a historian before your son passed?"

"I had studied with the guild, but had not been apprenticed."

"Does that matter?"

Urik looked up. "You know nothing about the guild, do you?" It was a question, rather than an accusation. There was none of the heat or malice to the words, not as there had been before.

"I don't. Novan doesn't speak of the guild."

"He wouldn't."

"Why not?"

"Novan serves in a different capacity. He is unique among historians."

Endric snorted. That seemed an understatement. Novan was unique, and Endric thought that he had only barely begun to understand how—and why. It had something to do with the Conclave, though he suspected there was more to it than that. Novan had a role that Endric didn't fully understand.

"How did you join the guild?"

Urik sighed. "After I lost everything, the guild granted me an apprenticeship. It was offered out of pity, but I was determined to make the most of it."

"How long were you with the historian guild?"

"Until I joined the Denraen."

"Have there ever been other historians who became soldiers?" Endric didn't know of any, but if anyone would, it would be one of the historians.

"Typically, the reverse is true. Soldiers decide they've seen enough and choose a life less violent. Few have come this way."

There was a mournful tone to the way that Urik spoke that was almost enough to make Endric feel bad for the man. Almost.

It was difficult to let go of what Urik had done, and all the people he had betrayed as he had pursued his vengeance. There might have been a good reason when he had started; then he might have actually been hurt, possibly even enough to have an understandable reason to act the way that he did, but he had taken it to a place where it should not have gone.

Endric stood, but when he reached the door, Urik stopped him. "That's it?"

Endric looked over his shoulder. "That's what?"

"I thought you would push harder. I expected that your father had asked you to pressure me to share more with you."

Endric shook his head. "My father didn't pressure me to do anything. He gave me an assignment, and that was it."

Urik grunted. "Knowing Dendril as I do, I suspect there was more to it than that."

Endric didn't say anything. He knew his father as well, and there was something more to it, even if he wasn't entirely sure what it was. He was to have somehow gotten more information out of Urik, though he wasn't entirely sure what he was expected to get from the man. Was it only about discovering more of his history? Was there more to it?

"He's glad you're back," Urik said.

"Who?"

"Your father. He may not say it, but he's pleased that you returned."

Urik turned his attention back to the book he'd been reading and left Endric staring after him for a moment. Could he actually have been attempting to console him?

That seemed too much credit to give to Urik, especially after everything he'd done. Endric expected there was some ulterior motive, though he was at a loss to come up with what it might be.

He stepped into the hall and closed the door behind him, trying not to let Urik's comments get to him. He knew that was what the man wanted, and he couldn't allow it to bother him.

It was difficult. He had a hard time shaking the questions in his mind as he left Urik in his room, sitting alone, studying his books. Endric had a hard time feeling as if there were a significant difference between himself and Urik. Both had acted in their best interests, wanting only to find information that would bring them a sense of personal peace rather than focusing on the needs of the Denraen.

He pushed those thoughts away as he hurried along the hall.

7

The gate leading into the university remained closed. Two men stood stationed on either side of it, both wearing the dark brown robes that signified university scholars. Endric wore his own Denraen dress, the crisp, gray uniform with the crest signaling his rank. His sword was sheathed at his side, though he didn't expect to need it here.

"Why do you think we should allow you passage?" one of the men asked. He had a long face and a hooked nose. His eyes were sunken, but there was a brightness to them and he shone with intelligence. The man might seem unassuming, but Endric knew better than to believe there wasn't more to him.

"I am Endric Verilan, en'raen of the Denraen."

The man met his gaze unblinkingly. "The Denraen don't have jurisdiction on university grounds."

Endric nodded. Tradition had long held that the university patrolled itself and that the Denraen did not—and would not—interfere. There were times when that tradition was superseded by the needs of the city. During the miner rebellion, when the

Deshmahne had attacked, the Denraen had assumed control of the entire city. Their patrols had increased, and even the university had not been off-limits.

"Not jurisdiction. We aren't claiming the need… at this time."

He hesitated, leaving the words hanging in the air. It was enough that it should raise a question. These men weren't in a position to challenge him. They were simply guards, men assigned to prevent unauthorized access to the university. How would they know whether there was anything more taking place in Vasha?

"What is it that you need?" the man asked.

"I need to see one of the scholars." This was the way he should have approached from the beginning, rather than thinking to sneak in, but coming directly like this would create more questions—especially from his father—but not nearly as many as attempting to wander through the teralin mines in the dark.

"Which scholar would you request?"

Answering it the wrong way would raise suspicion. His presence would arouse a certain level of suspicion, especially as word got out that one of the Denraen came to the university. Not only one of the Denraen, but a ranking member. It wouldn't take long for a connection to be made between Endric and Dendril, and he doubted that much time would be wasted connecting the two, making his father aware of the fact that he'd come.

He wanted information before that occurred. He wanted to be in—and then out—before his father discovered that he'd come here.

"Elizabeth Greln."

The man's eyes narrowed a moment but then he nodded. "I can send word to her that you seek her for questions."

"Sending word isn't good enough. I need to see her."

"I can't guarantee that she is even available. Master Greln often keeps herself busy."

"I am quite certain that she will see me. If she does not, you can tell her that I threatened you."

The man started to smile when Endric unsheathed his sword.

"Don't make me threaten you."

"The Denraen don't have—"

Endric stepped toward the man and grabbed him near the neck. He twisted, preventing the other gate guard from intervening. "Don't we? The Denraen have jurisdiction everywhere. That is our purpose. Do you think the university is somehow excluded? I don't intend to ask again. Now. Take me to her."

He released the man's robes and pushed him back. The scholar stumbled toward the gate and cast a hateful glance at the other man. It could just as easily have been him, had he been the one to speak. Endric didn't care which of the two he threatened. He had no intention of harming anyone, but he did have every intention of passing through the gate and reaching Elizabeth. It was time for him to have answers. Time for him to know what had taken place in the city while he'd been gone.

Something had occurred.

His father had trusted Urik when he should not have. That told Endric that there had been enough of a danger to the teralin for him to need about to seek help from a man who had betrayed them. Endric wasn't even certain that Urik had done as needed. Perhaps he should discover what exactly Urik had charged and double check whether he had somehow influenced things in the wrong fashion.

The scholar motioned for Endric to follow, and they passed through the gate.

The inside of the university had less activity than outside. The streets outside the university were bustling with travelers, people who came to Vasha seeking the knowledge and wisdom of the Magi. Some came to Vasha seeking the temple here, thinking that the priests who served within Vasha somehow rivaled those who served in Thealon. Endric didn't know whether that was true or not but doubted that a proximity to the gods mattered, just as he doubted that having a temple sitting atop the mountain made a difference in reaching the gods.

Some came to Vasha simply to see it. It was something of a rite of passage, a journey many made as they sought to understand where they fit into the world. It made the city increasingly busy, far busier than it should be considering how difficult it was to reach.

Inside the university grounds, they were surrounded by scholars. Almost everyone wore the solid brown robes, and most hurried from place to place, not staring up toward the third terrace as they did outside the university.

The man guided him through the streets, leading him away from the central complex of buildings. Endric scanned the buildings, searching for something that would stand out, but there was nothing. He hadn't expected to see anything. When he'd come with Pendin, he hadn't noticed anything then, either, and that time he had come during a choosing, a time when the university selected new scholars. If they were to see anything, that would have been the opportunity.

They meandered down a few side streets, heading toward the wall that rose up to the second terrace, before the scholar stopped. He rapped on a heavy wooden door and waited.

Was this the same place Endric had come before? Was this the strange gallery to which Pendin's father had brought them as they had made their way through the city?

When the door opened, an unfamiliar face greeted him. It was an older woman who had dark gray hair and steely gray eyes. Her gaze swept up from the scholar to Endric before turning back to the scholar. "Why have you brought him here?"

"The Denraen seek Master Greln's counsel."

The woman *tsk*ed. "You take him at his word? Anyone could

come to the university and claim they were Denraen and demand access to one of the Masters."

"He wears the crest of en'raen."

Endric resisted the urge to glance at his uniform. He hadn't expected the scholar to recognize the marking of his office. He should have. The university scholars were nothing if not incredibly gifted. It was the reason so few were granted access each year. They were even more selective than the university in Thealon.

"Anyone could re-create that crest."

Endric realized that the woman's objections were not meant for him but for the younger scholar.

"He claimed himself to be the son of Dendril."

Had he? Endric didn't recall announcing himself as Dendril's son, though he had given his last name. Perhaps that was enough to reveal himself.

"Any man could claim himself to be Dendril's son." The fight in the old woman had faded, and Endric had the sense that she argued now simply to see what reaction she might get from this man.

"And he carries a teralin sword."

This time, Endric did unsheathe his sword slightly. How had they known that he carried a teralin sword? He had unsheathed briefly, for the barest amount of time, but certainly not long enough for the man to have recognized a teralin blade—hadn't he?

Maybe he had. Many of the scholars were related to miners. He wouldn't have put it past Pendin to have recognized the teralin blade. It was a unique sword, one that he'd found within Urik's quarters long after the man was gone. He didn't know the significance of the sword, or whether he was meant to find it, but he had carried it—and used it—in the time since then. It had become as much his sword as any that he'd ever used.

The blade was simple, but finely made. The hilt fit his hand nicely, and there was a weighting to it that felt right. He had often wondered at its making, wondering who would have forged such a weapon. Perhaps Urik, or perhaps Urik had discovered it somewhere within the teralin mines. That was equally possible, Endric realized.

"Many carry a teralin sword."

The man shook his head. "Few carry a teralin sword. Doing so affects the bearer."

Endric glanced at the man, who seemed to pointedly avoid his gaze.

"Indeed. Perhaps you are right to bring him to her. She would have words with him."

She waved a crooked hand and the man nodded before disappearing along the street, heading back toward the gate. How much trouble would he be in for allowing Endric access to the university? Had he satisfied this old woman by answering her questions? Would there be other questions asked of him? Not that it mattered to Endric—at least, not too much. He had questions, and he would find answers.

"Come. Come." The woman waved him to follow her, so he did, trailing after her as he headed into the room.

She shut the door behind him, leaving him with a faint, pale white light that emanated from two lanterns that hung near the door. The woman headed down the hall, and Endric followed. She turned a corner but when he followed after her, she was gone.

He paused. Where had she gone? There had to be some door that she had disappeared behind. Every question that she'd asked the scholar had seemed a test. Was that what she did now? Did she test Endric?

If that were the case, he wasn't certain what he would say that would help him pass whatever they might have of him. He wasn't certain what he might be asked to do to prove that he belonged.

He continued along the hall, listening for sounds of the old woman, but heard none.

The last time he had come to Elizabeth, there had been teralin involved. She had implanted it into the stone of the hallway, leaving it so that he had been forced into darkness, leaving him and Pendin wondering what was happening. He still wasn't entirely certain what had transpired, but wondered if perhaps she used teralin on him now.

He tried to focus on it, but there was no sense of it around him.

Endric decided to try a different tact.

He sat.

He waited in the hall, sitting there with his knees bent, his sword within easy reach. He wasn't certain how long he remained in such a position. Time passed, moments or hours, long enough that he lost track. Eventually, he noted a sense of pressure around him that reminded him of teralin though it was not.

That sensation passed, and when it did, he saw Elizabeth standing at one end of the hall.

She was short and petite. She had dark blue eyes that seemed to pierce him, as if seeing deeper within him than she had a right to. In spite of her short stature, she carried herself as a much taller and commanding person.

"Have you returned to destroy my son's career further?"

"Destroy his career? When I was raised to an officer, I brought him with me as steward."

"And then you disappeared. You left him without an officer to serve, and without any other rank."

Endric stood slowly, holding Elizabeth with his gaze. He hadn't considered how his disappearance would have affected Pendin. He had assumed that his father would have allowed Pendin to continue to serve, but Pendin had only been Endric's steward and had not had any other responsibility. Had Endric continued to gain rank, he would have brought Pendin with him, but without Endric, Pendin would not have such opportunities.

"I did not intend to abandon him."

"And Senda? Did you abandon her?"

"I didn't intend to abandon anyone."

"What do you need, Endric?" Elizabeth asked.

She was direct, and there was irritation in her voice. Endric suspected he deserved it, especially if she perceived him as someone who placed her son in danger and had potentially impacted his career in a negative fashion. Endric had not been the best influence on Pendin, and had not provided him all the opportunities that he deserved. Pendin was far too skilled to be held back by Endric's incompetence. He felt the same way about Senda, but at least she had not been held back by him.

"I need to know what happened to Tresten."

Her eyes narrowed and she looked past him, seeming to scan the hall. She stared into the distance for a moment before shaking her head and then waved for him to follow her.

She hurried along the hallway, taking a few sharp turns and then heading down a series of steps. Endric took them cautiously, remembering when he'd been trapped in a strange room the last time he'd followed one of the scholars down a series of steps. This time, Elizabeth guided him to a formal office, one that reminded him of the room he had occupied the last time he'd found her, though he suspected it was not the same one.

She motioned to a chair, and he took a seat.

"Is that why you traveled the tunnels? Is that why you ended up in the Lashiin ruins?"

"You knew?"

Elizabeth chuckled. "There is not much that happens within the mines that we aren't aware of. They might be shuttered, and the Magi might have seen fit to ensure that we don't have the same level of authority over them that we once did, but we still have our knowledge. That will not change."

There was likely more to it, but Endric didn't expect her to share that with him. Whatever secrets the miners had of the mines, it would remain confined not only to the miners, but to the university and those who controlled it. The Magi thought they controlled the mines, but even closed, they did not control them at all.

"What do you know about his death?"

"Death?"

"I had word that Tresten slipped and fell," Endric said.

Elizabeth watched him, her nostrils flaring as she took steady breaths. "I'm not entirely certain what happened."

"Then you know that he slipped and that he's gone."

"Gone. Perhaps that's a better way of putting it than dead."

"You don't think Tresten is dead?"

A hint of a smile spread across her mouth. "Tresten is far too capable to have slipped and fallen to his death. I think a more likely scenario is that he needed a way of maintaining his anonymity. That is something I would expect of Tresten."

Could that be why he had sent him the summons to return to Vasha? "It seems as if you know him well."

"There is no knowing Tresten. He is a force of nature."

Endric laughed, thinking of what he remembered of the Mage the last time he'd seen him. He was unlike any other Mage that Endric had encountered within the city. Most were reserved and barely came out of the palace. Not Tresten. He had come to the barracks several times to speak to Dendril and had ventured outside of the city to help them defeat Urik. Without Tresten's involvement, Endric wasn't sure that they would have managed to defeat Urik. He didn't think that he'd ever thanked Tresten for all the Mage had done.

"I'm trying to find out what happened."

"And what has your father told you?"

Endric shook his head. "He told me that he slipped and he fell."

"That much is true. If he has disappeared, he's done so for his own purposes."

"His disappearance has forced my father to use Urik to help him with the teralin."

Her mouth twisted in a frown. "Yes. That's an unfortunate consequence. I am surprised that your father would utilize Urik in such a way. I'm surprised that Urik would agree to help them."

"The last time I saw you, you made a statement that made it clear that you supported Urik. You agreed with what he did."

"Not what he did, but the intention behind it. Urik wanted the Denraen to confront the Deshmahne. There was little doubt in my mind that had he not, the Deshmahne would have continued to gain strength and the Denraen would have ignored them for much longer than they should have."

"There are other ways of facilitating what needed to happen," Endric said.

"With your father? I'm not sure that there were. Dendril can be… stubborn. It's a trait I believe you share?"

Endric sat back in his chair. It had a hard back and was otherwise uncomfortable, not the kind of chair he would have wanted to spend hours sitting in, not at all like the plush chair Elizabeth sat upon. Hers reminded him of the chairs within the officers' hall, the kind that he could sit in for extended periods of time. They were comfortable enough to relax within, comfortable enough that he could even fall asleep, were he given the opportunity.

"Why would Tresten have disappeared?" Endric asked.

"That is a very different question, isn't it?"

"Do the Magi believe him gone as well?"

Elizabeth shrugged. "If Tresten has decided to disappear, he would not do so lightly. He would make sure that there were no loose ends, and he would not have any who could claim that he still lived if he intended to be gone."

"But you believe he's alive."

"Belief and proof are different things. I believe that he lives, much as I believe he is connected to the world in ways that I don't fully understand."

He had the sense that admitting that was difficult for her.

"Why do you think he has disappeared?" Endric asked.

Elizabeth shrugged. "There are many reasons he might have chosen to disappear. He could have been working on something that he considered dangerous for him to remain exposed. It could be that he has decided that it simply was his time to disappear. It could be that he was simply tired." She smiled and spread her hands across her desk. "He wouldn't be the first Mage who has decided that he's had enough of the world and decided to separate from it."

"I've never heard of any others disappearing like that," Endric said.

"No? Are you so well connected to the Magi that you would have heard of this?"

Endric frowned. "I suppose not."

Elizabeth nodded. "Then do not suppose that you know all that the Magi might do."

The idea that Tresten would have disappeared troubled him. It was nearly as bad as thinking that Tresten had died, though perhaps not quite as unsettling. Thinking that Tresten had fallen had bothered him if only because he found it unlikely. It was almost as if someone intended to play a prank on him, to try and hide the Magi's disappearance. If he wasn't dead, if he had only disappeared, then Endric would have to be content with that.

Worse, he didn't think there was anyone he could talk to about it. Could he share with his father that Elizabeth believed that Tresten still lived? Would his father care?

Probably not. He would have told Endric to leave the Magi alone, to let them do whatever it was that they felt they needed to do, to avoid involving himself in the machinations of the Magi. It was good advice, but it was the kind of advice that Endric didn't think that he could heed.

Yet, he would have to.

"Is that all?" Elizabeth asked.

Endric sighed. "I suppose that it is. I came looking for answers. You've given me what you know."

"I've given you what I can," Elizabeth said.

"Does that mean you know more than what you shared?"

She stared at him, saying nothing.

Endric barked out a laugh. "You're much like my father, do you realize that?"

"Dendril does as he sees necessary. In that way, he and I probably are the same."

"And what do you see as necessary?"

"Only turmoil within the Denraen."

"Turmoil?"

She leaned forward and fixed him with her intense gaze. "You've been gone a long time, Endric. Many things have become unsettled in the time that you've been gone. Survey your men, discover what bothers them. Understand. Then you might begin to recognize what role you could play now that you've return to Vasha. It is one that is greater than simply ensuring Urik doesn't attack the Denraen again."

Endric waited for her to say more, but she didn't. He shook his head, realizing that was all he was going to get from her. It was more than he had before he'd come, but also less than what he needed.

8

Endric patrolled the yard, making a slow circuit as he observed the Denraen. So far, the men moved in formation, drilling with an intensity that they had not had when he'd been here before. Endric stood off to the side, watching the soldiers as they marched, noting the precise movements. Every so often, one of the sergeants would pause and make a few corrections before continuing.

Watching rather than actually leading led him to wonder if this was this all he was destined to do. He felt as if there should be more—that after what he'd been through, that there *would* be more—but maybe this was it for him. He had returned to the Denraen, thinking that he would take on a greater role with them, that after what he'd seen, he *needed* to take on a greater role, but since returning, he'd felt as if he weren't needed. Since returning, he'd been treated the way the Antrilii viewed his father.

Sound nearby caused him to turn.

He noted men practicing and was dragged toward them, as he so often was when sparring took place. It compelled him and he wanted to be a part of it, even knowing that he should keep his distance. They didn't want Endric working with them. Perhaps when he was outside of the city on patrol, there would have been a desire for him to remain with them, but inside the city, men practiced with who they wanted.

As he watched, he noted one of the men—a younger recruit he'd not met—used his sword sloppily. It was more about the technique than anything else. He didn't keep his movements as controlled as he needed.

The other man, an older soldier named Olivar, was much more careful with his attack. He used a steady sweep, each movement controlled, and had an easy time of defeating the other man.

Was this all they did?

There needed to be more to sparring. It had to be about learning, not simply going through the motions. That was how *he* had learned, first from Andril and later from his father, and how he had taught when they had been outside the city on patrols.

When the men were finished, Olivar replaced his practice stave on the rack. He nodded to Endric but said nothing.

The younger man watched Olivar as he departed. He had a dejected look in his eyes, one that Endric recognized. He had started to turn away when Endric decided to step forward.

"Your form is all over the place," he said.

The man paused and turned to Endric. He took in Endric's crisp, gray uniform, but no hint of recognition flashed in his eyes. Endric decided that was for the best. Maybe it was better that he not be recognized by Denraen soldiers. He could work in relative anonymity.

"What do you know about my form?"

A bit of attitude. That might serve him well. It reminded Endric of him when he had sparred with Andril. He had a streak that required him to challenge as well. It had gotten him in trouble more often than he liked, but it had served him as well.

"I know that you bring your hand back too far when you're moving through your patterns. I know that you open yourself up too much. It's wasteful."

The man pressed his mouth together, likely trying to decide whether Endric was high enough ranking that he needed to worry about offending him. Endric suppressed a grin. Had he been concerned about that, he would have chosen his words more carefully from the beginning.

"You think you can show me better?"

Was that a hint of interest?

Endric nodded and grabbed one of the practice staves from the rack. He swung it once, moving through a series of movements to loosen himself up, and then stood across from the young Denraen, holding himself at the ready.

"I think I can show you better, if you're willing to improve."

It was a similar thing that had been said to him before. Most of the ranking Denraen wanted only to help the soldiers improve. Few willingly faced anyone with real rank, something that did nothing to improve the skill of the overall Denraen.

"All I want is a chance to improve. They plucked me out of Gomald and brought me here but haven't been willing to teach me anything."

"Well, I'm willing to teach."

The man nodded and brought his practice stave up, preparing to attack.

The young Denraen, Bem, leaned forward, resting his hands on his thighs. Sweat streamed down his face and he looked at Endric with something that seemed almost appreciative. The man had improved. Endric had returned to the barracks yard each day over the last few, a way to break up the monotony, and had practiced as he promised with Bem.

"You keep pulling your shoulder back too much," Endric said.

"I have to. Otherwise your longer reach would sever my arm."

Endric sniffed. He was barely winded, though a trail of sweat did stream from his forehead, nothing like it did with Bem. "You have to trust the catah. If you don't, you will have your arm severed."

Bem had improved over the last few days, gaining more confidence if nothing else. His footwork remained jumpy and he continued to be sloppy with the sword, but overall there had been improvement.

He nodded to Endric and his jaw clenched, moving as if he seemed to want to say something.

"Get on with it," Endric said.

Bem stood and jabbed at him with his practice stave. "I know who you are."

Endric chuckled. "Is that right? And who is that?"

"You're the general's son."

Endric could only nod. Was that what he was now? Was he Dendril's son once more? Before leaving Vasha the last time, he had taken on his own role and had begun to serve in a leadership capacity. Had all of that changed since he had gone north?

He'd tried to push away the comments that Urik had made to him. It was difficult, especially as he made a valid point. As much as what Endric might have learned traveling through the north and working with the Antrilii, his departure had created a separation.

"Endric," he said.

Bem nodded. "That's what I said."

Endric replaced his practice stave on the rack and noted that a few other Denraen watched him. Each day there had been a couple, but today there were nearly two dozen Denraen who tried to remain unobtrusive, but they each watched.

Endric scanned the barracks, looking for sign of an instructor, but there was none. Where was the sword master? There should be someone—ideally, someone other than Olivar—who would work with the Denraen, especially the new recruits, and ensure that each of the Denraen was given similar levels of training.

"Work on keeping your elbows in."

He nodded to Bem, dismissing him.

The young Denraen hurriedly replaced his practice stave and joined a pair of the Denraen watching him. They spoke quietly and Bem glanced over his shoulder and motioned to Endric.

Dendril's son.

He had thought that he had moved past that, but perhaps he hadn't. Perhaps he never would. Maybe it didn't matter.

He turned away, thinking that it was time for him to go to Urik again and question him, when one of the other Denraen separated from the group and came toward him. "Are you willing to work with anyone?" the man asked. He had a high-pitched voice that cracked as he spoke. How young *were* these recruits?

As young as he once had been. Hopefully not as cocky.

Endric grunted. "Anyone who's willing to learn."

"I'd like to learn. I'd like to improve."

Endric glanced over at Bem, but the young soldier had already started away. Endric shrugged and grabbed another practice stave, tossing it to the soldier. He caught it out of the air and licked his lips, swallowing nervously.

"Show me what you know," Endric said.

The man nodded. He was more advanced than Bem, but his knowledge was somewhat stilted, his movements stiff.

Endric led him through a series of catahs, demonstrating first the movement and then the defense, the same as he had learned and the same as he had taught when they were outside the city on patrol. It seemed to him the best way to learn.

This man caught on quickly, and Endric progressed through increasingly more complicated catahs.

He lost himself in the patterns. There was a certain peace in flowing through the movements, the mindlessness that he fell into when he worked with his sword. It was relaxing, and the sword became a part of him, an extension of his arm, one that allowed him to strike and retreat before striking once more.

After a while, the man was replaced by another, and Endric continued to practice. He lost track of how many of the men came to him, content simply to work with the sword, demonstrating the patterns.

There was value in what he did.

He hadn't felt that way about everything in the time that he'd been back in Vasha. Watching over Urik might be beneficial for whatever his father planned, and it might be necessary given what had happened with the teralin, but it didn't help the rest of the Denraen, not in such a direct way. Teaching these men how to become better soldiers did.

After a while, the line of men dwindled to nothing and the last of them replaced his practice stave. Endric stood in the yard for a moment, watching patrols practicing their march and noting the way the men spoke quietly to each other, most laughing at each other, every so often glancing back at Endric.

He recognized that look in their eyes. It was the same way men had once looked at his brother. Andril had earned that respect. Endric wasn't entirely certain that he had—not yet.

Now that he was back in Vasha, he would. If he were to remain, he needed to.

Unless he didn't stay in Vasha.

That had never been a consideration before. While staying with the Antrilii, he had always planned to return to Vasha, but now that he was here, a part of him wished he would have remained. The merahl cub wouldn't have nipped at him for leaving the way that he had. There were always more groeliin to kill. And he could help. He felt that while there.

He had once felt that here.

Would he ever again?

With a sigh, he replaced his practice stave on the rack and headed back to his quarters.

9

Endric sat at the end of the hall. A few lanterns glowed along the walls, giving off a flickering light. He felt good. For the first time since returning to Vasha, his body felt invigorated, no longer stiff and sore from the travel back to the city. He'd been working with the Denraen in the practice yard, serving as something of a sword master, for the last few days. More and more men came to him, willing to face him. None gave him much of a challenge, though there was much he learned simply demonstrating the catahs for them. It required a preciseness to his movements and forced him to focus on what he demonstrated. It gave him purpose.

"Why here?"

Endric glanced over at Pendin. Since his return, Pendin had been quiet and had not spent much time with him. Endric assumed it was that his friend had other responsibilities. Since he'd gone away, Pendin would have been reassigned. He hadn't even bothered to ask what rank—and position—Pendin had taken on during his absence. Hopefully they could reconnect, and if Endric were to reestablish his commission, he could take Pendin on as his steward once more.

"You don't have to come with me," he said.

Pendin rubbed his eyes. They were slightly bloodshot, and he blinked. "You've been gone from the city for nearly a year, Endric. Then when you return, you're more interested in serving as sword master to the new recruits than you are in spending any time with your friends."

He shrugged. "You've been watching?"

"Watching? I don't need to watch. Most of the Denraen stationed in the city are aware of what you're doing."

"What are they saying about it?"

"That it's your penance for having so much time away."

Endric chuckled. Perhaps it was his penance. If it was, it was one that he deserved. More and more, he'd begun to think that he needed to pay a penance. He had left the Denraen for selfish reasons. They were necessary reasons, but no less selfish. He had broken his vows—his oaths—and so a penance was deserved.

"That's your reaction? You laugh at it?"

Endric glanced over at Pendin. "I didn't know that I needed to take them seriously. Besides, it's better than the last penance I served."

"You could at least attempt to be the person you were before you left."

"But I'm not the person I was before I left," Endric said. He wasn't sure that he knew how to be that person anymore. That man had still been selfish. There was much that he had done, thinking that he had needed to do it. Chasing Urik had been done for selfish reasons. Hunting the groeliin had been partially selfish, but there had been something more to it as well. It had been necessary, necessary for him to understand who he was and what he was meant to do.

"I can see that."

An uncomfortable silence fell. Endric thought about telling Pendin how he had gone to see Elizabeth, but decided against it. If Pendin was already upset with him, telling his friend how he had gone to his mother might enrage him even more. They were not close, though Endric didn't know what had happened between Pendin and his family. Whatever it was had kept them apart. It had something to do with the fact that Pendin had joined the Denraen, but it wasn't about that entirely. There was more to it than Pendin would acknowledge.

"I'm sorry," he said.

"Sorry?"

"I didn't think about how my departure would impact your career. I haven't asked about it since I returned. For that, I'm sorry."

Pendin grunted. "Your absence has made it difficult for me. When you were here, I was your steward, and that granted me certain freedoms."

"I'm aware of what that granted you."

"No. I don't think that you do."

Endric waited, but Pendin didn't elaborate.

"Senda could have looked out for you."

Pendin shook his head and laughed bitterly. "Senda? When she was promoted to Raen, she made it clear that she would not allow any favoritism."

It was almost enough to make Endric smile. He could imagine Senda being quite determined to prove herself, and part of that would likely have been wanting to avoid any illusion of favoritism. The easiest way to avoid that would be by not showing any to her closest friends.

"She would have asked you to prove your merit," Endric said.

"I think I've proven myself enough, don't you? She saw me when we fought in Thealon. She knows what I went through and what I was willing to do on behalf of the Denraen."

He sensed resentment in Pendin's voice. "Whatever happened, I'm sorry."

"Sorry." Pendin shook his head, letting out a heavy sigh.

"You don't have to sit with me," Endric said.

"I don't, but I was hoping…"

Endric waited for him to finish, but he didn't. Pendin looked at him and then rubbed his bloodshot eyes again before shaking his head and leaving Endric standing in the hall by himself.

What had happened to his friend in the time that he been away?

It wasn't only Tresten who had been lost. It seemed that Pendin had as well. Was that what Elizabeth had meant when she had referred to Endric's actions? Did she know something about what had happened to Pendin?

It seemed as if it was more than anger, but he wasn't sure why that would be.

He needed to find Senda and would need to ask her what she knew about Pendin and what had changed for him. And he would, but first he had other things that he needed to complete.

He pushed open the door and stepped inside.

The room hadn't changed much since he had been here over a year ago. It was Urik's old room, one that had been left untouched in the time that they had been searching for the man. Endric had been surprised to learn that Dendril had left the room alone, and that he hadn't given it back to Urik to use.

Dust covered much within it. There were a few books stacked on the desk and the bed was unmade. The wardrobe against the wall had not been opened in quite some time and cobwebs covered the front of it.

It seemed a waste having a room like this untouched and unused. There were many ways that this room could have been used, and he imagined that there were many Denraen who would be pleased to have such accommodations.

His father must have some reason for leaving it empty like this.

Endric wasn't certain what it was, and Dendril had been difficult to find over the last few days, making answers he wanted unable to be obtained by the general's absence.

Why had he come here?

Maybe he'd come because he wanted answers, but maybe he'd come because he was frustrated with what had become of him. He wanted answers, wanted to know more about what he had been asked to do.

The wardrobe was where he had discovered the teralin sword. It had been placed there after Urik's departure and Endric still didn't know why—or how—it had ended up there.

He pulled open the door. Dust drifted away as he did, clogging his nostrils. He wiped his hands on his pants, clearing the dust.

The wardrobe should have been empty, but it wasn't.

There was a roll of parchment propped against the far corner. Had that been there the last time he had been here?

He couldn't recall. It was possible that it had been, but he didn't know.

Endric grabbed the parchment and unrolled it. The words written on the surface were in the ancient language and he didn't recognize them. He stuffed the paper into his pocket and closed the wardrobe, standing in place for a moment.

As he turned to leave, he discovered Urik standing in the doorway.

"I saw the door open and thought…"

Endric straightened, gathering his thoughts and giving himself a moment to adjust to the suddenness of Urik's appearance. "Does it bother you that my father hasn't given you access to this room again?"

Urik sniffed. "I don't deserve to have access to this room. I am no longer Denraen. The quarters he's given me are more than I deserve anyway."

The comment surprised Endric. He would have expected more

agitation out of Urik, but this was a tone of regret. "We spent months searching through your room, searching for anything that would help us understand why you betrayed us."

"Months searching when the answers should have been clear, if only you'd been listening."

Endric frowned. "You don't think anyone was listening to you?"

"We've had this conversation before, Endric."

"We've had a conversation where you seemed determined to place the blame on my father and his unwillingness to do as you wanted."

"After what you've seen of the Deshmahne, do you still believe that I was wrong?"

Endric held Urik's gaze for a long moment before looking away. "I don't know what to think. It's possible that the Deshmahne would have attacked anyway." Endric wasn't convinced of that, though there seemed no point in arguing with Urik over that. Whether or not the Deshmahne planned an attack no longer mattered. The Deshmahne had only attacked because of Urik's influence. "How did you coax them into attacking?"

That had never been clear. He knew that Urik had a hand in the attack, but not what it was, not entirely.

"It was easier than you would think. They have a deep desire for all things teralin."

Endric grunted. "I think we've seen that, don't you?"

Urik shook his head. "It's more than the negatively charged teralin swords. They used teralin in their ceremonies. They use it for other purposes."

"What other purposes?"

Urik shrugged. "I never was privy to that. It was something that I wanted to understand, but I never managed to find the answers in spite of my studies."

"Studies. That's what you would have them called?"

"Would you call it something different? I studied the teralin and I searched for its importance."

"You knew that the Magi didn't need to use it to reach the gods."

Urik held his gaze for a moment. There seemed to be something he wanted to tell Endric, but he refrained. Instead, he said, "Yes. I knew it was not entirely necessary to reach the gods."

"Novan claims the metal is of some historical significance."

A smile tugged at the corner of Urik's lips. "Some?"

"More than some?"

"Teralin has been known through the years as a metal of power. There was a time when wars were fought over it. Men died to gain access to it."

"Because it could be used the way you intended to use it?"

Urik clasped his hands behind his back. "There was a time when teralin was better known. Even today, we know so little about it. What is known is gleaned from the past from those who had more expertise with it than what we possess today. The Magi know very little about teralin, though they would claim understanding they do not possess."

"How do you know that the Magi know little?"

"Think of the decorations throughout the city, Endric. Before the attack, most of the teralin sculptures were neutral. Had they known—and had they recognized the danger—they would not have left it in a neutral state."

Endric remembered Tresten making his way through the city, changing the polarity of the metal. Why had he waited until then to do that?

Maybe it was only what Urik claimed. Maybe there was no reason to charge it until it was necessary.

Or maybe there was another reason.

The negatively charged teralin influenced the bearer of it, which led Endric to wonder whether the positively charged teralin would have a similar effect. He'd been carrying a teralin forged sword for months, and though he wasn't sure if he had changed, he no longer knew whether that was true.

"How did you learn about charging teralin?" Endric asked.

"The knowledge is there if you know where to look."

"And you knew where to look?"

"The guild has access to such knowledge, even if they have never acted on it. None have ever wanted to act on it."

"Maybe they didn't act on it for a reason. Maybe they recognized that they shouldn't be, and that the knowledge of teralin, and the way that it can be used, was far too dangerous."

"Knowledge is only dangerous when you're ignorant of it."

Endric wasn't certain that he believed that. The knowledge that Urik possessed was dangerous. He had used it in ways that had harmed too many others. That was more than simply danger that stemmed from ignorance. It was danger that came from understanding.

"Has the guild attempted to punish you for your role in all of this?"

Urik sniffed. "The guild would love to have an opportunity to seek whatever revenge they think they deserve, but they aren't willing to risk your father."

Endric wasn't sure what to make of that. He had the sense that Novan and Dendril worked together, and they would have agreed upon whatever penance that Urik needed to pay. If Urik was here, it was because both had agreed on it.

Why, then?

There seem to be too many questions, and they all surrounded Urik and the reason that he remained unpunished and in the city. It bothered him, though he knew it should not. He should trust that his father knew what he needed to do, and trust that he understood what the Denraen needed to do, but he'd seen his father make mistakes, which made all that difficult for him to do.

"Why did you come here?" Urik asked.

Endric sighed. A hint of honesty would be the only thing that would convince Urik. "I'm troubled by Tresten's accident."

Urik sniffed. "You're still on that? He was old, Endric. That is all."

Endric smiled to himself. Tresten might have been an old Mage, but he was more than that, and if Urik didn't know, then he wasn't the one to reveal it.

"Why come to my quarters?" Urik asked.

"I thought you were accepting of the fact that this was no longer your rooms."

The corner of Urik's eyes narrowed. "They were my rooms for the duration of my time here. No one else has claimed them. What else would they be?"

Endric glanced around, noting the empty wardrobe, the bed that now had a layer of dust, and the stack of untouched books on the desk. He started out of the room, forcing Urik ahead of him. He closed the door behind him, locking it. "They are an example of a mistake made by the Denraen. It is one we will not make again."

As Endric made his way past, he felt Urik watching him and made a point of ignoring the other man. Had he pushed him too hard? Would he ever be able to find what his father wanted of Urik?

When he rounded the corner, he hesitated, waiting to see if Urik would follow, but he didn't. Endric wished he hadn't felt relieved and was embarrassed that he did. Why was it that Urik still unsettled him? Why *didn't* he unsettle Dendril?

10

Endric leaned over the desk in his room, the roll of parchment smoothed open in front of him, the words difficult to interpret. He had a book of the ancient language spread open next to him, but it had been little help in determining what had been written upon the parchment.

The lantern light in his room flickered, making him wish for one of the strange lanterns they had used within the teralin mines. Those had a steady light and required little oil, burning brightly with minimal smoke. As a ranking Denraen, he had access to the cleanest burning oil the Denraen possessed, but there was still a small haze that came off the lantern.

He sat up, rubbing his eyes.

He was more and more certain that the parchment had not been in Urik's room the last time he'd been there. Why now? And why was it written in the ancient language, one that only a few would be able to translate?

He suspected that Urik would have been able to understand what it said. Perhaps he should have given the former historian a chance to translate it, though depending on what was written on the page, he might not want Urik to have that opportunity.

There were others he could ask. He could return to the university and ask Elizabeth. He suspected she had some facility with the ancient language, and if she didn't, she might know someone who would. Doing that might open him up to more questions. And he had the same issues with Elizabeth that he had with Urik. He wasn't entirely certain where her allegiances lay. After her comment regarding the Deshmahne, and the fact that she believed Urik's attack had beneficial effects, he didn't know whether he should trust her.

It left him attempting to sort through it on his own.

The book he'd pulled from the Denraen archives was helpful, but using it to translate the ancient language was slow. The language itself was difficult, not only to read, but to speak, and he found his mind struggling through it.

There was a knock on his door. He looked up.

The door cracked open and Senda poked her head inside. "Are you busy?"

Endric shifted the book on the ancient language so that it covered up the roll of parchment. "I'm not too busy to see you."

She pushed the door open and stepped inside, closing it behind her. She wore her hair parted in the middle and braided on each side. Her eyes had a certain tension to them and her jaw was set, giving her an almost angry demeanor. He knew better; at least, he had. Endric no longer knew whether Senda was angry or whether this was a mask she had to wear as she led.

She took a seat across the table from him and crossed her hands in her lap. "We haven't spent much time together since your return."

Endric smiled. "Between you and Pendin—"

"Pendin. Yes. That's part of the reason I wanted to find you."

"I know he's angry that I was gone. The same way that you're angry that I was gone."

She arched a brow. "Is that right? You know this?"

"Pendin was my steward. My leaving placed him into a position of..." Endric wasn't entirely certain what position his departure had left Pendin in. He would have been allowed to continue to serve in some capacity. His knowledge of the inner workings of the Denraen would have been valuable, and Pendin should have been able to serve as steward to one of the other en'raen, though Endric wasn't certain who had been promoted. He hadn't taken the time to look into it.

"Pendin was demoted, Endric."

"Demoted?"

She frowned at him. "You didn't know?"

He looked down at his hands for a moment before looking up and meeting her gaze. "How was I to know? He won't talk to me, and now that you serve as Raen, it seems that you won't talk to me either."

"You could ask your father."

"If I could find him."

"Dendril has been busy."

"I imagine that he is. He's so busy that he can't even spend time with his son, especially after I was gone as long as I was."

"Dendril has more concerns than only his son, Endric. I thought you moved past that misconception when you were last in the city. If you haven't, then let me help you see that you are only a part of the Denraen. The general must lead all of the Denraen, which means that he must find a way to be more than any single soldier."

It was strange for him to have Senda speaking to him in such a way. It was strange for her to chastise him for selfishness. She had always wanted him to be more than what he was, and always wanted him to be the soldier that she saw in her mind when she looked at him, but she had never chastised him in such a way. It wasn't that he didn't deserve it. The gods knew that he deserved every bit of harassment that Senda could provide.

"What happened with Pendin?"

A debate warred across her face. Finally, she sighed. "It should be Pendin who shares this with you."

"He might have tried."

"Might have?"

Endric shrugged. "He met me outside of Urik's quarters, and I had the sense that he wanted to tell me something."

"Why were you outside of Urik's quarters?" She shook her head. "Maybe it doesn't matter. What did you discover?"

"I think he's still mad at me."

"Why would Pendin be mad at you?"

"Because I left. Because he wasn't able to serve as my steward when I was gone. Because he lost the opportunities that I afforded him."

Senda shook her head. "Oh, Endric. Pendin didn't lose anything because of you. When you were gone, your father offered him the opportunity to serve as his steward. Dendril had never taken on a steward before, but with Listain's death"—her voice caught, and he recognized the difficulty that she still had, talking about Listain —"he was willing to use more help. Since Pendin didn't have you to serve, Dendril offered him the chance to work with him."

Endric stared at her. If Pendin had been given the chance to work with Dendril, then it wasn't a demotion at all, but a promotion. "What happened?"

"Pendin happened."

"I don't understand."

Senda snorted. "You don't, because you have been gone too long."

"Help me understand. If there's anything I can do to help Pendin—"

Senda shook her head. "Pendin needs to help himself. He's been given every opportunity. If he's not careful, he may wash out of the Denraen."

"Wash out? This is *Pendin* you're talking about."

"And I care about him as much as you do."

Were it anyone else, Endric would challenge them, but he knew Senda *did* care about Pendin. They had been friends for a long time.

"He's made mistakes, Endric. He was lucky Dendril didn't demote him even further."

"What kind of mistakes?"

"The kind that nearly got men killed."

Endric took a deep breath. What had he been missing since his return? His friend needed him, and he hadn't been there. He had been focused on his frustration in finding Urik freed, and his need to understand what happened to Tresten, but he'd neglected the relationships that were important to him. Were it not for Pendin—and for Senda—Endric would have ended up as something else. He would never have managed to find himself the way that he did. His friends had stood by him, and they had supported him.

It was Endric's turn. Whatever had happened with Pendin, Endric needed to be there, needed to help his friend.

"You're telling me this because you think there's something I can do."

Senda nodded. "I've tried getting through to him, but I think it might mean more to him coming from you."

Endric thought back to the conversation in the hall outside of Urik's rooms. He wasn't sure that it would mean more to Pendin, but he was willing to do whatever he could to help his friend.

"Thank you for telling me."

"If you were more observant, you might not have needed me to."

Endric sighed. "I'm sorry." He fell silent for a moment, staring down at the book that he had pulled from the archives. Senda looked at it and glanced up at him, a smile on her face. "It's been hard returning," he said. "I hadn't expected that."

"What did you expect?"

"I expected that I would return to Vasha and I would be allowed to serve as en'raen once more. Instead, it seems that my return has only caused more problems."

"Your return hasn't caused the problems, Endric. The problems were there before you returned. You're only seeing the changes that happened in the time that you've been away."

He sighed. There had been many changes. The Denraen had changed, though maybe that was more about him than it was about the Denraen. After his time with the Antrilii, he had thought it would be a simple matter to return and to resume his place. He had thought that he had to come to terms with who he was as Antrilii, but maybe it was more about coming to terms with who he was as Denraen. That might be the more difficult transition.

"I've seen you working with soldiers in the yard," she said.

"Are you going to harass me about that as well?"

"Who harassed you about it?"

He shook his head. Senda already seemed to have a negative opinion of Pendin. That bothered him. It had been Endric who had been the one to have the negative opinions about him. Pendin had always been the one he wanted to emulate.

"It doesn't matter."

"I think it's good that you work with them. Sometimes the new recruits tend to get lost within the Denraen. Having someone with your skill to work with them, to demonstrate what's possible, is valuable."

"I'm not sure that I'm the one they should seek to emulate."

"Why not? You've gone from a simple soldier to an officer."

"I think my connection to the Antrilii gives me an advantage."

"Why would it?"

Endric met her gaze and realized that Senda didn't know. He wouldn't be the one to tell her the secrets of the Antrilii. "Only that I learned from my father, an incredibly skilled swordsman. While I was gone, I studied with the Antrilii."

She smiled. "That only proves that with hard work, even someone who's given a place of authority can rise to deserve it."

Endric laughed. It was nice sitting with her, having this quiet time. There remained something of a wall between them—an uncomfortable sensation—but he doubted that would go away anytime soon. When he'd spoken to his father, he'd left thinking that perhaps Senda had moved on. In a way, she had. She had been promoted and moved out of Listain's shadow. She had become a competent—and skilled—leader. He had seen the way the other Denraen looked at her, the respect that filled their eyes. He understood it well. Senda was worthy of such respect.

"What are you working on here?"

She grabbed the book and revealed the sheet of parchment beneath it.

Endric tried reaching for it, but she had fast hands and scooped the page off the table. Considering how quickly she reacted, he suspected she had seen it when she'd entered the room.

Senda flipped through the book before setting it back down. She held the parchment out in front of her, studying the page.

Endric was tempted to grab it, but he was in a strange situation. Senda outranked him.

"Where did you find this?"

"It was in Urik's room."

"We catalogued everything in Urik's rooms. There wasn't anything like this."

Endric unsheathed his sword and set it on the table. "Even after we catalogued everything, this appeared in his wardrobe before I left."

The teralin had a slight warmth to it, but less than neutral teralin did.

Senda considered the sword for a moment before her eyes turned back to the parchment. "Do you know what is said here?"

Endric patted the book that rested on his desk. "No. That's the reason I have this."

"It speaks of an event, but I can't translate it well enough to understand."

Endric frowned. "An event?"

She looked from the parchment over to Endric and nodded. "That's about the only part of it that I can translate."

It was more than he had managed. He had struggled through the language, able to capture a word here or there, but not enough to make sense of what was written there, not with any real context.

"It's odd, don't you think?" she asked.

"That it's written in the ancient language? Yes, that is odd."

"That's not it. In Vasha, there's much that's written in the ancient language. Listain wanted me to learn it, but he continued to assign the other responsibilities that detracted from time needed to understand it."

"What's odd, then?"

"The fact that you discovered it in Urik's room. Why would it be there, of all places?"

"You think it's a message to Urik?"

"Only if someone thought that he might be there. Otherwise, why would there be a message in his quarters?"

"We could ask him," Endric said.

Senda arched a brow at him. "Is that wise?"

"I don't know what is wise when it comes to him. If it were up to me, I would never have granted him such freedom throughout the barracks. My father obviously feels differently."

"Because your father had no real choice."

"There's always a choice, Senda."

She stared at him. "Yes. There is."

An uncomfortable silence hung between them. Endric shook it off. "What happened with the teralin? Why did my father need Urik?"

Senda stared at him unblinkingly. Endric wondered if she might not answer, but she took a deep breath and rested her hands on the armrests of the chair. "The teralin became unstable."

"Unstable?"

She nodded. "In the mines. There was… an accident. I don't know much more about it than that, only that several miners died."

Elizabeth hadn't shared that with him. He suspected she knew the answers to both and had not shared either because she wanted him to discover on his own or because she was angry with them. If she was so angry, she wouldn't have met with him. That meant there might be another reason.

"Teralin doesn't get unstable like that."

"Are you sure?"

Endric took his sword and ran his finger along the edge, feeling the heat. There was a sense to the teralin that he couldn't explain, much as he couldn't explain how he was aware of the negatively charged teralin when he was around it. "I can change the polarity of teralin."

"So I've heard," she said.

Endric didn't remember telling her directly, which made it likely that she'd heard from Listain. Or his father. "Having that connection to teralin allows me to understand it. I feel it, almost as if it's alive." He held his hand on the hilt of his sword, the connection to the teralin filling him. "Urik says that wars were fought over teralin. He claims men thought it was a metal given to them by the gods, a part of creation."

That explanation of teralin made the most sense. Teralin did have strange characteristics, and it was strange that it could be both positively and negatively charged. Why would that be? Why would a metal like that exist, one that seemed as if it cared not who held it or who used it?

It made him wonder what purpose the gods had for teralin. Why had they placed it throughout the mountains beneath Vasha?

"I've never known teralin to be unstable. It's either neutral or it's charged."

Senda shrugged. "Something changed. The metal became unstable. One of the mines collapsed."

"What did Pendin say about it?"

She shook her head. "Pendin had been demoted by that time. Your father wasn't willing to involve him."

"And Tresten had been gone by then?"

Senda nodded. "It happened several weeks after Tresten fell."

Endric stared at his desk. "Did anyone ever find Tresten's body?"

"His body? What kind of question is that?"

"Only that you've met Tresten. You know that he's uniquely gifted."

"He was observed falling."

Endric frowned. "Observed? By who?"

"By me."

Endric stared at Senda. If she had seen Tresten fall, then there could be no question that he had. "Where was he? Where did he fall from?"

Senda watched him for a moment. "Does it matter? All that matters is that he fell, that he's gone."

Endric resisted the urge to say that Tresten was simply missing, rather than gone. Hearing Senda's description made him believe even more what Elizabeth had shared with him. Maybe Tresten hadn't died. If any Mage could find a way to conceal their disappearance, he could see Tresten doing it. And what better way than to have Senda be the one to witness it.

"We need to get this page translated."

Endric nodded. "I suppose we could go to the university. Elizabeth would probably help."

That was not where he wanted to go with the parchment, but it was the place that made the most sense.

"I doubt your father would be too eager to utilize the resources of the university."

"Why? Elizabeth would help."

"Possibly. Even if she were to help, I'm not sure that we should accept her help."

"She was involved in your training."

"Which is why I know that she can't be entirely trusted."

"Senda—"

She shook her head. "I know that she's Pendin's mother. More than anyone else, I understand the difficulty that we have with not trusting her. I want to be able to trust her. I want to be able to use those connections that I once possessed. Especially now. I think that those connections would be valuable. But... I can't."

Endric watched her for a moment. "Then what?"

"You're not going to like what I'm going to say."

He shook his head. "If you mean Urik, I've already thought about it and decided that it wouldn't make any sense. If he was the recipient of a message, how can we trust him?"

"We don't have to trust him. We just have to trust that he will translate it close enough. We can always confirm whether it's accurate or not."

Endric didn't like it, but it made the most sense. He hated that they were pulling Urik deeper into the role of the Denraen, especially after what he had done, the betrayal that he had made to the Denraen. Yet with Listain's death and with Tresten missing—not dead, not that Endric would admit to—what choice did they have?

"Would my father know anything about the ancient language?"

"Probably, but he's gone."

"Gone?" Where would he have gone? Did it have anything to do with why he'd asked Endric to question Urik? "For how long?"

"Long enough that I'm not comfortable waiting for his return."

Endric wished that she might explain more, but he could see from Senda's face that she would not. He recognized that set to her jaw and the tension to her eyes. She had made up her mind. Now that she outranked him, he would just have to go along with it, regardless of how difficult that might be.

"When will we go to Urik?"

She shook her head. "Not we."

"But I'm the one who found this."

"And I'm thankful that you did."

Endric stared at her. So much had changed in the time that had been gone. He had changed. Going through what he had when he was with the Antrilii, there had been no choice. He was a different person, altered by everything that he'd gone through, and now at least partially serving the Antrilii. He knew their secrets, and he would not share them.

He had never considered the fact that Senda would change.

"Will you share with me what you discover?"

She pressed her lips together and nodded slightly.

At least there was that. He had to take solace in the fact that she might still confide in him. She was the Raen. She outranked him.

Hopefully, she was still *his* Senda.

11

The inside of the tavern was dim and run-down. A lutist at the back of the room played a mournful song, and a fire crackled in the hearth. The tavern was not full and those within it spoke softly, leaning over their tables.

Endric stood in the doorway, surveying the room. This was the eleventh tavern he had stopped in on the first terrace. None of the others had any sign of Pendin, and he was determined to find his friend and to understand what had happened in the time that Endric had been away. Senda had told him that Pendin would be found in one of the taverns, but had not known which one. Maybe she had, but she hadn't wanted to share.

The tavern stunk. This was one of the less reputable places along the terrace, one where the Denraen rarely visited. It was filled with people from the city, no travelers, and most of them were poor.

He noted a man sitting by himself along the wall. He leaned over a mug of ale, and two other empty mugs rested on the table.

Endric made his way over to the table and sat across from Pendin. “This is the tavern you choose?” Endric asked.

Pendin didn’t look up from his mug. “How many did you have to stop in to find me?”

“Most of them.”

Pendin grunted and tipped back his mug, taking a long drink. “Then I should have hidden better.”

“Why are you here, Pendin?”

His friend grunted again. “It’s a tavern, Endric. Why else would I be here?”

“Why this tavern?”

Pendin stared at his mug. “The others have asked me not to return.”

Endric sighed. Was that what this was all about? Senda had been so vague about what had happened to Pendin that when she told him to find their friend in the tavern, he hadn’t known why or what she was trying to hide from him. It turned out that she wasn’t trying to hide anything, that she wanted only to allow Endric to see the depths to which Pendin had fallen.

“What did you do?”

“Nothing more than you ever used to do.”

“I was stupid and young.”

“You’re saying I’m not either of those?”

“I’m saying that you should know better.”

Pendin grunted and finished his mug of ale. He set it down on the table and waved to one of the waitresses, who made her way over to him with another mug.

Endric grabbed it, pulling it toward him rather than letting Pendin claim it.

Pendin waved to the waitress again and turned his attention back to Endric. “If you’ve come to drink with me, then drink with me.”

Endric met his friend’s gaze, debating whether there was

anything more that he should say. How had it come to this? How had Pendin descended to this point?

"What happened?" Endric asked.

"You left."

Endric shook his head. "No. This isn't my fault."

The waitress returned, setting the mug on the table. Pendin grabbed it quickly and brought it to his lips, drinking deeply. He set the mug down and wiped his arm across his sleeve. "Now who's deflecting the blame?"

"I went to understand the Antrilii."

"You abandoned the Denraen. You abandoned me."

"My father made you his steward."

"Which opened me up to more scrutiny."

Endric stared at him, shocked at the accusation in the words. "You don't think you would have had the same scrutiny had I been here?"

Pendin took another drink, finishing the mug. This was not the man Endric remembered. Pendin was never the one to get lost in his ale, was he?

But then, Endric remembered seeing Pendin drinking too much in the time leading up to their departure from the city. And Pendin had brought a flask with him, one of the few of the Denraen who had snuck some out of the city. Endric hadn't thought of anything at the time, but now that he saw what had happened to his friend, he realized that there must have been more to it. Could it all have begun that long ago?

And had he been here, would he have been able to intervene? Would he have somehow managed to prevent Pendin from descending to the point where he had become little more than a tavern drunk?

It was a wonder that he hadn't washed out any more than he had.

"Why would you have cared, when you were doing the same sort of things?"

"When I took my commission, I wasn't doing those things," Endric said.

Pendin grunted. He reached for Endric's mug but Endric caught his arm, forcing it down. Pendin had always been strong, but either Endric had grown much stronger over the time that he'd been gone or Pendin had atrophied.

"Sure you were. You just weren't doing it out in the open anymore."

"You were with me. Do you really think I had an opportunity to drink when I was trying to understand my role within the Denraen?"

Pendin didn't meet his eyes.

"Tell me about your demotion," Endric said.

"You heard?"

"How long did you think to keep it from me?"

Pendin shrugged. "As long as possible. It's not something that I'm particularly proud of."

"What happens if you wash out of the Denraen? What do you intend to do?"

Pendin's brow furrowed and his eyes darkened. "I'm not going to wash out of the Denraen."

"Are you certain? To hear Senda tell of it, you nearly did already. Were it not for my father, you might have."

Pendin glanced up before looking back down at the table. "Had you been here—"

Endric shook his head. "Had I been here, I wouldn't have tolerated it either."

"But we're friends."

"Does our friendship mean that I should let you become something that you are not?"

Pendin didn't look up. He remained silent for a while, and when he did look up, his gaze lingered on the full mug sitting across from Endric. "Is that why you came here? Did you want to harass me?"

"I wanted to understand what happened to you. I wanted to see if there was anything that I could do to help my friend."

"If you wanted to help me, you never would have left the Denraen."

"I don't know that I could have."

Pendin looked up. His eyes were bloodshot and he rubbed at them.

"But that doesn't mean this is my fault. I have made my own mistakes."

"When you returned…"

"Did you think that you would be promoted back to my steward?"

Pendin took a deep breath and nodded. "I thought you would resume your position and that you would pull me back in to serve you."

"Even if I do resume my position, I'm not sure that you can serve as my steward."

"Why not?"

"I need someone that I can trust."

Pendin barked out a bitter laugh. "Trust? That's ironic, considering everything that you've done over the years."

"You're right. I've made my share of mistakes. I've made several men's share of mistakes. That doesn't make them any better. All I can do is try to make amends."

Pendin offered a sardonic grin. "If you want me to make amends, I'm happy to tell you whatever it is you need to hear."

"I've been gone long enough that I don't think it's what I need to hear that matters."

"What does that mean?"

Endric shook his head. "It's not me that you need to convince."

He pushed the mug of ale back across the table, and Pendin took it. Endric had a moment of hope that his friend would simply set it aside, but that passed when Pendin took a long drink.

"I'm here for you when you're ready to change," Endric said.

"The same way you've been here for me the last few months?"

Endric met his gaze. "No. The same way you were there for me when I needed it."

He stood and considered trying to drag Pendin with him, but it would do no good. He remembered how he had been when he was angry at his father and his brother, angry at everything that had happened to him. His friends had supported him and, because of that, he had finally managed to break free of the person that he'd been and had been able to grow.

Could he do the same for Pendin?

He had to. His friend needed that from him. Pendin had been there for him, no differently than Senda had been.

He clasped Pendin on the shoulder. "I'm here for you when you need it."

Pendin didn't look up. Endric didn't need him to but wished that he would have. He wished that Pendin would have stood, and would have followed him from the tavern, and would have returned with him to the second terrace and the barracks.

But he didn't.

Endric made his way out, hating that it felt as if he was abandoning his friend.

12

The steady clacking of swords filled the air. Endric moved crisply through his movements, demonstrating another catah for Bem, moving first through the pattern and then demonstrating the defense. Bem picked up on it, albeit somewhat slowly. He had improved in the days since Endric had started working with him, his skill gradually increasing to the point that Endric suspected he would become a competent Denraen. He would never be an outstanding swordsman, but that wasn't necessary. Not all men could be amazing swordsmen. Competence was enough.

He caught Bem on the arm twice, forcing the man to drop his practice stave. Endric stepped back, remaining ready, and Bem picked up the practice stave, shaking his head. "You're too quick."

"It's not always about speed. It's about recognition."

"Then your mind is too quick."

Endric laughed. "That's about familiarity. The more you practice, the more that you see the catahs, the easier it is for you to recognize them."

Bem tipped his head, nodding to Endric. He replaced his practice stave and started away before pausing. "Tomorrow, then?"

"I'll be here if I can," Endric said. There was no reason that he couldn't. He had no assignments. He tried finding Senda, thinking that she might have discovered something from the scrap of parchment, but he hadn't been able to find her, either.

A line of men waited for him and Endric nodded to the next, preparing for another attack. It was good to work with these men. The more that he did, the more he saw them regarding him with respect. Was that a secret his father had intended for him to learn on his own? His brother had always taken time to work with the men, though he had never made himself nearly as available as Endric had the last few weeks. Then again, Andril had more on his plate. His father had trusted him with real responsibilities, not at all like Endric and his lack of responsibility.

He worked with the next man, going through a series of catahs, noting the man's strengths. Every so often, he would pause, make a few corrections and suggestions, and then begin again. The man improved even in the short session, much as each of the soldiers improved. Many of them came on a regular basis. Perhaps not daily, but often enough that faces were familiar. He didn't know everyone's names—not yet, but he intended to learn them. He might not lead, not as en'raen as he once would have, but he could try to understand them.

When he was finished, another man stepped in front of him.

Endric blinked. "Pendin. You don't have to do this."

"You seem to welcome all comers."

Endric sighed to himself. "You're welcome to practice with me, but maybe not so publicly?" he asked, pitching his voice low.

Pendin sneered at him. It was unusual to see such anger on his friend's face. "Are you afraid that I might beat you?"

"No."

The bluntness of the answer nearly forced Pendin back a step.

"Listen. I'm happy to spar with you. I'm happy to do whatever it takes to help you. But if you do it publicly, I will treat you no differently than these men."

"You haven't lost that arrogant streak, have you?"

"This isn't arrogance, Pendin. This is understanding my abilities as well as understanding your limitations."

Pendin's sneered deepened. "Limitations?"

"You attack with strength, rather than focusing on technique. You have incredible skill, but you force it, thinking to overpower your opponent. Sometimes, strength is necessary, though oftentimes fluidity would overwhelm your opponent. You become predictable. You tend to fall into the same patterns, and though you learn quickly, you hate the fact that someone might be better than you."

"The last could describe you as well."

"It does."

Pendin swung the practice stave and Endric thought that he might attack, but he tossed it off to the side, stalking away.

Endric watched him disappear. He shook his head. He hated that this was the Pendin he had returned to. With everything else that had gone on, he needed his friend more than anything else. He needed to have him not only to bounce ideas off of, but he needed to know what really had happened within Vasha during his absence. Now that Senda served as Raen, he couldn't count on her to be quite as honest with him as he needed.

Endric sighed, tearing his gaze from the spot Pendin had last occupied. There was a line of Denraen to work with, men who were eager to work with him, who wanted to improve, and to had not sunk into self-destruction.

He would help them, but that didn't mean he could stop trying to help Pendin. If anything, Pendin needed him more than ever. Somehow, he had to find a way to reach his friend and get through to him so that he could become a useful soldier once more. If

Endric couldn't, it was possible that Pendin would actually wash out of the Denraen. That had seemed impossible only a year ago.

Endric motioned to the next man in line, welcoming him, and prepared for sparring. As he did, he couldn't shake the feeling that Pendin needed him and there was something he wasn't offering his friend, but how was he supposed to help him if Pendin didn't want help?

"Did you discover what it says?" Endric asked Senda.

They were alone in the officers' hall, the table laden with food tempting him, but when he'd seen her in the room, he'd decided to focus on getting answers. He wanted to know what she might have learned.

She turned toward him, her face an unreadable mask. Endric wanted to go to her, to touch her, to have that familiarity again, but there had been a distance between them since his return. It wasn't quite as great as the distance between him and Pendin, but it was distance just the same.

"Urik has given me his attempt to translate it."

"And?"

"Endric, this isn't something I can share with you."

He snorted. "You can't share? I'm en'raen—"

"You *were* en'raen."

Endric blinked. "Are you saying I've been demoted?"

"I don't know what you've been. Your father hasn't given guidance. He hasn't said that you can be brought back into the fold, but he hasn't restricted you either."

It was the clearest answer he'd gotten. Endric had felt a distance since his return, but had not expected that Dendril would exile him from the Denraen. Why would he, when Dendril had been the one to allow him to leave the Denraen? But Dendril hadn't wanted Endric to leave. He had wanted him to remain, to continue to train with the Denraen rather than head to the Antrilii, only Endric didn't think that he could be the Denraen that he needed had he *not* gone to the Antrilii to understand what he was.

"I'm still Endric. And you're still Senda."

He took a step toward her and cringed when she stiffened. Had so much changed for them that she was unwilling to give him the chance to be with her?

"I'm the Raen now. I have responsibilities—"

"And I was en'raen when we were together last. That didn't change anything for us. I've returned to the Denraen, Senda. I'm not going anywhere again."

She sighed and met his gaze. "If you've returned to the Denraen, then you will go where you're called."

"I will," he agreed. He didn't expect it to lead him anywhere—at least not for a while. He'd been gone long enough that he needed to remain in the city and to understand what had changed with the Denraen and why there was a strange sort of tension that he felt within the barracks. "What did it say?"

He stopped in front of Senda and wanted to lift her chin, to kiss her as he once had, but he sensed the reluctance within her and knew that if he did—or attempted to—she would resist. That wasn't the welcome that he wanted.

"It was a message," Senda said.

He stopped moving toward Senda and frowned. "Who would send a message using the ancient language?"

"You see the difficulty."

"I don't see anything. If someone wrote a message in the ancient language, it would be directed to someone else able to read it."

"Yes."

Endric took a step back and studied her. What was she not

sharing with him? When she'd served under Listain, he'd grown accustomed to her keeping things from him. Listain didn't want her to share everything, and even as en'raen, his rank didn't entitle him to knowing everything that Listain knew.

This felt different.

"Senda. What did it say?"

She sighed. "It should have gone to your father, not to Urik."

He grunted. "That's not surprising." What *was* surprising would be the fact that his father could read the ancient language well enough to be able to translate a message written in it. There were few who had such knowledge of the ancient language, and he had figured it would be confined to scholars like those in the university or the historian guild, or to the Magi.

Magi?

A message in that room, directed toward his father.

"Tresten?" he whispered.

Senda studied him. "How did you know that?"

"Who else would use the ancient language to send a message? And there's a reason it was in Urik's old quarters."

But Dendril wouldn't have gone to Urik's old quarters, and if Tresten knew that Urik wasn't there, he wouldn't have left it for just anyone.

It was where Tresten would have expected Endric to look and no one else.

"It was for me, wasn't it?"

"Endric—"

"What did it say?"

"The message was directed to you, but I can't confirm what it says."

"You don't have to confirm. If it came from Tresten and was directed to me, I need to know what it says."

"No."

"No?" That wasn't what he expected.

"I'm not going to argue with you on this, Endric. In the general's absence, I'm leading the Denraen. I can't have you disrupting that."

"I don't want to disrupt it. I want to know what message Tresten left for me."

If there was a message, then it meant Tresten really *wasn't* dead. It meant that what Elizabeth had told him was true. It meant there was another reason for the Mage's absence.

But if there was a message and it was directed at Endric, he needed to know why… and what it said.

"You have to wait for Dendril to return. I'll let him decide what to do with the message."

"And you won't tell me when that might be."

"I don't know when it might be."

He stared at her, frustration rising within him. He took a step back and crossed his arms over his chest. "Why won't you tell me? If the message is directed at me, I deserve to know."

"You'll have to trust me that I can't share with you."

"Trust?"

"Fine. A command. Is that what you wanted to hear?"

He frowned. It wasn't what he wanted to hear. What he wanted was for them to have the same connection they once had shared. What he wanted was for them to work together, and for him not to feel as if he'd returned to something he didn't know and didn't fit in.

Instead, he felt there was a greater distance between them than ever.

"I will follow my command," he said.

Her brow furrowed and she nodded. "I know you will."

13

Endric waited for Urik on the edge of the barracks. He finished his sparring session, having worked with each of the men willing to face him again, and now remained hidden in the shadows, scanning the barracks. He'd seen how Urik tended to wander. He was confined to the barracks level only, though even that confinement wouldn't restrict him from leaving were he to really try. He knew ways through the mines, which meant that there was nothing they could do that would completely restrict his movement.

Senda had asked Endric for patience, but that was never his strong suit. If the message was for him, if Tresten were somehow trying to get word to him, Endric needed to know. Senda might think that she were protecting the Denraen by not telling him, but there were things she didn't know.

Could this be about the Conclave? That had been his first thought after leaving Senda, after she had refused to share with him the contents of the message, but if this had to do with the Conclave, he would have expected the message to have been directed to his father and not to him. Dendril was an integral part of the Conclave and would be better suited to whatever secret Tresten thought he needed to share with the Conclave.

Unless it was something he didn't feel he could share with Dendril.

Endric didn't know where Dendril sat with the Conclave. When the Deshmahne had attacked and Dendril had been separated from them, he recalled a conversation where Tresten had chastised Dendril, making it clear that he needed to take a greater role with the Conclave once again. Maybe it was all tied to that.

He saw no sign of Urik.

He could wait. He needed to be patient, and that patience would be the way that he would eventually find Urik and discover what he'd learned from the message.

As he waited, he noted Pendin staggering across the lawn.

He was clearly intoxicated, and it was early. Was this the sort of thing that Pendin had been doing? Was this how he had been spending his time in the days that Endric had been gone?

With a sigh, he hurried across the lawn and grabbed Pendin, dragging him across the yard, propping him upright.

"Endric?" Pendin asked, slurring his words.

"What are you doing?" Endric asked.

"I was trying to find my way to my regiment."

"You're in no shape to find your regiment."

"No shape? I'm fine." He started to stumble, but Endric held him upright.

If anything, the time spent wandering the mountains with the Antrilii had made Endric much stronger. He had thought himself well conditioned before, but spending time there had disabused him of that notion. Compared to the Antrilii, he had not been well conditioned.

"I'm going to get you away from here."

"If you do that, I'm going to be docked for behavior."

Endric grunted. "I think you already deserve that, don't you?"

Pendin tried to pull away, but Endric held on to him. "Don't do this, Endric. Just let me go."

"The same way you let me go when I was acting like an ass?"

Pendin looked over at him. His eyes were bloodshot and his breath stunk of ale. It wasn't only his breath. Everything about Pendin stunk. It was a foul odor of stale sweat mixed with vomit.

They reached the gate to the barracks and Endric nodded to the soldiers watching it before guiding Pendin out and down the sloping ramp leading away from the second terrace. He had to fight against Pendin the entire time, struggling to keep him from falling over, but managed to keep him propped mostly upright. The farther they got from the barracks, the less Endric was concerned about discovery. What did it matter if others saw him escorting his friend away?

"Where are you taking me?" Pendin looked around and seemed to realize that they had reached the first terrace. "If you wanted to go drinking, you could have just told me. I know the perfect place—"

"You don't know any perfect place. You've been kicked out of all of those places."

Pendin made a face at him. "Then what are you doing? Where are you bringing me?"

Endric remained silent. He wasn't certain that this plan would even work, that they would even accept Pendin, but he needed to get him away from the barracks and needed to keep his friend safe somehow. Endric couldn't watch him, not with the level of intensity that he needed.

That left him with only a few options, but really only one good one.

As they neared the university, Pendin seemed to recognize it. "What do you think you're doing?"

"I'm bringing you someplace where you can't cause as much trouble."

"You're bringing me to my father?"

Endric glanced over as they reached the gate and shook his head. "No. I'm bringing you to your mother." He turned and nodded to the two scholars waiting at the gate. Neither had been here the last time. Endric pulled himself upright, thankful that he wore his Denraen uniform, thrusting his chest forward and hoping that his insignia of rank would draw attention.

"I need to see Elizabeth."

"No, he doesn't," Pendin said.

The two scholars glanced at each other before frowning at Endric. "The Denraen have no—"

Endric stepped toward the man who'd spoken. He was shorter and slender. "I'm very aware that the Denraen don't have jurisdiction. Or at least, that the university convinces themselves that they do not have jurisdiction. Either you're going to open the gate for me or I'm going to force myself in. If you think you can stop me, you're welcome to try."

"You wouldn't know—"

Endric ignored them and pushed past the two men. They tried to holler at him but he ignored them, hurrying through the streets of the university, making his way toward the same nondescript building Elizabeth had occupied the last time. When he reached it, he knocked, stepping back and waiting.

"You're a bastard, you know that?" Pendin asked.

"I'm a bastard who cares about you."

"I would never have done this to you."

"You would if it meant saving me."

"Saving me? Is that what you think you're doing? Bringing me here, to my mother of all people, isn't saving me. You're tormenting me."

"If that's what you think, I'm fine tormenting you, especially if it means that you're going to get the help that you need."

"My mother doesn't care enough to help me."

"I think you're wrong."

"And you know her so well? The one time that we came here has given you such insight into my mother's feelings about me?"

Endric shot him a look. "What makes you think that was the only time I've spoken to your mother?"

"When else did you speak to her?"

Endric sighed. "It doesn't matter."

Pendin tried to pull away, but Endric held on to him. Pendin fought until it became apparent that Endric wouldn't loosen his grip, and then he relaxed.

Endric knocked on the door again, waiting for Elizabeth.

He hadn't given much thought to what he would do if she weren't here. He supposed that he could find Pendin's father, though that would be a little more difficult. His father would be surrounded by others of the university, which made passing through more noticeable. The advantage of going to Elizabeth was that there wouldn't be many people to recognize them.

"See? She doesn't care enough to even answer the door."

"She'll answer," Endric said.

"And if she doesn't? What you intend to do then?" Pendin tried jerking away but Endric held firmly. "Just bring me back out. We can go to a tavern. You can drink and I'll watch."

"No more drinking."

Pendin grinned. "None? I don't believe that you will abandon drinking entirely. You like the ale is much as I do."

"I don't think there are many who do."

Pendin sneered at him. "You're just doing this because you're upset that Senda outranks you."

"If that's what you think, that's fine. If you were sober, you would recognize how ridiculous that comment is."

"Is it because your father released Urik? Are you mad that everything we went through means nothing?"

"It means something. We stopped the Ravers from attacking. We maintained peace in the north. And we managed to capture Urik and prevent him from spreading knowledge of teralin, knowledge that he intended to use for dangerous purposes. I know you better than this, Pendin. I know that you see how much we were able to accomplish."

"I see my friend abandoned me. I see another friend ignoring me now that she's reached the rank she's always sought. And I see a traitor roaming the barracks freely."

Endric glanced over and sighed. "If that's all you see, then it seems the drink has clouded your vision as well."

Pendin laughed. "It is ironic that you're the one who is chastising me."

"You said that before. I doesn't change the fact that I am the one here with you. The same way that you were there with me when I made mistakes."

Pendin opened his mouth but quickly clamped it closed.

Endric knocked again, this time pounding with more force. He needed to get Elizabeth to open the door, needed her to help him.

The door opened slowly and Endric expected the old woman to answer, but it wasn't her. This time, it was an older man, the same one Endric had seen when they first came to Elizabeth, guided by Pendin's father.

"You shouldn't be here," the old man said.

"I didn't know where else to bring him."

The man studied Pendin. "You're here for him?" He leaned in and his nose pinched as he took a breath. "Follow me."

The man guided them into the room. Somehow, it had changed from the last time Endric had been here, just a few weeks prior. How was that possible? It was a wide hallway, with portraits hanging along the walls. They weren't quite like the portraits that he'd seen the first time he'd been to visit Elizabeth. Those had a strangeness to them, a quality that made them seem as if they wanted to draw him into the picture, as if something were attempting to pull on him.

When they reached the stair, Endric grabbed the man's arm. "No games this time. I need to see Elizabeth."

The man frowned at him. "Games?"

"I don't need to be trapped in some hallway with teralin. Whatever test she thought she needed to use on us, I don't have the patience for it."

The man watched Endric for a moment before nodding. "No games."

They made their way down the stair. At the bottom, there was a massive teralin door. It was the same door that they'd seen when they'd come before. The man tapped on a few spots on the door and it slid open.

Endric waited, motioning for the man to lead him.

"I'm not allowed beyond this point."

"And I'm not going to go through here until I know this isn't some sort of trick again."

"No tricks."

Endric turned to see Elizabeth standing with her hands on her hips. She wasn't dressed like one of the scholars, but then again, she never had been. She wore a simple gray dress with a locket around her neck. Her eyes darted from Endric to Pendin before she nodded.

"Thank you, Petra. You may leave us."

When the man departed, she turned to Endric. "Why did you bring him to me?"

"I didn't have anywhere else to bring him. He's drunk."

"I can see that."

"It's not even noon."

"I'm aware of the time."

"Then you're aware that he's far enough gone that he needs help."

"Just bring him somewhere that he can dry out."

"Dry out? He's drunk and it's not even noon. He needs more than just drying out. He needs help."

"And what do you expect me to do?"

Endric was shocked by the response. He had expected that she would offer to help and that she would do whatever it took to get Pendin what he needed. He hadn't expected that she would refuse. That thought hadn't even crossed Endric's mind.

"You're his mother. I expect that you will try to help him."

"He left to join the Denraen. The Denraen should be responsible for rehabilitating him."

"If he stays with the Denraen, and if he remains intoxicated like this, he will wash out. Now, that might be what you want, but I know that's not what Pendin wants. He's a good soldier and he deserves help."

Elizabeth considered Pendin for a long moment, and Endric wondered if she would refuse again or if she would take pity on her son. He wasn't certain which it would be. Even if she decided to keep Pendin here, Endric wasn't certain that his friend would get the help that he needed. If Elizabeth was convinced she wasn't able to help them, there might not be anything he could do to convince her otherwise.

"He wouldn't want my help," Elizabeth said.

Endric recognized the hurt in her voice. Pendin's parents had been disappointed that he'd left the university and had gone to become Denraen. That didn't mean they didn't care about him.

"He doesn't want anyone's help right now. That's just the problem. He doesn't know what he needs. That's why we need to show him. He can't be given the choice."

Elizabeth sighed. "I will do what I can."

"That's all I can ask."

"How will you explain it?"

Endric hadn't given enough thought of that yet. He could claim that Pendin had been reassigned, but that would require Senda's cooperation. Would she help?

It troubled him that he had to even wonder. Senda cared about her friends and cared about Pendin, but she was far enough invested in her role that she might not feel as if she could help.

"I'm en'raen. I'll find some way to explain it."

"From what I understand, your rank means little since your return."

He frowned and nodded. "Maybe that's true. Maybe my rank does mean little, but that doesn't mean that I won't still serve as I'm needed to."

"And what does that mean?"

"I'm Denraen. I will do as I'm directed."

Elizabeth smiled. "From what I hear, you're more than Denraen. Perhaps it's time that you remember that."

Endric glanced around the room. Her office appeared the same as it had when he'd been here before. A stack of books on the desk looked recently shuffled through. He noted a map, though didn't recognize any of the lands pinned on it. A fire crackled brightly in the hearth, lending the room a sense of warmth.

"I don't know how to be more than just Denraen."

"Don't you? When you ventured north, what did you do there?"

"That is secrets of the Antrilii."

Elizabeth snorted. "Do you think the Antrilii are the only ones who know those secrets?"

"No." Novan and Brohmin knew about the groeliin. Brohmin in particular had fought them, though Endric still wasn't certain how he had been able to see them. There was supposed to be some trick to the Antrilii that allowed them to see the groeliin, a trick that Endric shared by his heritage. He wasn't certain why Novan was able to see them, but there was something different about Novan.

"As you've seen, there are those who share knowledge."

He stared at her. Was she telling him that she was a part of the Conclave? When he'd first met with her, he'd had suspicions, but there had been nothing to confirm it. And when he'd first met with her, she had suggested that Urik had been right in forcing the Denraen to confront the Deshmahne.

"I have seen that there are those who share knowledge. Are you trying to tell me that you sit among them?"

"There are many who seek understanding of the mysteries of the world, Endric."

It wasn't an admission, but it wasn't a denial either.

It wasn't Endric's place to share anything about the Conclave. He was not a member, and wasn't certain that he wanted to be one, even if it were offered to him.

"How do you suggest that I use my Antrilii connection while serving as Denraen?"

"What is the purpose of the Denraen?"

"The Denraen served to maintain peace. We serve the Urmahne ideals."

"Very well. Don't the Antrilii do something similar?"

He supposed they did in their own way.

"There are many ways to serve the ideals of peace. Don't think that what you've been taught, and what you've seen, are the only ways."

She stood and waved Endric away.

With a sigh, he turned from Pendin, who had remained silent during the entire interaction. Endric hurried up the stairs, making his way from the university, not glancing at the two scholars standing guard at the gate, and hurrying back up to the second terrace. It was a lonely walk, made all the worse by the fact that he felt as if he had abandoned Pendin.

Hopefully he had helped. That was all that he could do.

When he reached his room, he settled himself on the bed. Endric stared up at the ceiling, troubled thoughts rolling through his mind. Somehow, he would have to find a way to mix the two parts of him—both Denraen and Antrilii—but he wasn't sure he knew how. Maybe there wasn't a way. His father certainly hadn't managed to do it.

He glanced over and noted a note propped on his desk.

He grabbed the note, reading it quickly. When he was done, he frowned. What would Urik want with him?

14

Endric followed the instructions on the note that had been left to him, amused by the detail within them. Urik required that he follow specific steps, turning in certain places, and required that he pause to ensure that no one followed him. The level of suspicion in the note was funny, especially coming from Urik. Yet Endric's curiosity was piqued. He would know what Urik intended for him. He would find out why he'd sent him the note and requested a meeting, even if it meant following the strange steps.

The path led him behind the barracks. The instructions asked him to climb the wall around the barracks, and Endric glanced around before doing so. When he'd been younger—when he'd been more interested in breaking Denraen rules—he had climbed the walls many times. Never had he done so while trying to be mysterious. There had always been an intent to reach the first terrace without getting caught.

Had Urik known?

Likely he did. Otherwise why would he have asked Endric to come this way?

If Urik had known, it made it likely that Dendril had known.

And here he thought he'd been so clever back then. He thought he'd managed to sneak behind his father's back, to break out of the barracks.

According to the note, there would be a rope. Endric found it and climbed quickly, leading to the third terrace.

Once he was there, he jumped over the teralin gate and stood with the palace of the Magi gleaming above him. He didn't feel the same sense of awe that so many others did when in the presence of the palace, but that was more to do with the fact that he had grown up in Vasha, and though he recognized the power of the Magi, he didn't see them as nearly as intimidating as others did.

He followed the rest of the instructions and shook his head when he reached the Lashiin ruins.

"You could've simply told me to make my way to the ruins," Endric said.

He saw Urik outlined against the night. The man hadn't made any attempt to conceal himself. "Had I done that, you wouldn't have paid attention to whether or not you were followed."

"I think I can conceal myself."

"Can you? You remain close to Senda. She's like a spider."

Endric grinned. That was the first time he'd heard anyone refer to Senda in such a way. Listain had often managed to carry such a reputation, but Senda had avoided it for the most part. "Are you afraid of spiders?"

"Only when their webs are spread everywhere."

"And you think that Senda's webs are everywhere?"

"I know they are."

"I suspect I know way of reaching the ruins that Senda would not."

Urik arched a brow. Endric shook his head. "I'm not sharing any secrets with you. You're still a traitor."

Urik grinned. "A traitor that you felt compelled to come see in the middle of the night."

"I want to know what you told Senda about that note."

"Senda had no interest in the contents of the note. When she learned that it was directed to you, she pulled it back, thinking that I wouldn't have had a chance to read the entire thing."

Senda hadn't shared that with him, though he wasn't surprised that she would try to conceal the contents of the note from Urik. That made him feel somewhat better.

"It was from Tresten."

Urik nodded. "From Tresten. Directed to you. Interesting, don't you think?"

"Tresten and I had an understanding. I recognize the role that he plays, and he…" Endric shook his head. He didn't know how to explain why Tresten had grown to trust him. There had to be a reason, though whatever it was remained mysterious to him.

"That Mage is more talented than most. I suppose you know that as well."

"I had an opportunity to spend quite a bit of time with Tresten. I recognize what he was capable of doing." Endric shifted so he wasn't staring at Urik but instead looked up at the palace. "This is where I first met him."

Urik frowned. "In the ruins?"

Endric sighed. "After the Deshmahne attack. When they—when *you* allowed them to attempt an attack on the palace."

Urik grinned. "Yes. An attack that you thwarted. There aren't many men who would have been able to disrupt the Deshviili."

"Why were you willing to attack the Magi?"

"The Magi were never in any danger. Even had the Deshmahne succeeded in their attack, the Magi—and the palace—were protected."

"But the rest of the city was not. I lost a friend in that attack." He hadn't thought of Olin that often since then. They had once been close. Olin had always been quiet and somber, and Endric had appreciated his dry sense of humor. And now? He missed him.

"One life is a small part of a larger war."

"There was only war because you brought it to us," Endric said.

Urik studied him for a moment. "If that's what you believe, then perhaps there is no reason for me to share what was in the note."

"The Denraen would have eventually faced the Deshmahne."

"Your father was never clear about that," Urik said. "As I've told you, I tried to convince him of the threat, but they would not see. That is his failing. Sometimes, he does not look beyond what is directly in front of him."

Endric hadn't felt that way about his father, but then again, he couldn't deny that Dendril had been reticent to confront the Deshmahne. Even after Andril's death, he hadn't wanted to openly confront them. Urik bringing the attack to Vasha had forced a change in perspective and had forced the Denraen to recognize the depths of the danger the Deshmahne posed.

"And the teralin throne? What was the purpose of that?"

Urik's brow furrowed. "I needed information from Listain."

"But you didn't get it."

"No. He was... stronger... than I expected."

Did Urik know that Listain was descended from the Magi? For that matter, did he know that Senda was descended from them? Listain had been her uncle, and he had welcomed her in after her parents had died. Maybe Urik didn't know, and if he didn't, that was a secret Endric would hang onto.

"What was the throne?"

"Many of the artifacts stored in that chamber are felt to be remnants of a time before the city was here."

Endric glanced at the ruins. "You mean the gods?"

Urik shrugged. “I’m not saying that it’s true, only that some feel that those artifacts are the remnants of that time.”

Endric thought about all of the teralin artifacts that he’d found there. There had been neutral teralin, but there had been others that had polarity to it, hadn’t there? The throne… which polarity had it possessed?

It was negatively charged.

“Why would the gods have a negatively charged teralin throne?”

“Why indeed?”

“You don’t think these were from the gods, do you?”

Urik smiled. “You pay attention. That’s something your father lacks.”

“My father listens, but he does what he thinks is necessary. It may not be what you, or what I, think is necessary.”

“You don’t have to defend him. He’s not here.”

“And not in the city.”

Urik stared. “No. He’s not in the city, is he?”

“What was the throne?”

Endric felt the answer to that was important, and felt as if Urik were keeping it from him for some reason. Either he didn’t want to share or he didn’t know the answer. Either way, Endric wanted to know. He hadn’t seen the throne since they had rescued Listain from it and suspected that Tresten had done something to it, securing it and hopefully changing its polarity. Considering how few were able to impact the polarity of teralin, it would at least offer some protection.

“A way to torment Listain. Nothing more.”

“I don’t believe that’s true.”

“You can believe what you want, Endric. I don’t have all the answers. I didn’t have them then, either. I recognized the power that the throne offered and knew that I could use it to confine

Listain. I needed answers from him so that I could allow the Deshmahne into the city."

"All you would have done was destroy the Denraen. He would have destroyed those who had the ability to stop them."

"No. Those with the ability to stop them would have recognized their danger. They would have been galvanized." His gaze drifted to the Magi palace.

Endric followed his eyes and chuckled. "You intended to convince the Magi to act against the Deshmahne?"

"The Magi would be the only ones capable of acting against the Deshmahne. I believe you've seen them fight?"

Endric thought back to his time with the Antrilii, and their battle with the Deshmahne. Armed with the negatively charged teralin swords, they were incredible swordsmen and would have been deadly to the Denraen, perhaps deadly enough that there might have been nothing that the Denraen could have done to stop them.

"The Magi wouldn't have done anything, either."

"Perhaps not at first. Most forget that the Magi were once warriors. They need to be reminded of that."

It was something that he would have to ask Tresten about, if he could ever find the man again. What would Tresten's response be to Urik claiming that the Magi had been warriors and that they should become warriors once again?

"How many would have suffered?" Endric asked. This wasn't the conversation he had intended to have with Urik, but they were questions that he had anyway. He wanted to know why Urik had been so willing to sacrifice as much as he had. Why had he been willing to destroy all of Vasha for his revenge?

"As I said, it would have been a small sacrifice in a greater war."

Endric stared at him. "You have served both the historian guild and the Denraen, and you feel this way?" He had thought that Urik had been tainted by the dark teralin, but if he had been healed as

Endric suspected, the teralin wasn't the reason for this attitude. This was all about Urik.

"It's because I've served the historian guild in the Denraen that I feel this way. I have a perspective that so many lack."

"Why did you summon me here? You could have taunted me like this in the barracks, or you could have simply found me somewhere else. What is it that you wanted me to see here?"

"See? What makes you think that I wanted you to see anything?"

"You called me to the Lashiin ruins. We sit at the base of the palace of the Magi. And you're here, in the dark, wanting to conceal the fact that you called me to you. I think that there is something here that you wanted for me to know. What is it?"

Urik considered him for a moment. "I remember the day that your father sent you to me. I thought you brash, a skilled soldier, but never expected you to amount to much."

Endric snorted. "If you called me here to insult me, you could have done that in the barracks as well."

"Then you challenged your father. That surprised me. I thought I had everything well-planned, but I had not accounted for you, Endric. Your brother was so rigid in his beliefs and his viewpoint. He was easy to remove, and he had to be removed. Whether he survived the attack and returned with word of the truth threat or whether he died, either would have afforded me my goal."

Endric squeezed his hands together, fighting back the surge of anger rolling through him. "Do not speak of my brother in such a way."

"I respected your brother. Don't get me wrong."

"Are you going to tell me why you called me here?" Endric asked.

Urik smiled at him. "You keep coming back around to that, don't you?"

Endric breathed out, suppressing the frustration that threatened to rise within him. Urik was pushing on him, needling him in ways that he knew would cause Endric to react. He couldn't allow himself to be so predictable.

"Why here after Tresten left a note?"

"Now you begin to ask good questions."

"I don't believe that Tresten is dead," Endric said.

"As well you shouldn't."

"What do you know?"

Urik nodded toward the palace. "It's an impressive structure, isn't it? The Magi managed to create something quite amazing here in Vasha. It's almost enough to believe that they have the ear of the gods, as they claim."

What was Urik trying to tell him in his roundabout way? There had to be something to it, though Endric didn't know what the man was trying to reveal. Maybe it was nothing. Maybe there was no answer to what he intended to share, other than a way of taunting him and attempting to drag him away from the barracks. Yet he suspected there was something to what Urik was sharing. The man had his own particular way of doling out information. Endric had to be patient, and he had to keep from letting his frustration get the best of him.

"The stories claim the Magi pulled the palace out of the mountain itself," Endric said.

"Yes. There is a mystical quality about it, isn't there? But the stone is too white and practically glows in certain light. It's almost as if..." He shrugged. "That's not why you've come here, is it? You want answers."

"I'd like answers, but I don't get the sense that you are interested in sharing anything," Endric said.

"What answers would you prefer? What do you think I might have for you that might be revealed that you did not already know?"

It was a game. Endric could tell that to be the case, but that didn't make it any easier for him to stomach. "I think that I will take the slip of paper that Tresten left for me."

"Ah, you are mistaken if you think your friend allowed me to maintain possession of it. She feared what I might do with it."

"And what might you do with it?"

"This."

He launched himself at Endric.

It happened faster than Endric could react, and Urik's fist collided with Endric's temple, dropping him. Everything went black.

15

His head throbbed. Endric awoke to pain that pulsed through him, radiating through his head and down his body, trailing throughout him. Thoughts were difficult. It seemed as if awareness came to him slowly, as if from a great distance, and he recognized that it was because of the pain.

Urik had attacked him.

He blinked, looking around, but there was only darkness.

There was more than darkness, though. Endric felt a warmth, and he felt a strange pressure on him, one that was familiar and that he recognized.

Teralin.

Was he in the mines?

He would have to be, if Urik attacked him in this way and intended to somehow use him. He had let his guard down around Urik, a mistake that he should have known better than to make, and yet he had still allowed himself to do so. He had known that Urik was a planner and likely had been anticipating that he would grow increasingly complacent, which was exactly what had happened. Endric swore to himself. It was a mistake, and now he would pay the price.

He tried to move and found that his wrists were bound, as were his ankles. He was trapped. In the darkness of the mine, he wasn't sure that even if he weren't bound that he could find his way free.

The sense of teralin was all around him. It came from the walls of the mines but it also came from something else.

Were the artifacts nearby?

As far as he knew, the teralin throne remained somewhere within the mountain. Urik had some use for it—something that was more than merely for torture. He wasn't certain what that was, and wasn't certain that Urik would share, but there had been something to it, some use that he had intended for Listain. It was more than about torment.

He heard a soft scraping and turned toward the sound. A lantern glowed in the distance, the soft white light that he'd attributed to the miner's lanterns. They were Urik's creation. Tresten had shared that when they had arrived in the temple in Thealon, a gift of knowledge that Urik had offered.

The figure that approached became clear and Endric glared at him. "How long do you intend to keep me captive?" he asked Urik.

He chuckled. "Is that what you think this is? Do you believe that I've captured you to ransom you for something?"

"You waited until my father was out of the city. You used the note from Tresten as a way of summoning me. I think that you do intend to ransom me. I doubt the Denraen will offer much for me."

Urik chuckled and took a seat across from Endric. He had a lump of bread in his hand and tore off a piece, stuffing it into Endric's mouth. He had no choice but to chew. It was surprisingly sweet, and his rumbling stomach betrayed his hunger. Urik grinned at him and tore off another piece when Endric had finished chewing the first.

"I don't have any misguided belief that the Denraen will offer much ransom for you. Perhaps before you went on your little jaunt to the Antrilii lands, your father might have placed more value on you then. Now?" He shrugged. "You have value, but it's a different sort of value."

"What sort of different value do I have?"

Urik flicked his gaze around the tunnels. "I told you the truth when I said that you surprised me. I had not expected you to have a connection to teralin. When you challenged your father, you gave me an opportunity. I had not anticipated that you would turn that opportunity into a way of overriding my plans."

Endric grunted. "I'm sorry that I was the reason that you failed to overthrow the Denraen."

Urik shook his head. "No. Don't be sorry. I'm not disappointed that you revealed the secret of the teralin. I'm only surprised that it was you who managed to do so. And yet, because of that, you gained the attention of Tresten."

"So?"

Urik leaned toward him, a grin spreading across his face. "You don't know much about him, do you?"

"I know that he is a powerful Mage. I know that he possesses knowledge that few other Magi managed to possess."

Urik's grin widened. "Powerful, yes, but perhaps not for the reason that you believe."

"Then for what reason?"

Urik shrugged. "When we find him, you will understand."

"You know how to find Tresten?"

He nodded at Endric. "I don't, but he seems to think that you do."

Endric shook his head. "I haven't seen Tresten since we defeated you. Why would I have any way of finding him? I've spent the last few months in the northern mountains with the Antrilii."

"Why, indeed? I admit that it is a bit surprising, and I had not expected you to be the connection to him. I thought that perhaps your father might lead me to him."

"I don't understand."

"You will. I think that you are much brighter than you're given credit for." Urik stood and grabbed Endric's wrists, jerking him to his feet. "Now. I'm going to cut the bindings free from your ankles. You will walk, and if you think to try anything different with me, you'll find that I'm more capable than you suspect."

Endric glared at him. This was his father's fault. He had trusted Urik and allowed him to wander freely. But it was also Endric's fault. He had answered the summons, knowing that it was from Urik and knowing what he did about the man and the fact that he could not be trusted. That mistake had led to his capture, and now… Now he wasn't entirely certain what else would happen to him. What did Urik plan?

Urik cut the bindings and Endric staggered forward. They hadn't been tight—at least not too tight, but now that he was free, he was tempted to kick, to lash out, but he was curious.

What did Urik know about Tresten?

Then again, he wasn't sure that he wanted Urik to find Tresten. He didn't know what the man wanted with the Mage, but he had an unsettled feeling that whatever reason it was, it likely meant something dangerous for him.

Urik marched him along the tunnels. The lantern lit the way, guiding them as they made their way. Urik navigated easily, following some unseen pathway, managing to move through as easily as any of the miners would have.

"Where are we going?" Endric asked.

"When you discovered the note, it gave me an idea." They were descending now, a slope leading them gradually downward. "Your father freed me from my cell and forced me to charge the teralin for him, which I was more than happy to do, especially as it seemed to grant me some measure of freedom. I hadn't learned that Tresten was missing until much later."

They turned a corner, veering off what Endric suspected was the primary shaft. "Why did it matter for you?"

"Why? Because with Tresten in the city, I didn't dare attempt to escape."

"You fear Tresten more than you feared my father?"

"Feared might be a bit strong. I certainly respect Tresten in ways that I don't respect your father."

They squeezed through a narrow opening and Endric felt the pressure of the hot teralin upon him. All of it was neutral here, none of it charged, and he was tempted to leave a trail of positively charged teralin to follow if he were to manage to escape. He resisted the urge to do it, anticipating that if he tried it, Urik would know.

"Why now? Why did you wait until now to attempt to break free?"

"It was because of Tresten. When he sent that note, I knew that there was a way for me to use you."

"I'm not sure there's anything that you can use me for," Endric said. "Tresten helped me, but he did so because he was asked..." He wasn't about to reveal anything about the Conclave, not to Urik. Yet, from the hint of a smile on Urik's face, he wondered if the man didn't already know. It was possible that he had already learned something of the Conclave and that he had discovered that there were those who had a different sort of power and sought a different sort of purpose.

"Go on," Urik said.

"What is there to go on about? You've already made up your mind."

Urik grinned at him. "This has nothing to do with making up my mind."

"Then what does it have to do with?" Endric asked.

"You will see."

They continued walking, and it became clear that they were heading deep into the mountain, making their way through tunnels that Endric might have passed through when he had been chased by the Deshmahne. Then, he had run out of fear, hurrying to reach Vasha so that he could warn the Denraen. These mines were supposedly closed and he saw no sign of any miner and no sign of lanterns—not as he had the last time he'd come through here.

What would Senda think of his absence?

Would she believe that he had disappeared? Would she have thought that he'd taken Pendin with him? The timing was terrible. He understood how it would look. Not only would he be gone, now it would be Pendin with him.

That wasn't at all what he wanted for his friend.

They walked for what seemed an incredibly long time. Urik seemed content to remain silent and barely spoke, only motioning from time to time as he showed Endric which direction they needed to follow. They made their way steadily downward. Urik navigated the tunnels with expertise, and Endric marveled at how much the man must have had to study to master these tunnels.

Eventually, they reached an opening with light spilling out. Endric blinked against it and rubbed his eyes. Had they traveled all night? It had been dark when he'd gone to find Urik, and he wasn't sure how long he had been out, lying unconscious after he'd been struck. The throbbing in his head had eased the longer he had walked.

They emerged from the mine and out into the daylight. The air smelled crisp, mixing with flowers scattered in a field nearby. A few of the towering pines that grew along the mountains added their aroma. A cold breeze gusted out of the north and mixed with the warmth that radiated from the teralin, warmth that was both unsettling and comforting.

Urik stood for a moment, surveying the landscape around him. They had to squeeze through a pair of towering rocks to get free, and when they did, Endric couldn't believe how easy it was to access the mines. They were supposed to have been closed off, but what he saw was nothing closed off. Navigating through the mines would have been difficult, but it was not impossible to reach them.

That surprised him. His father should have secured them better, especially knowing what they did.

"What now?" Endric asked.

"Now? Now we continue to walk."

Endric grunted. "You won't make very good time on foot."

"We won't have to walk for long. Laurent isn't far from us."

"There are regiments of Denraen who patrol in Laurent."

"I'm quite aware, Endric."

That was what made Urik dangerous. His knowledge of the Denraen was extensive. He'd served in a role that had granted him access to knowledge and understanding, and he had taken that and twisted it, and now he was using it against them.

He had already used it against them when he had attacked, guiding the Ravers against the Denraen. This time, it was only Endric who was in any danger. None of the other Denraen were at risk.

He would rather it be him than anyone else, and would rather be the one to potentially suffer, than have others—new recruits like Bem—be dragged into a fight that they were not yet equipped to handle.

If Endric ever did manage to regain any significant rank, he would need to improve the training of the new recruits. Too many of them were unprepared for the dangers they would face. They were plucked from choosings, the best soldiers from each country, taken to be a part of the Denraen, but many still had so much to learn.

They walked until darkness fell once more.

When they stopped for the night, it was near a small copse of trees. Urik tied Endric's ankles, binding them so that he couldn't walk. He was then secured to a tree, in such a position that he wouldn't be able to cut himself free. Then Urik settled himself and fell quickly asleep.

Endric lay awake, his mind racing, trying to understand what had happened and how he had been captured, as well as what Urik might want from him.

Answers didn't come and he fell into a fitful sleep.

16

Endric awoke to a faint streak of light on the horizon. Urik sat upright, running a stone across Endric's sword, sharpening it. He glanced up the moment Endric awoke, as if he somehow were aware of it.

"I'm sorry if you didn't sleep well."

Endric grunted. "You could have cut me free and I would've slept better."

"I'm sorry that I couldn't do that, either."

"You have my sword."

"Is it yours? I seem to recall hearing that you found this blade in my quarters. That would make it mine."

"You would have had nothing to do with a positively charged teralin sword."

Urik chuckled. "Perhaps you're right. I've never been able to benefit from the positively charged teralin. I suppose that says something about me, though it could be only that I haven't yet learned the secret."

"Do you intend to change the polarity of it?"

Urik stared at the sword, running the stone across the blade. "I would never have guessed that the polarity could be changed. It was my understanding that once the metal was charged, it was permanent."

"Novan seemed to think otherwise."

"Novan always was the best historian."

He said it with a hint of disgust. What had happened between Urik and Novan?

"Do you intend to reach Laurent today?"

"We'll reach Laurent, and then we'll secure horses, and from there…" Urik grinned. "From there, you will have to wait to find out."

"Do you intend to torment me the entire time?"

Urik frowned. "Other than when I struck you to secure you, I've done nothing to torment you."

"Yet."

Urik smiled. "Perhaps you're right. Yet."

He stood and grabbed Endric by the wrists, jerking him to his feet again. They started off, walking through thick grasses, damp morning dew brushing against Endric's boots, darkening them. The air had a fragrance to it, one that was pleasant and familiar. He wished he'd brought his cloak and noted that Urik had one.

"Tell me about your family," Endric said.

"I don't talk about them," Urik said.

"You know about mine."

"Because I served with them."

Endric resisted the urge to call him out and resisted the urge to say something that he might regret. "Why won't you tell me about them?"

"I've tried to forget them."

"You'd forget your family? I would think that you would want to honor them and that you would want to do anything that you could to remember them."

Urik's jaw clenched and they walked for a while in silence. Endric was tempted to push him, to see if he could coax him into revealing more, but he didn't want to anger the man. Urik had proven himself deadly with the sword, and he was at a disadvantage, bound as he was. He needed to wait for the right moment, and when he found it, he would attack.

"You had two children?"

Urik glanced over. "Is it your intention to continue to question?"

Endric shrugged. "You've got me captive. What else is there for me to do?"

"Silence."

"Consider this my way of tormenting you."

"I could stuff cloth into your mouth."

"I think you enjoy talking to me," Endric said.

Urik snorted. "Enjoy might be a bit strong."

"How old would they be?"

Urik let out a frustrated sigh. "Josiah would have been twenty-two. Camira would have been twenty."

"And your wife?"

"She would be the same age as me."

"What happened with them?"

They passed a stream and Urik paused, leaning to take a long drink. He stared into the water, as if watching his own reflection. What did he see when he did? Did he see a traitor? Did he see a man who had betrayed the family that he sought vengeance for? Or did he see nothing like that? Endric couldn't imagine such betrayal, living with it day after day, and how that must have changed him.

Perhaps that was the reason positively charged teralin would not respond to Urik. He had changed himself, which in turn, changed the way that he could respond to the metal.

"I've told you. The Deshmahne."

"You've told me that the Deshmahne were responsible for their deaths, but you haven't told me how."

Urik wiped his arm across his mouth and stood, looking over at Endric. His eyes had hardened, taking on a dangerous glint. "And I won't. Do not ask me about them again."

Endric held his gaze and then shrugged. He leaned forward and cupped water to his mouth, taking a long drink. His stomach rumbled. The bread that he'd eaten in the tunnels had only been enough to take the edge off his appetite, but barely more than that. He needed more food. When they reached Laurent, would Urik get them anything to eat? Did he have money for supplies?

How much had he planned for this?

"Why are you so determined to reach Tresten?" Endric asked after they had walked for a little while further.

Urik glanced over. The hard edge to his eyes remained, but it had softened somewhat. "Tresten holds the key to something that I need."

"How?"

"So many questions. I would have expected that you would know the answers by now, but perhaps you were not as close to Tresten as I believed."

Endric laughed. "I could've told you that we weren't particularly close."

"Yet he left Vasha to help you. That tells me you were closer than you realize."

"Believe what you must, but I'm not sure that I know anything that will help you find him."

Urik grinned. "Perhaps you know more than you realize. We will see in time."

They walked in silence. In the distance, Endric saw the shape of Laurent come into view. He wondered if Urik would bring him into the city. If he did, Endric suspected he could raise enough noise to get himself free.

Urik answered that by tying Endric to a tree near another stream.

He hurried into the city, leaving Endric bound by himself. He tried to break free of the bindings, but Urik had tied a secure knot, and there was nothing that Endric could do to get free.

He watched the sun continue to climb in the sky and ticked off the time as he sat alone, waiting. Either Urik would return or some other traveler would come by. If they did not, he could linger here. How long could he last if Urik decided to abandon him here? Endric suspected that it was no more than a few days.

Late in the day, Urik returned, guiding two horses. One of them had a heavy pack and Endric couldn't help but be impressed with Urik's ability to obtain supplies. Had he paid for them or had he stolen them?

Urik knelt in front of him and removed the ropes from his wrist. "Up."

"I don't want to," Endric said.

Urik smiled. There was a hint of darkness in his eyes that reminded Endric of the teralin influence. After handling the negatively charged teralin, Urik had become more like the Deshmahne than the Denraen soldier he had wanted to be.

"What you want is no longer of any importance. Now get up before I decide to force you up."

"If you wanted a fight, you could have said so."

"I don't think either of us wants that, now do we?"

Endric glared at him. There were many things he wanted to do to Urik, and all included fighting. After what he'd done, a knife across the neck would have been the best. Maybe Endric should have done that before, ending Urik rather than leaving him to cause more trouble. Now he had to deal with all the ways Urik might cause him more problems, and that was *if* he managed to escape. That wasn't certain.

He stood, rubbing his wrists. The rope had cut into the skin of his arms, leaving them burning. He tried rubbing sensation back into his hands, massaging them until feeling returned. When he had an opportunity, he intended to attack Urik.

"I see what you're planning," Urik said.

"You see nothing."

Urik snorted. "You look at me the way I looked at you when I was trapped in Vasha. Why wouldn't I know what you were thinking?"

"I looked at you with pity in Vasha. No longer."

"Pity? Is that what I deserved from you?"

"You lost your family. I felt sorry for you with that."

"I never asked anyone to feel sorry for me. All I wanted was to convince the Denraen to recognize the dangers in the south. Had your father been willing to do that, none of this would have been necessary."

"Now you want to blame my father?"

"Should I not? Should Dendril be given a pass?"

"My father serves the Denraen. He's sacrificed more than you would ever understand."

There was a time when Endric wouldn't have understood how much his father had given up in order to serve the Denraen, but traveling to the Antrilii lands had given him perspective. He had gone thinking that he would gain understanding for himself, but he had gained an appreciation for his father as well. It would have been difficult for him to have made the choice to leave the Antrilii and serve the Denraen. It meant the appearance of an oathbreaker, something that his father might claim meant nothing to him, but Endric knew how valuable his father felt that his word was.

And now that Endric was an oathbreaker—though only to the Denraen—he understood how difficult it was to attempt a return. That had to be why his father had never returned to the Antrilii lands.

"Because of his ties to the Antrilii?" Urik leaned toward him, his hand drifting toward the sword. Endric resisted the urge to leap at Urik and reach for it. He *would* do it, but the timing had to be right. First, he would see the reasons Urik claimed he needed to drag Endric with him on this mission outside the city. What could he think he would find that would be worth the risk?

"You know nothing of his ties to the Antrilii," Endric said.

"No? Do you so quickly forget the time I spent with the historians? The Antrilii believe they have hidden themselves from the world, but there are those who observe and see, those who know what they have done. The guild recognizes and documents."

Endric climbed into the saddle of the horse, ignoring Urik. "The Antrilii know that the guild watches, and they have limited what they share. The only person who might be able to claim to know anything about the Antrilii would be Novan."

He glanced over to see what sort of reaction that might get out of Urik.

Novan had searched for Urik, wanting to punish him for what he'd done to the guild, but Dendril had been the one to hold Urik. Would Novan eventually come for him again? If he did, would Novan be able to free Endric? He didn't fear Urik attacking him. Had he wanted to kill him, Endric would already be dead. He did worry about what Urik intended for him and how he would use him.

What reason was there, though?

"You hold him in higher esteem than he deserves," Urik said.

"Why? Because he's managed to learn what you could not?"

"He knows nothing."

"He knows how to change the polarity of teralin. That's something you never managed to do. You were only ever able to charge it negatively."

Urik jumped atop the second horse and nodded toward the south. "And Novan only ever charged it positively. Did you ever think to question why that would be?"

"No."

Urik snorted. "Because he *can't* charge it any other way. That's the secret he didn't want to tell you, the same one that Tresten never wanted to share with you. They can change it from negative to positive because of what power *they* can access, but they can't take it the other way."

"Why would they want to?"

Urik shrugged. "There is more power than what you understand, Endric. You believe in the Magi and the powers they possess, and you've seen the way the Deshmahne claim power, but there are others—greater powers—that you have never witnessed. The world is full of mysteries."

"Is that why we're here? Do you think that you can find the answer to some of the world's mysteries? Is that the next place you think to pursue in your quest for power?"

"You say that as if there is something terrible about searching for power, but power by itself is not dangerous. It's what one does with it that makes it deadly."

"You only want it because of what happened to your family. For you, power is about vengeance."

Urik rode alongside him, forcing him to veer toward the south. Endric realized that Urik had given him the heavier mount, and the one that had been laden with supplies. He could attempt to dump the supplies and make a run for it, but even if he did, the size of the horse meant that it wouldn't be fleet enough to make a serious escape.

Once again, Urik had outthought him.

That had been Elizabeth's warning about Urik the first time she had seen Endric. She had wanted him to anticipate the ways that Urik might outmaneuver him. So far, Endric still wasn't able to manage it. Urik was a planner, and he had skill in thinking and anticipating. He would anticipate anything that Endric might do.

But he hadn't always anticipated.

Endric *had* beaten him… twice.

He could do it again.

First, he would have to discover what Urik might be after, and when he did, he could begin to plan for what he might do that would prevent Urik from gaining it. It was something of power, and it had to do with Tresten, but what? And why did Urik think that Endric could help him?

"Power is not a right. There are too many who have it who should not," Urik said. "I want to take it from those who do not deserve it."

"And who decides who deserves to have power? You?"

"Yes."

"What makes you think that you're the right person for that task?"

Urik rode in silence for a while before answering. "Because I have suffered and survived. I know what it means to have lost everything… *everything*… and still move on. I know what it's like to have nothing and long for *something*." Urik looked over at Endric. His eyes were haunted, still holding that hint of darkness that made Endric uncomfortable. "Why should I *not* be the one to decide who gets power? Why should it be the Deshmahne or the Magi?"

"What about the gods?" Endric didn't really expect Urik to answer, and he didn't, keeping his gaze fixed straight ahead.

17

They reached the plains of Saeline that night. The last time Endric had been here was when he'd been chased by the Ravers. Listain had been lost here. He doubted Urik had forgotten that.

Was there something he wanted Endric to see? Was that the reason he'd come here?

Endric had been watching Urik for the last hour, hoping for a sign of fatigue, but the man showed no evidence of slowing. Eventually, Endric hoped to stay awake longer than Urik and gain the upper hand.

When they stopped, Urik unsheathed and motioned with his sword for Endric to dismount. "Don't get any thoughts about escape into your head, Endric," Urik said.

Endric climbed out of the saddle and glared at Urik. "You think I haven't had them already?"

Urik chuckled. "Oh, I know that you have. I've seen the way that you're watching me. You think that I'll grow tired and that you can overpower me, but I've been waiting for this far longer than you will understand. Now, over here." Urik tramped down a section of the grasses and motioned for Endric to take a seat.

Urik gathered dried branches from a few of the scattered trees and piled them in the center of the trampled section. Within a short while, he had a crackling fire burning.

Endric welcomed the warmth. If nothing else, his time in the northern mountains, time spent wandering alone—often cold—had taught him to take advantage of times of comfort.

"What is your plan?" Endric asked as they sat there for a while. Urik had handed him strips of jerky, likely procured from Laurent.

"You're a part of my plan."

Endric looked around at the plains spreading all around them. The hills undulated away from them, a flowing grassland. In the daylight, it was quite lovely, a change from farther south where the landscape flattened as it headed toward the southern peninsula. A rocky coast surrounded everything there, but not so rocky and treacherous that the city of Gomald couldn't serve as one of the massive ports and a vital point of communication between the northern continent and the southern one.

"I gathered that I'm a part of your plan, but what exactly *is* your plan? You're after something with Tresten, though I don't know how I can help you."

Urik chewed on a strip of meat, tearing a portion of it free. "You're more a part of this than you realize. Tresten entrusted you with knowledge that he did not with anyone else. Perhaps you didn't even know that he had."

"Tresten didn't entrust me with any knowledge. He helped me stop you, but that was the only thing he did."

Urik chuckled. In the darkness, the sound was eerie and carried out into the night. A soft howl echoed distantly, far enough away that Endric didn't fear for his safety, but near enough that he was reminded of being tormented by the lacas while lying injured and near death a few days from the base of Vasha.

"Tresten helped you more than he has helped anyone else. That fact alone tells me that you have more knowledge than you realize."

Endric's gaze drifted to his sword, which Urik now wore. "Tresten didn't tell me anything about changing teralin's polarity."

"No, I suppose he didn't. He only showed you how it was possible and allowed you to do it on your own. Interesting that he would do that. Even more interesting is the fact that he knew how to do it, something that has been lost for countless generations."

"Maybe to you, but he's one of the Magi. Why wouldn't he know of it?"

Urik shrugged. "How many of the Magi have you seen spending time in the teralin mines? Most of them prefer to remain in the palace and only ventured out when it was necessary. Few bother to even make their way to the second terrace, and fewer still venture down to the first. Why would any of them bother to go into the mines, especially if it placed them into some sort of danger?"

Endric fell silent. He had no sense that going into the mines placed the Magi into any danger. Certainly, Tresten had not been in danger, and had gone there of his own volition, choosing to enter the mines and use what he knew to change the polarity of the mined ore.

Had Tresten shared anything with them? Endric didn't think so. Tresten had helped him learn what it took to change the polarity of teralin, but he seemed to believe that Endric would have had that ability regardless. It likely stemmed from his connection to the Antrilii, as so many things about him did.

What else could there have been? What other secrets could Tresten have shared that Urik wanted to know?

"I will manage to get away," Endric said.

Urik laughed. "I have no doubt that you will try, but whether you will succeed is a very different thing. You might be able to overpower me with your sword," he said, incredulity in his voice making it clear that he still struggled with how Endric had defeated him before, "but without your sword? You're less without it, Endric. Face it. You're a soldier. That is all that you will ever be. You're a skilled soldier, and have grown incredibly talented, but..." He smiled and shrugged.

The words stung more than any attack would have. Endric wanted to be more than only a soldier and had thought that he was becoming so, but if Urik was able to overcome him and out-plan him, then how would he ever be anything more than a soldier?

He fell silent and leaned back, looking up at the stars. A cool breeze gusted, taking with it the smoke from the fire. The wind carried a mournful whistle, one that reminded Endric of the sounds he had heard through the mountains near Farsea. Maybe it would have been better to have remained there, to have stayed with the Antrilii and continue to serve there. Maybe it would have been better for him—and the Denraen.

"If I'm nothing but a soldier, why do you care about whether I'm with you?"

"Because there are times that even soldiers hear things not meant for their ears. I think that you have observed many things above your station. Now sleep."

Endric avoided looking at Urik, staring at the sky instead. The stars shone brightly, light that some had called a reflection of the gods, a sign that they still watched over the people in the world below. Some believed the stars *were* the gods, that each one represented one of the ancient and nameless gods.

Endric doubted that, much as he doubted his role in the world. There had been a time when it had all been so easy for him, a time when he didn't question what he was to do, leaving him with a confidence in knowing that he was meant to serve as a soldier, but he'd begun to allow himself the belief that he could be more, that he was meant for more. And maybe he still was. He wasn't about to let Urik dictate what he was to do. Endric didn't often know what role he was to serve, but one thing he did understand was that Urik had betrayed the Denraen as well as the historians.

"When I'm free, I will make certain that you suffer."

Urik looked over at him, his eyes catching the shadows, making him appear haunted. "What makes you think that I haven't suffered?"

He scooted away from the fire and left Endric.

Could it be that all of this was still about revenge? The man had lost his family and he blamed the Deshmahne, but Endric didn't know the details about what had happened or why he had lost those that he had. Even though he had lost his family, it was the choices that he made that had turned him into a traitor. Urik had lost. He had suffered, and he had pressed on, determined to not let those tragedies define him. That was the way of the Denraen.

Which meant that Urik never had been Denraen. He had only pretended to be a soldier.

Endric took a deep breath, letting the cool night air fill his lungs. Those thoughts stayed with them as he drifted. He would escape. Eventually, he would find a way to free himself, and he would have to decide whether to get revenge for what Urik had done to him or return him to Vasha. He didn't know what he would choose.

He awoke from a deep slumber. It had not been dreamless. Endric had flashes of memories, images that came to mind while he slept, things that reminded him of his time while wandering the Antrilii lands. The dreams had been real and terrifying, but they faded the longer that he was awake. Why should he dream about the groeliin? Why should he fear them and a man with tattoos much like the Deshmahne—but who did not appear to be one of them?

There had been other dreams. He had flashes of memories, visions of challenging his father and wandering through the mines as he attempted to reclaim Vasha from Urik and his attack. There had been others as well, those like the Raver attack where Listain had died and the priests had been influenced by teralin. When Endric awoke, he suspected those thoughts were his way of working through what Urik had done, his way of trying to come to terms with the fact that Urik had betrayed the Denraen.

Maybe there was something else to it. Maybe it was his mind's way of sending him a message. What message was that?

Urik was already awake by the time Endric arose. He had put out the fire and buried it, shifting the grasses on the plains so that evidence of their passing would be concealed. It was a Denraen technique, and he was not surprised that Urik would fall into and do everything that he could to mask their passing.

As the dreams faded, Endric thought he knew their purpose. It was a new day, and he was determined to get free of Urik, regardless of what that required. He would spend no more time in this man's captivity. Urik had harmed the Denraen too much, and Endric would not be a victim to it any longer.

"You don't sleep like a soldier," Urik said.

Endric sat up and rubbed the sleep out of his eyes. "Is that meant as an insult?"

Urik grunted. "An insult? Maybe it is. I expected you to be up when the sun first crossed the horizon."

Endric glanced at the sky. The sun was well up and had already begun to burn off the morning haze. He had slept longer than he normally would. It was longer than most men of the Denraen would sleep, longer than Endric typically slept.

He stood, determined to ignore Urik and his insults and determined to discover what Urik intended. There had to be something that he planned and some way that Endric could turn it to his benefit.

How could he do it?

He needed to unsettle Urik, much as he had unsettled him in the past. He had the sense from his conversations with Urik that Endric managing to overwhelm him annoyed the man. If he was annoyed—preferably angry—he would make mistakes. That was one of the first lessons of the Denraen.

"Which direction?" Endric asked.

Urik glared at him. "You'll find out the direction we travel when you need to know."

Endric laughed, meeting his eyes, making a point of holding his attention. "I'll know the direction we travel a moment we climb on the horse. Unless you somehow plan to blindfold me? Even then, I'll feel the warmth on my skin."

Urik kicked at the ground as he reached the horse. He climbed into the saddle. "I don't intend to blindfold you. You'll be no good to me then."

Endric laughed again. "I'll be no good to you anyway."

"Now you think you have me figured out? You sleep through the morning and somehow you think this has given you the upper hand?"

Endric shrugged. "I know you."

He said nothing else, letting that sink in, letting the comment alone be enough that it could unsettle Urik. And he knew that it would. Urik had proven himself a man of pride, a man who believed himself superior. He was a man was so different than the one Endric had believed he had known when Urik served the Denraen. That Urik had been unassuming and quiet, a servant of the Denraen and a servant of the Urmahne. If teralin still painted him, and if teralin were responsible for the way he behaved, Endric would play upon that.

"You know the man I allowed you to know," Urik said.

Endric grunted. "Isn't that true of all of us? We're a different person to ourselves than we are to the outside world."

"Now you would philosophize? Men are defined by their actions. Your actions tell me all I need to know about you."

Listain had once believed the same thing, but Endric hoped that the old spymaster had discovered something different before his passing. "Then your actions would make you a traitor several times over. Is that the way you want to be defined? Is that how you want the gods to perceive you?"

Urik leaned toward him. "Do not *dare* question me about the purpose the gods have for me. I have a greater understanding of the world than you will ever possess."

"In spite of that, I've stopped you twice."

"Through luck. It was not through any skill of your own."

Endric looked down at the sword. *His* sword. "Luck? Did luck grant me the ability to defeat you the first time because it placed me in contact with the Antrilii, or was it my father?"

Urik's brow furrowed. "Your father had no idea what he was doing. Had Dendril known, he would have seen my plan long before."

Endric shrugged. "Perhaps he was caught off guard, but I don't think you surprised him the second time."

"Your father allowed me to bait him into a challenge. You are much like him. Impulsive. No foresight. No ability to plan and anticipate. Nothing."

"And you possess these qualities?"

"More than you will ever understand."

"What are you after? If you have me trapped as well as you think you do, and if you are planning the way that you claim that you are, what is it that you propose to do?"

"You're so certain with what you know, aren't you?" Urik said.

Endric shrugged. "I'm certain that I've seen more of the world in the last year than I ever knew existed. I suspect I know even more about some things than you do, despite your claims to the alternative. I believe that my Antrilii heritage connects me to the past—and to the gods—in a way that you can only dream of." Endric twisted so that he could fix Urik with a hard glare. "And I am certain that I will escape, and that you will suffer for what you have done to the Denraen."

"Only if I let you live."

"Your threat's an empty one. If you had any intent to end my life, you would have done so long ago. No. You need me for something."

Urik grabbed the reins and pulled, leading the horses away. They traveled south, veering across the thick grass, occasional blades scratching at Endric's legs. Dew dampened his pants and boots.

"You have it all figured out, don't you?" Urik asked. "Everything other than the fact that you know nothing. You think that you know so much more than you do. Ignorance can be dangerous, and in your case, it might be deadly."

"For who?"

Urik glanced over. "For you. For the Denraen. For everyone."

Endric watched him, thinking that he was boasting again and that Urik intended to torment him, but he sensed no boasting from the man, nothing that would make Endric believe that he was anything other than honest.

That might be even more concerning.

18

Endric thought he figured out which direction they headed by the end of the third day of captivity. They traveled south, but also easterly. When they reached the Rondall River, Urik wandered upstream until they found a passable bridge. On the other side of the bridge, they would pass from Gom Aaldia and into Thealon.

Each place they traveled left him with memories of people he had lost. Endric had come through here, facing the Ravers, and had lost Denraen who had agreed to travel with him, men who were good soldiers, skilled warriors, and who had given up their lives in service of an ideal. Endric had nearly died countless times on that journey, but only once had he done so because it would have served the Denraen. The others had been a sacrifice he had been willing to make on behalf of his friends—and Senda in particular.

His father had believed that he served the Denraen and that he had fought honorably, but Endric knew the truth. He knew that he had been selfish. Had he not, and had he been willing to make the necessary sacrifice, one that may have resulted in the loss of Senda, the Denraen may have held onto a valuable leader in Listain.

They paused at the river's edge, letting the horses drink. Urik granted Endric a reprieve, long enough for him to quench his thirst as well. Endric was reminded of a conversation he'd had along the river, when he had first learned of Senda's connection to Listain, and to the Magi.

He looked up to see Urik watching him. Endric wiped his hands on his pants and straightened his back. "Did you know Listain was descended from the Magi?" he asked Urik.

Urik blinked. "That's the question that comes to your mind as we stand along the edge of the Rondall?"

Endric shrugged. "It's one of the questions that comes to mind. Did you know?"

Urik's mouth tensed and his jaw opened and closed before he finally sighed. "Not while I was in Vasha. Listain managed to conceal his connections to the Magi. I should have known. He would have had to have connections to the Magi in order to know about the tunnels beneath the city."

"Not necessarily." Urik frowned. "The miners might have guided him otherwise. Especially the master miners in the university. They would've had access to any of the tunnels and would have known how they interconnect even more than the Magi."

Urik flashed a half smile. "There is a difference between the mines and the tunnels Listain used. His were older than those of the mine. Those connections were there from the very beginning, built at the time of the city's construction."

"How did you discover them?" When Urik frowned again, Endric pushed. "You had to have learned about the tunnels somewhere. You used them to attack Listain and drag him off."

"Did I? Or was it the Deshmahne who did that?"

Endric shook his head. He stood at the edge of the water,

scratching the toe of his boot in the sand and making an absent-minded pattern as he did.

Urik pushed him back and sent him staggering. He caught himself and considered lunging at Urik, but decided otherwise. If he would have, he might have sent Urik into the river, but he would still be bound. He didn't want Urik to escape. He wanted to ensure that he captured the traitor and that Urik would be punished for what he had done.

"What was that—"

Urik stared at the ground. "Where did you see that pattern?"

Endric stared at him incredulously. "What pattern?"

Urik pointed toward the ground where Endric had been dragging his toes through the sand. "This pattern. Where did you see it?"

Endric approached slowly, cautiously. He looked at the ground, trying to figure out what it was that had unsettled Urik the way that it had. The pattern was a strange one, one that appeared to be an incomplete triangle, with one line bent in, crossing the other. An eye was made around that line.

Why *would* he have made a shape like that?

He must've seen it somewhere. Was it something he'd seen in the Antrilii lands? There were plenty of patterns that he had observed there, and the Antrilii used shapes—and languages—that no longer were utilized. "Probably in the north," Endric said.

"This isn't a pattern of the Antrilii," Urik said.

"If not the Antrilii, what is that?"

"You really don't recognize it?"

Endric shrugged. "I don't know why I would be expected to recognize that."

"You don't know... You *drew* it. That's why you would be expected to recognize it."

Endric snorted. "I must've seen it somewhere."

"That's what I'm trying to get out of you, Endric. Where did you see this?"

Endric studied Urik. Whatever this shape was, it was important to him. He could use that and try to get information out of the man. "Tell me where we're going."

Urik stalked toward him. One hand was near the hilt of the sword, but he left it sheathed. "That's not how this works. You will tell me what I want to know."

"For what?" Urik's brow furrowed. "If you kill me, you won't find out what you want to know and you won't be able to use me for whatever purpose you intend by bringing me into Thealon. It seems that bargaining is the only way you'll find out what you want." He held Urik's gaze, making a point of not looking away.

Urik's jaw clenched but he said nothing. He grabbed the reins of the horses and led them along the edge of the river, toward the bridge.

The bridge crossing the Rondall was made entirely of stone. It had been constructed long enough ago that the stones had weathered and faded. It was solid and had withstood countless storms over the years, and it remained one of the safest places to cross the river outside of cities like Chrysia and Riverbranch. The Denraen used this crossing frequently.

In times of war between Thealon and Gom Aaldia, the bridge was contested. The last war between these nations had been dozens of years ago, though there was always an edge between them. Endric had read books about how to best defend the bridge, and there had been entire war plans drafted on maintaining access between the nations. It was a safer way to cross than trying to go through one of the cities.

"Why do you care so much about that symbol," Endric asked as they neared the edge of the bridge.

Urik looked over, glaring at him. "You will tell me where you saw that."

"I've told you my price."

"It is not a negotiation."

Endric shrugged. "Everything is a negotiation."

He pursed his lips. "Is that something your father taught you?"

Endric sniffed. "No. Listain."

Urik glared at him for another moment before leading the horses across the stone bridge. When they reached the peak of the arch, Endric saw movement in the distance. Even from his position, he could see horses and the gleam of the sun off metal armor. Soldiers.

In Thealon, soldiers could be either the Denraen or the Ur. Both patrolled widely, and Endric would receive a different welcome from either.

Urik noted it as well. "Don't get any ideas about escape."

"You mean don't get any *new* ideas?" Endric asked. "I can assure you, I've had plenty of ideas about escape. In fact, I might even leave that symbol burned into your flesh when I escape."

Urik sneered at him. "I thought I was the one with the edge of darkness to him."

"All men have darkness within them. It's how much they let it out."

"Another thing that Listain told you?"

Endric shook his head. "Not Listain. That was my brother."

He held Urik's gaze, forcing the man to focus on him. Speaking of Andril was always difficult for Endric, and it always left him with an unsettled feeling and an emptiness. So much had been lost through Andril's death, but no longer could Endric deny that he had gained as well. That made him uncomfortable and left him wondering if Andril's death had been something desired by the gods all along. He had no idea why that should be, but would he have accomplished half of what he had if Andril still lived?

That was the dark line of thinking and not a way that he wanted to consider his brother. Maybe if his brother had lived,

Dendril would have forced Endric to the north to meet with the Antrilii regardless.

Urik hurried along the bridge, reaching the other shore. From the shoreline, it was difficult to tell whether the soldiers they had seen from a higher vantage had noticed them. If they were any kind of soldier, they would have.

Urik must have had the same thought. He urged the horses across the ground, kicking them forward at a faster pace than they had ridden before.

They traveled east, which meant that if they continued in this direction, they would eventually come across the city of Thealon and the Tower of the Gods. Was that where Urik brought him? He had been housed by the Urmahne priests before and had been given safe passage, but that had been when he had used negatively charged teralin to influence them. Without that, would the priests be as welcoming as they had been before?

They rode until the soldiers were no longer visible in the distance.

Urik finally slowed, and though they took a slower pace, tension was evident in his posture and the way that he scanned the horizon.

"A Denraen patrol will be more than you can manage," he told Urik.

"We won't encounter any Denraen patrols," he said.

"The Denraen patrol in Thealon as much as they patrol anywhere else. Perhaps more."

Urik grunted. "Not more. The Denraen rely upon the Ur to patrol in Thealon. Your father thinks that they can extend their reach more by allowing the Ur to provide that coverage."

Endric laughed and shook his head. "My father wouldn't do that, not after the way that you showed the Ur were so easily influenced. He'd prefer to have soldiers under his command."

"I've spent more time with your father over the last few months than you have. I know how he thinks, much like I know how you think."

"You keep making assumptions that you know about me, but I don't think you know nearly as much as you believe. If you knew what you thought that you did, you would have known what that symbol meant."

Endric was determined to use that symbol to his advantage. Urik wanted to know about it, and he might be willing to offer up information in exchange for it.

Something motivated Urik to head toward Thealon. He wasn't certain what it was, and whether it was only a matter of trying to reach the priests, or was there something else that he hoped to gain?

What else would there be in Thealon for him?

Endric tried to think about what else would be in Thealon. There was the Tower, which lent credibility about the gods' proximity to the city. There was the head of the church, the High Priest of the Urmahne who remained in Thealon. And there was the university.

Urik couldn't reach the tower and he'd already been to the temple, which left Endric wondering if there was something at the university he hoped to procure.

Why would he need Endric, though?

It had something to do with Tresten, though whatever connection it had was not anything Endric could think of. What had Tresten shared with him? He'd shown him how to change polarity of teralin, but that didn't seem to be something that would be of much importance to the university. Besides, anything that had to do teralin would be less valuable at the university.

"I know what that symbol meant," Urik said softly.

"What was it?"

"I saw the symbol the day my family died," Urik said.

Endric blinked, almost unable to respond. He hadn't expected Urik to answer him, hadn't thought that he would say anything.

"I thought the Deshmahne killed your family," Endric said.

"They did."

"Then why is that symbol important to you?"

"You've faced the Deshmahne. Think about what you know about them."

They fell into an uncomfortable silence. "Their markings?" Endric asked.

"Markings. Tattoos. Symbols of power that the Deshmahne place upon their flesh." He looked over at Endric. "There was one marking that I will never forget. It was on the man who took my wife."

Endric's breath caught. At least he understood why Urik had reacted as strongly as he had, even if he wasn't sure why he had made the symbol. Where *had* he seen it before? It didn't seem like one of the symbols he'd seen on the Deshmahne, though Endric couldn't be certain.

Thunder rumbled in the distance.

Endric had been staring at Urik when it happened, and the man stiffened, scanning the horizon, looking out toward the north, as if he expected to see soldiers riding down on them.

He lunged.

It happened out of instinct. He jumped toward Urik, slamming into his back, and reached for the sword, pulling it from the sheath before Urik had a chance to react. Even bound as he was, as soon as his hands gripped the hilt, he felt a surge of hope and victory wash through him.

Urik kneed him in the side as they rolled, but Endric had the sword. Urik kicked and Endric fought against it, trying not to double over, not grunting or making any other noise, needing to hold on.

He slipped his arms forward, slicing the ropes holding him, trying to avoid cutting himself as well.

His hands were free.

Urik lunged to his feet, but he was too slow.

Endric slipped the sword underneath the ropes holding his legs.

Jumping to his feet, he faced Urik with the sword. "You should have killed me if that was your intent."

"My intent? Do you really think to know my intent?"

"Why Thealon?"

Urik grunted. "You still don't get it, do you?"

"Then tell me. Help me understand what you think I need to know."

"You've been searching for answers about what happened to Tresten. I thought you would have uncovered this before now."

"Uncover what?"

"Tresten didn't die in Vasha."

"Then where did he?"

Urik grinned at him.

The other man's legs twitched.

Endric slipped off to the side, avoiding the kick, swinging his arm around as Listain had once taught him. He slammed the hilt of the sword on the side of Urik's head, dropping him to the ground, where he stopped moving.

Endric let out a relieved sigh as he began to bind Urik's arms and legs. It was time to return to Vasha… except there was something that Urik had known about Tresten, a reason that he had wanted to bring Endric to Thealon.

He could return to Vasha, but would it matter if he took a brief detour? Couldn't he take the time to travel to Thealon and see what it was that Urik was after? From here, it would only be another day or so to reach the city.

They would return to Vasha, but Endric would return with more answers than he had left with. Was that what he wanted?

He propped Urik over the saddle of one of the horses, fixing the rope so that he couldn't attack Endric in the same way that Endric had attacked him.

"I'll take you to Thealon," Endric said. "But it will be on my terms. I *will* find out what happened to Tresten and why you seem so intent on taking me to Thealon."

Urik groaned but didn't say anything else.

Endric smiled as he climbed into the saddle of what had been Urik's horse and started guiding them toward the distant city of Thealon.

19

The massive city of Thealon rose before Endric. He stood on the hillside overlooking it, taking in the sight of the enormous wall surrounding the city. Wind gusted and carried a hint of rain. Was it a portent of what was to come?

Somehow, he would have to get through the soldiers guarding the entrance to the city.

He glanced over at Urik and checked the bindings holding his wrist and ankles. Endric had tied them tightly and knew that they were well secured, but habit forced him to double-check.

"The priests will release me," Urik said.

"I don't think they will. They know how you tainted them with teralin when you were here last. They won't be swayed like that again."

Urik laughed, a bitter sound. It was times like this that Endric wondered if he were still under the influence of the negatively charged teralin, or if this simply was Urik's nature. The man had a darkness about him. Was that from losing his family? Or was the darkness something he had been born with, something that was a part of him and would have been there regardless of what had happened to his family?

"They see me as faithful. When they discover what you've done—"

Endric slammed his fist into the back of Urik's neck, forcing the man to crumble. He'd heard enough from him during the ride toward Thealon and was tired of it.

Urik fell silent, slumped over the saddle of the horse, and Endric was tempted to tie him so that he couldn't move, but that would only draw more attention. He wanted to avoid attention and wanted to get into the city and determine whether Tresten had come to Thealon or whether his disappearance meant that he had gone elsewhere. Urik seemed to know something, but the damned man had been unwilling to share. There was only so much that Endric had been able to force out of him.

It was better that Urik was unconscious anyway. Were he awake, he might alert the Ur and raise an alarm that Endric did not want roused. Not yet, at least. He didn't want attention until he was prepared for it. He wasn't entirely certain what he might find in Thealon.

Last time he'd been here, he had helped rescue the priests and their soldiers from the influence of the negatively charged teralin. Did they appreciate what he had done or would they be angry about the fact that they had been influenced by teralin in the first place?

The wind gusted again, carrying the scents from the city. Thealon was one of the great cities and was better than most places that Endric had visited. Most had an undercurrent of filth. Even in Vasha, the first terrace often had an odor to it, one that reminded him of the dark side of the city. There were thieves, and drunks, and other criminals found throughout the city. It was something the Denraen tried to keep hidden from the Magi, but

Endric had long suspected they understood their city was not the perfect place they tried to present it as.

Maybe Thealon would be like that as well. Endric had not spent enough time in Thealon to know whether that was the case or not. His time in the city had been limited to reaching the priests and, from there, trying to free them from what Urik had done.

Sitting here brought him no closer to answers, and answers were the reason that he was here. He needed to know what had happened to Tresten. He needed to find his father and get word to him as well, and then... Endric needed to return to Vasha. He'd been gone long enough that questions would be asked. How would he explain the fact that he had been gone for months, only to disappear once more after he'd returned? How would he explain what had happened to Pendin?

Endric tapped the horse's flank and started forward. He could ride, but it was better to walk. Besides, after his time with the Antrilii, Endric had been conditioned so well that he no longer struggled with walking such distances. Not that he ever had struggled, but he had grown quite a bit stronger than he had been before.

He reached the line of people heading into the city. As he did, Endric pulled a blanket from one of the saddlebags and draped it over Urik, concealing the bindings around his ankles at least. He doubted that he would be able to conceal those around his wrists, at least not as well as he wanted, but he could conceal Urik's arms with his own body, at least well enough to obscure the fact that he was bound to the saddle.

Surprisingly, Endric entered the city without any confrontation. The guards waved him through along with all of the others making their way toward the city.

That surprised him. Considering what had happened when he had been to Thealon last, he expected the city to have been closed, and if not, at least limited in who could access it. Instead, there seemed no limitation and a freedom that surprised him.

Inside the walls, Endric paused, looking around. There was a general bustle of activity that reminded him of every other great city he'd visited, but there was an organization to it. The road he entered led straight through the city, heading toward the massive Tower of the Gods rising over the city itself, casting a long shadow over much of it. In the time that he'd been heading toward Thealon, he'd noted how the shadow moved, shifting with the changing position of the sun. How many people were under the shadow of the gods at any given time? How many more never were?

Men guiding wagons hurried along the street, traveling between shops. People of all different dress made their way along the street, and in that, it reminded him of Vasha. Vasha was a place that all people wanted to visit, thinking the proximity to the Magi would bring them closer to the gods. Thealon created an even more direct connection. While in Thealon, people could actually see the evidence of the gods. They could see their Tower and what they had created. He could not deny feeling a hint of awe at the site.

Where should he begin looking?

Urik thought Tresten would be in the city, and Endric believed that he might actually be here. Finding him was the challenge. He could try to reach the priests, but doing that opened him to questions. He would need to be prepared for those questions and be prepared to provide whatever answer that he could. Would the priests even be willing to see him? When they'd come the last time, the Ur had run off, checking with the priests before ultimately sending them away.

Maybe it would be better to send word.

And Endric didn't want to show up with Urik in tow. If he had access to the priests once more, he wasn't certain what he might do, or what influence he still might exert over them. Maybe it would be better to leave Urik somewhere.

Endric looked along the street and noted the row of taverns. He would have to find a place here to leave him within. That would be the best—and the safest. Somehow, he would need to find a place where he could leave Urik confined.

Endric started along the road that intersected the main street leading through Thealon. In this outer section of the city, it seemed as if there were dozens of taverns. Most had signs out front indicating their name, often some reference to the gods. None of those felt quite right. He didn't need a place that was striving to demonstrate its devotion to the nameless gods.

What he needed was a place where he could move unencumbered and wouldn't raise the attention of the tavern owner, especially if Urik awoke and began making noise. He could keep his mouth gagged and could silence him as much as possible, but if Endric were to succeed in confining Urik, it would be done in a way that didn't expose him too much.

As he circled the row of taverns, he began to doubt that he would find the right kind of place. What he needed was someplace where the tavern owner didn't care quite as much about the outer appearance. He needed a place that some of the more disreputable people in the city might frequent. Without knowing Thealon well, he had no way of finding that.

Maybe this was a mistake.

Should he return Urik to Vasha?

If he did, he might never learn what happened to Tresten, and Endric had a growing suspicion that he needed to know.

He continued to circle and eventually found a place far away from the main entrance to the city. The sign was faded and had what appeared to be two crossed swords as a marker. Loud music radiated from inside, loud enough that he could hear it easily along the street. There was an occasional shout and he slowed, listening before he approached too closely.

The longer he listened, the more he decided that this had to be the place.

He hadn't found anywhere else that would work, not nearly as well as a place that sounded as bawdy as this. Endric made his way around until he reached the stables and flipped a copper coin to the stable boy, jerking Urik off the saddle.

"Take good care of them," he told the boy.

The stable boy caught the coin and bit into it. He shrugged. "I take better care of them for two coppers."

Endric glared at him but suspected that the boy would do exactly that. He might have need of the horses to return quickly to Vasha so if he didn't pay the boy, how well would he care for them?

Endric flipped another coin to him. The boy caught it and smiled.

"See that she's fed and watered and brush her down."

The boy shrugged. "Food and water's included, but brushing…"

Endric took another copper from his pocket and tossed it to the boy. "As I said, see that she's brushed."

Now he knew he had the right kind of place. For them to keep a stable boy like this, it had to be the kind of place that he needed.

He propped Urik against his side and made his way into the tavern. There were more people than he would've expected from the street outside. Several lingered near the back of the tavern, where the musicians were playing, dancing or singing along to the music, while others sat at tables scattered throughout.

Endric paused, holding Urik up. At least he could make it seem as if Urik were drunk and pretend that he needed Endric's support. He scanned the tavern, noting the hint of grime to everyone and the way that more than a few were already intoxicated.

This was definitely the right kind of tavern.

After the cleanliness of Thealon, and seeing how everyone else in the city seemed to be well-dressed and put together, he was a little surprised to find a tavern like this. This kind of tavern was even more ribald than what he would find in Vasha.

He dragged Urik through the tavern until he found a serving girl. She wore a tight-fitting dress that enhanced her cleavage. She had a round face and her hair was braided with three ribbons: one blue, one green, and one red. Her cheeks were flushed. Whether that was from the heat of the effort her work required or whether she wore rouge, the effect was the same.

"I'm looking for the proprietor," he said.

She held two mugs of ale in each hand and studied him a moment. "Why do you need the proprietor? He's a busy man."

"I'm looking for a room for the night."

"The night? Most men come here looking for room for a few hours."

Endric grunted. He hadn't realized it was that kind of tavern. It made it even less likely that he would be noticed—or reported. "For the night."

The woman frowned at him and then nodded toward the back of the tavern. Endric followed the direction of her gaze and noted an older man sitting at a table by himself. He had a pile of cards that he stacked, flipping them over one by one on top of the table.

"Jester is over there. He can help you."

Endric nodded. He considered saying something more, asking for a mug of ale, but changed his mind. Pendin's trouble jumped to the forefront of his mind when he thought about it.

Endric dragged Urik until he reached Jester. He leaned Urik along the wall, less mindful of the fact that he had him bound and had just dragged him through the tavern. Once done, he pulled out the empty chair sitting across from the man and took a seat. "You're Jester?"

"So they tell me."

"I need a room."

"The women negotiate their own time."

Endric shook his head but Jester continued to flip his cards, not looking up. "For the night."

This caused Jester to look up. He glanced from Endric over to Urik, a hint of a smile tugging the corners of his mouth. "That kind of thing is frowned upon in Thealon."

Endric glanced over at Urik. "There's no kind of thing. I need a room."

"The room will be two silvers."

"For how long?"

"A night."

Endric fixed him with a frown. Two silvers would buy several weeks in most taverns. Especially in Vasha. He couldn't believe the man asked for so much per night. "Two silvers for one night? Are the beds gilded?"

"The two silvers are to pay for what my women will lose out on."

Endric chewed on the inside of his lip. Jester went back to flipping his cards, his long face focused downward at the table, ignoring Endric completely.

He had money. Service in the Denraen was nothing if not good pay, but was he willing to pay as much as this?

If things went well, he would only be here one or two nights. He didn't need to spend that much, but he did need to have a place where keeping Urik bound and confined to his room wouldn't draw attention. This was that kind of place.

Endric reached into his pocket and slid two silvers over to the man. Jester flicked his gaze to them before looking up at Endric. "Three night minimum," he said.

Endric didn't know whether to be angry or amused. "The stable boy. Is he yours?"

"My son. Why?"

Endric grunted and fished out four more silvers from his pocket and slid them across the table to Jester. "Only that there's a resemblance between the two of you," he said.

Jester chuckled. "There's not many who notice it."

"I suppose not." Most who came to this tavern likely weren't interested in the quality of the ale or the amenities available in the room. Most likely wanted to remain anonymous, at least as much as they could. "Which room?" Endric asked.

"Top of the stairs, last room on the right. Darla can lead you to it. Tell her you paid for the king's special."

"Which one is Darla?"

Jester flicked his gaze to a slender woman making her rounds through the tavern. She carried her tray laden with food and had a heavy sway to her hips as she walked. She had a prominent jaw and when she glanced over at Endric, he noted an intensity to her eyes.

"How is Darla related to you?" Endric asked.

"Darla's not."

Endric smiled. He found that difficult to believe, especially considering that Jester employed his son as a stable boy. How many of the people working in the tavern were related to him? And how could he allow his daughter to sell herself?

Endric stood, jerking Urik to his feet and dragging him along until he reached Darla. "Jester told me to inform you that I paid for the king's special."

She flashed a hint of a smile. It was one that reminded him very much of the way Jester had smiled. "He did now, did he?"

Endric nodded.

"Well then, come with me."

She led him to the back of the tavern and up a narrow staircase. An equally narrow hallway at the top of the stair had several doors on either side. There were no other decorations in the hall and no lighting. Endric's hand went to the hilt of his sword, concern that he might be swindled rising within him. Jester had already seen how willing Endric had been to part with his coin. A man like that would be equally as likely to forcibly part him from even more.

She reached the back of the hall and fished a key out of her pocket, unlocking the door. "Here it is. How many girls do you need?"

She handed the key to Endric and he gripped it, waiting for something else. Would she try to slip a knife into him? Did they have another key they intended to use in the middle of the night and break in, robbing him while he slept?

He'd have to block the door. It wouldn't be the first time.

"How many girls?" Endric repeated.

"King's special, you said. How many girls?"

Endric shook his head. "No girls."

Her gaze drifted to Urik and she shrugged. "If you say so. You paid for the king's special. All you have to do is let me know. I'll make sure you get all that you want."

"Including you?"

Her smile faded and she glared at him. "I'm not on the menu. Even if I were, you wouldn't have enough coin."

She turned, leaving him watching her depart. Endric waited until she was at the bottom of the stair before stepping into the room and closing the door. He locked it behind him.

Urik started to stir and Endric punched him on the back of the neck again, using a technique Listain had taught him, silencing him.

He glanced around the room. It was sparsely decorated. A massive bed took up the majority of the space, with neatly pressed sheets pulled up on it. Worry that there might not be a place to secure Urik was alleviated when Endric noticed two hooks set into the wall above the bed.

Endric chuckled. Those would be perfect for tying Urik into

place. They weren't the intended purpose, but they would do well enough for him.

He sighed and began securing Urik. The longer he was here, the more that he wanted to get this over with, see what he could find of Tresten, and return to Vasha as quickly as he could.

20

The street was awash with activity. Endric paused, looking around, searching for evidence of the Ur soldiers, but saw no sign. They would have to be here. In Thealon, the Ur were nearly as prevalent as the Denraen and Vasha.

It was late fall, yet a floral fragrance hung on the air. Was that from the flowers he knew to be planted around the tower? When he'd been in Thealon before, he'd seen the way the priests decorated the grounds around the tower, with dozens of species of flowering plants and countless trees dotting the grounds, creating an impressive decoration. It would be surprising for those scents to reach him this far out on the periphery of the city, practically near the wall that surrounded the entirety of it, but he detected something.

He needed to move quickly. If he didn't, Urik would awaken. The cloth he'd shoved into Urik's mouth to gag him might keep him silent for a time, but Endric didn't know how long that would last. If he made too much noise, would one of the other tavern workers come to check on him, or would they think him bound and gagged as some part of whatever games were common within the tavern?

It was a risk Endric wasn't willing to take.

Which meant he had to find information quickly. Then he had to find Tresten.

If he still lived.

Finding him would be difficult. Tresten could remain hidden with the priests or he could have gone anywhere else within the city. Endric assumed that he remained with the priests—especially as that had been his intent when they had been here the last time, but Tresten had proven somewhat difficult to anticipate.

If Endric could find one of the Ur, he thought he might be able to use them to bring him to the priests and see if Tresten was in fact still within the city. All signs Endric could find indicated that he was.

He weaved through the crowd, navigating between merchants pushing carts and clusters of individuals who made their way along the street. Judging by the way some were dressed—a formality to their clothing that Endric rarely saw in Vasha—he suspected they were heading toward the temple, choosing to worship. In Thealon, he suspected such worship would be common. The proximity to the Tower would draw people from all over.

Endric heard commotion along the street and veered toward it, his Denraen training taking over. As he did, he noted a cluster of people pushing their way forward. Most were men, most were dressed in tattered clothing, and none of them were armed. A few were larger than the others, muscular and brutish, though for the most part, they were scrawny and younger.

He lingered along the edge of the street and watched.

They continued to force their way forward and he realized they were making their way toward the center of the city—and the Tower.

Endric trailed after them. The two men—the larger of them—pushed their way through the crowd, forcing others to stagger off to the side. After a while, shouts gave enough warning so that others simply moved out of the way, avoiding the throng of dirty men.

They carried nothing with them.

Were they from Thealon? The leader had dark hair, and as they scanned the crowds, Endric noticed eyes so dark, they were nearly black. The men had light complexions, though with the dirt along their skin, it was difficult to tell.

These were not locals.

Most from the city had a hint of a tan and lighter hair and lighter-colored eyes. Many in the city felt that made them godlier, imagining that the gods had pale hair and bright eyes, though none would know for certain, as the gods had not been seen in countless generations.

As Endric followed, he paused at the street corner. A merchant pulled his cart to a hard stop and glared after the crowd making their way toward the tower. The man muttered softly. "Stupid miners," he said.

"Miners?" Endric asked without meaning to. He hadn't realized there were any active mines near Thealon. There was teralin here, but it was not mined, not as it had been in Vasha. Even that was no longer actively mined.

The merchant glanced over. He had a dark complexion and hazel eyes. From the cut of his cloak along with the embroidery along it, it seemed as if the man was fairly well off. His cart was covered and he led three horses with him. "Yes. Miners. They come out of the north, seeking the gods' approval. Most have never been out of their small mining towns, so that when they come to places like Thealon, they make a spectacle."

Endric had traveled through a few of the mining towns on his way back to Vasha after leaving Farsea. He didn't recall seeing men quite like that, though he hadn't stayed long. His visits had been brief, long enough to get a good night's rest and often a hot meal before continuing on his way. In many of those villages, men who were old enough to work went off into the iron mines, though some searched for silver and gold. Such valuable ore was rarely found in the north.

"Why do they come to Thealon?" Endric asked.

"The same as most men. The same as you, I suspect," the merchant said, eying up Endric, taking in his clothes before lingering on his sword.

Endric grunted. "The same as me? I doubt it."

"You don't think to join the Ur and gain the favor of the priests—and through them, the gods?"

Endric frowned. "Do you see many men come to Thealon seeking to join the Ur?" He hadn't realized that was how they recruited. The Denraen had it easier. Most soldiers wanted to be chosen by the Denraen. Choosing from each land enabled them to claim each nation equally, so that they would not be said to favor one place over another. In most places, being chosen for the Denraen was the highest honor a soldier could have.

"Men from the outer villages think they have some talent with the sword and they make their way to Thealon." The merchant shrugged. "Some of them probably do have a bit of skill. You grow up outside of the city, you get accustomed to dealing with bandits, and more than a few think that by joining the Ur, they will be able to direct the soldiers toward their home, finding a way to offer protection the Ur didn't otherwise grant."

"I take it you don't think that happens."

"I'm no soldier. I don't make any claims that I am. I'm a simple textile merchant."

That, at least, explained the quality of his clothing. "It sounds as if you have experience in what takes place in the lands around Thealon."

"You travel enough, and you see enough, you begin to make generalities." The merchant turned to him and considered him for a moment. "Take you, for example. You have a solid build and you're tall—I'll give you that. I suspect you grew up working a farm. Most men who have experience working on a farm are solid. Were you a little larger, I would have wondered whether you spent time as a blacksmith, but you don't have *quite* that build."

Endric smiled to himself. "Seems that miners have a similar build," he said, watching the men as they made their way along the street. They had slowed as they entered a busier section of the city, no longer forcing their way quite as aggressively through the crowd.

"Some do, though they're usually the ones who stole from others in their village to feed themselves."

Endric chuckled. What would Pendin have said were he to hear the merchant commenting on something like this? Pendin was not nearly as tall as Endric, but he was incredibly muscular, a build that came from his family's ties to the mine. Such strength would have been valuable when teralin was mined, but it was also valuable in serving the Denraen.

"And if I told you I didn't grow up on a farm?" Endric asked.

The man's gaze drifted back to his sword. "No farm? You don't have the dress of the Ur, so you're not a soldier already, and your accent would tell me that you aren't from the city itself. Maybe you *are* a blacksmith."

The men turned a corner, disappearing from view. Endric was drawn to follow, curious where they would go, and what they would do. He started into the street but the merchant grabbed his sleeve.

Endric turned and caught the merchant's eye. "I'm no blacksmith, either."

"What then?"

Endric turned away and started down the street. "I'm just a man looking for a priest, no different than those men."

He started to pull away but the merchant hung onto his sleeve. "Those men aren't going to reach any of the priests," he said.

"Why not?" Endric asked.

The merchant chuckled. "The priests don't visit with just anyone. You can find them in the temple, and anyone is allowed to worship, but to spend any time with the priests? That simply doesn't happen."

If that were the case, then Endric would have a harder time finding information about Tresten—or Tresten himself—than he thought. He had imagined finding the Ur, and convincing a higher-level soldier to help them reach the priests, but maybe that was unlikely. Without any of the Magi, simply serving as one of the Denraen would give him no pull to reach the priests.

"What if I have a message for a particular priest?" Why was he asking the merchant? It wasn't that the man had particular knowledge that Endric could utilize. He wasn't even connected to the city. He had already admitted that he was a traveling merchant and spent much of his time outside of the city.

"I suppose you could go to the temple, attend one of the worship ceremonies, and see if you were able to speak with the priests afterward. It would be unlikely to work, but…" The merchant shrugged.

Endric pulled his arm free and stared along the street. How long could he leave Urik bound in the room? If he left him too long, he risked the man somehow getting free. If that happened, it would be hard to recapture him. How much destruction could Urik cause if he managed to get free?

He would have to balance his needs with what he could realistically accomplish. He wanted to find what he could about Tresten—and he was convinced that he would find something here in the city—but he also needed to not risk Urik escaping.

As he started away, the merchant shouted after him, "You never told me what you did."

Endric paused and turned back to him, shaking his head. "I didn't."

The merchant left his wagon and hurried forward. His gaze lingered on Endric's sword once again. "You carry a sword and you have the build for a soldier, but you're not dressed like one of the Ur."

"I'm not one of the Ur."

The man smiled. "But you're a soldier."

Endric nodded. "I'm a soldier." That fit him better than any other title. His father had wanted him to serve in a leadership role and Endric had done all that he could to do so, but it remained an unnatural fit, despite how much he tried. He would serve, and he would lead if needed, but none of that would change the fact that Endric remained a soldier first.

"If you're a soldier, where do you serve? You've already told me you're not of the Ur, and I'd be surprised if Gom Aaldia sent men into the city… unless you were scouting. Is that it? Does the High King intend to attack Thealon again?"

"Not that I know," Endric answered.

"Then you are Gom Aaldian. I should have known it from your accent."

Endric chuckled. "I'm not Gom Aaldian, either."

"Then what *are* you? Where are you from?"

Endric flashed a grin. "Vasha."

"If you're from Vasha, that means…"

"That means," Endric agreed.

The merchant gasped. "Denraen in Thealon?" he whispered.

He glanced around, as if thinking to find other Denraen hiding along the street. Endric let him look, not wanting to disappoint him by letting him know that he was the only one here. Let the merchant believe there were dozens of Denraen in the city. And it was possible there were some. Patrols often passed through Thealon, and many would take time to stop and remain in the city. Thealon was safer than other places, and none would be blamed for wanting a warm bed and a hot meal.

"This one is."

Endric left the merchant and disappeared into the crowd, heading after the miners. When he reached the end of the street, he found that they were nowhere to be seen. He hadn't expected them to be, and now that he understood who they were—and what they likely were after—there wasn't any real urgency.

Had the chance meeting with the merchant given him some information? He understood that it would be unlikely to reach the priests on his own, which meant he had to find another way to get their attention. Perhaps if he had come with a regiment of Denraen, he might have had an easier time. Instead, he would have to find another way in.

Before he did that, he decided he had best check on Urik.

He hurried back toward the tavern until he saw the sign for the Shallow Scabbard, the oddly named tavern that he'd made his home while in Thealon. He hurried through the common room and up the stairs in the back to the quarters he been given—ransomed, really. He paused outside the door to the room, listening. He heard no movement, but with Urik, he didn't want to take it for granted that he wasn't attempting to deceive.

Endric grabbed the hilt of his sword and unlocked the door.

Hesitating again, he waited until he was certain that there was no movement.

There was nothing.

Endric stepped in and found the room exactly as he'd left it. Urik remained bound to the bed, his wrists held overhead and his legs strapped to the end of the bed. The gag Endric had forced into his mouth and tied into place still prevented him from making too much noise.

But Urik was awake.

He looked at Endric, anger flaring in his eyes, staring at him with an intensity that would make many step back. Endric only smiled.

"Good. You're awake."

Urik tried to say something, but Endric ignored it. If Urik was awake and had remained tied, unable to escape, the bindings would hold. Endric wouldn't rely upon them—not completely—but it was reassuring to know that he could be gone for stretches at a time and return to find Urik still here.

He made his way to the bed and unsheathed his sword. Urik eyed the blade as he did, and his eyes went wide when Endric brought it up before slamming it into the side of his head once more, knocking him out.

It might be that Urik couldn't escape, but he would have more time if he could rely upon Urik be no threat. He checked the knots, making sure that they remained well tied, before stepping back into the hall, pulling the door closed and locking it.

A slender woman in the hall, her cheeks painted a pale red, watched him, her gaze drifting past him and seeming to see through the door before she shifted her attention back to his face. He suspected many of the women had questions about why he had paid what he had and had no interest in any of the women. That question was in her eyes, but she didn't ask it.

Endric raised a finger to his lips and winked.

21

Endric sat at a table near the back of the tavern, listening to the music as it filled the air, a mug of ale resting on the table in front of him. There had been a time not all that long ago when he would have quickly drunk the ale, but so much had changed in that time. He had changed.

The tavern stunk. There was the familiar odor of ale, one he found pleasant, but there were other smells in the air, that of sweat and a foulness that he thought was particular to this tavern. He tried not to think about the source of the odor, preferring to ignore where it might come from, and struggled. Even the trays of food scattered around the tavern did nothing to overpower that stench.

He watched as women made their way from table to table, some taking men by the hand and leading them off and upstairs. Often times, they returned shortly after to the cheers of their companions. Some were away for longer, and there were more than a few who returned by themselves, without the woman.

Endric always wondered about that, worried what it meant for those who chose to sell themselves in such ways.

He told himself that it wasn't his concern. It couldn't be. He had other things he needed to do, especially if he intended to find anything he could about what had happened to Tresten.

Except… Tresten himself had wanted Endric to search for him.

Darla came over and took a seat in front of him. She had a round face and deep brown eyes that he once would have found appealing. She sat across from him and leaned forward, resting her head on her hands as she watched him.

"You're an odd one, aren't you?"

Endric smiled. "Am I?" he asked.

"You come to a place like this and you pay for days, but that's not what you want at all."

Endric gripped the mug of ale and pulled it toward him. "What do you know about what I want?"

Darla smiled. "I can see that you're barely touching your ale. You have it here to make it look like you're drinking it, but me and the other servers can see that you aren't. What is it? What are you after in Thealon?"

"Answers," he said.

She smiled. "Most who come to Thealon seek answers."

Endric shook his head. "Those aren't the kind of answers that I'm after."

"I never said what kind I was talking about."

Endric nodded toward a table near the front of the tavern. A man sitting there wore the heavy robes of the priests of the Urmahne and had a shaven head. "I'm not here for answers from the gods," Endric said. "I seek a man I once knew."

"A different man than the one you brought up to your room?" When Endric grunted, she shrugged. "We all know what you have up there. Daisy saw him in the room."

At least Endric knew the name of the girl who had seen him. "What has Daisy said?"

Darla shrugged again. "You have a man tied to the bed. That sort of thing isn't all that uncommon here, but you don't have the look of a person who enjoys such activities." Darla scanned the tavern and pointed to a thin man sitting near the hearth. "Him, on the other hand, enjoys tying and being tied. A few others like similar things. You," she said, turning her attention back to Endric, "have the look of a man with a purpose. I don't get the sense that you have him tied up there for your pleasure."

Endric grunted. "If it were my pleasure, his neck would have been slit open a year ago."

"What'd he do?"

He lifted the mug of ale and took a long drink. It was warm and had a dusty taste mixed with a hint of salt. A strange combination, and it burned his throat as it went down. "Led to my brother's death," Endric said.

Darla nodded slowly. "I probably would have slit his throat too."

Endric looked up. There was an earnestness to the way she spoke that told him she likely had lost someone and that she had suffered. "Who did you lose?"

Darla held his gaze for a moment before looking down at the table. "Most of us here have lost someone. You don't come to a place like the Shallow Scabbard if you have much of a choice, do you?"

"I had a choice and I came here."

Her eyes narrowed. "Did you have a choice, or did you only come here because you thought it would draw less attention than other places?"

She was smart.

"I don't intend to kill him here, if that's what you're concerned about."

"He wouldn't be the first man to die in this tavern."

"Are so many killed here, this close to the Tower?"

"The Tower?" she asked with a snort. "You think our proximity to the Tower makes men behave more godly? Most think that being here grants them a little more freedom, as if they will be forgiven for their behavior. Take that man," she said, nodding toward the priest. "I imagine in other cities he would be better behaved, but here? Here he's one of the worst. More than a few are left with bruises, or worse, when they spend time with him."

"Why do they spend time with them then?"

"Because he pays. For all his behavior, his coin is good. With everything that he's done, he gets charged a premium, and he willingly pays it. Women see that as an opportunity." She shrugged.

"Some opportunity. Risking themselves for money?"

Her gaze drifted down to his waist, where his sword was still buckled to his belt. "Are you so different? You have the look of a soldier, though I can tell you're not of the Ur. What are soldiers but men who prostitute themselves for different purpose?"

She stood and patted his hand. "If you do slit his throat, don't leave the sheets on the bed. It disturbs some of the women to find them like that. Throw them in the fire and leave a few extra coins for Jester so that he doesn't rage at us too much."

Endric shook his head. "I don't intend to slit his throat here."

"Then you do intend to do it at some point?"

Endric smiled. "You're persistent," he said. The matter-of-fact way that she spoke amused him, as did the fact that she seemed unconcerned about what he might do to Urik. There was something very much Denraen about her. What must Darla have seen to have hardened her in such a way? How could she have suffered so much, this close to Thealon, and this close to the gods?

"Persistence is the only thing that has kept me alive," she said.

She had started to turn away when Endric said, "I don't know if I will do it."

Darla turned back to him. "Why not? If he was responsible for your brother's death, why wouldn't you take his life?"

"He needs to pay the penance for what he's done, but there are times when death is too good for a man."

She watched him and then nodded. "Maybe you're right."

"You never told me who you lost."

"A father. My family."

"In Thealon?" Endric had a hard time believing that there would be such loss in Thealon, though there seemed to be more of an undercurrent of darkness in the city than he had realized. He had thought that Thealon would be clean—pure—but it was just like every other city he had visited.

Darla shook her head. "Not in Thealon, but near enough."

"Why did you come here?"

She sniffed. "Why does anyone come here? We come for answers, and we come for the hope that the gods might watch over us and bring us a sense of peace." She looked toward the door and Endric could tell that her gaze drifted toward the Tower of the Gods, which loomed over everything in the city. "The gods might watch over us, but they don't bring us any peace. They bring only heartache. Had they never Ascended, wouldn't they have been better able to observe and maintain peace? If they were still here, would my father and my sister still be alive?" She turned her gaze upon Endric. "Would your brother?"

She stared at him for a moment before spinning and leaving Endric watching her.

Endric had no answers. His gaze was drawn toward the priest sitting near the front of the tavern, a man who *should* have answers for those who sought them, but even he wouldn't have any, not if he came to a place like the Shallow Scabbard, and not if he was the worst of those who came here.

When he went to the temple, would Endric find any answers? He could search for Tresten, but if he was truly gone—dead, as everything that he'd heard would indicate—what answers might he find? Tresten might want him to look, but there seemed to be nothing for him here.

Maybe it would be best for him to return to Vasha, drag Urik with him, and resume his place, whether that was as soldier or as something else. No longer did he know quite what he was supposed to do to serve. It should bother him, but it didn't.

Returning had been about taking his place among the Denraen, but he still hadn't earned it, had he? It was no different than when he had been given the title of en'raen. All he had done for that had been revealing a plot against the Denraen. He had not worked his way up through the ranks, and he had not shown any real leadership, which made it easier for him to accept the fact that perhaps he was better suited to serve as a soldier.

Senda was a leader. She *had* earned her position.

When he returned to Vasha, that would be what he would do. He would gladly serve and willingly take patrols and be a dutiful soldier.

He stood, a smile crossing his face. It was strange that such peace would find him in Thealon, especially as he had arrived here for answers that he still had not acquired. Even if he never found anything about Tresten, the visit to Thealon had been valuable.

And now he would see if the priests hid anything that would be useful. If Tresten had remained with them before returning to Vasha, maybe there was something they knew, and something they would be able to tell him, about where he had gone before his death.

As Endric made his way from the tavern, he felt the weight of a gaze and found Darla watching him. She nodded, and he nodded in return.

Out in the street, he looked up, noting the Tower rising above everything, the shadow cast by its height stretching in this direction. The shadow moved over time, circling the city somewhat like a clock, so that everyone was eventually within the shadow of the gods. Endric suspected that was intentional, but was that what the gods would have wanted? Did they want to overshadow the people of the city?

Who was he to know? Who was he to question the intent of the gods?

And who was he to go to the temple searching for answers?

22

The temple was silent. The stink of incense hung over everything like a cloud, the haze of smoke filling the air. A few lanterns cast a flickering light, but not enough for Endric to see clearly. There were hundreds of people within the temple, more than he had expected at this time of day, and all remained perfectly still, their eyes fixed on the dais near the back.

The priest standing atop the dais wore flowing robes that brushed along the floor. He wore no adornments other than his robes. The priests believed in austerity and rarely wore any jewelry, nothing that would set them apart from each other. This man had a thin face and his head was shorn, but his voice had a deep and booming timber. It carried, easily filling the entirety of the temple as he chanted. He paused every so often, waiting for the worshipers to chant in return.

Endric had been raised according to the Urmahne faith and knew the proper words. He said them without much enthusiasm, careful not to draw any unwanted attention to himself.

It had been years since he'd attended a service. Despite having been born and living in Vasha, he had not spent much time in temple during his youth. Few of the Denraen made it a point to attend worship regularly. There simply wasn't time in between training. There were some who were devout, which made Urik and his devotion notable but not exceptional, but it was not all that common.

The temple itself was stifling, the humid air leaving a sheen of sweat across his skin. The incense and the smoke filled the air, making for an unpleasant experience. He kneeled, following the motions of the other worshipers around him, before getting to his feet and raising his arms in exaltation. He recognized the service, even though he had rarely attended them. This was one celebrating the Ascension, a time of great celebration for the Urmahne.

Could it be Ascension time already?

It was fall, which meant the season was right, but Endric didn't recall the calendar well enough to know whether they were that near the Ascension service or not. If it was, it explained the miners' presence in the city. Many people in outlying villages made their way toward larger cities—and larger temples—to celebrate the Ascension. Even in Vasha, there were thousands more people at that time of year. He imagined it had to be tenfold more in Thealon, especially because the Tower of the Gods was the place the gods had Ascended from.

The priest's chant ended and silence fell over the temple.

All around him, worshipers kept their arms raised. Endric followed them, not wanting to stand out but feeling somewhat deceptive in the fact that he was here, that he attempted to worship. He had no devotion and no belief, not as so many did. He believed the gods were real—at least, that they *had* been real—but how long had it been since they were a part of the world? How long had it been since they had any interest in influence?

To most of the people around him, none of that mattered. Most of the people awaited a time when the gods would return and rejoin the world. If they practiced peace long enough, and if they maintained that peace as the gods desired, the return would be expedited. Endric had a hard time believing that would happen.

For him, the gods were gone. They had abandoned the world. It was up to the Denraen—and the Magi, if they were interested—to maintain peace.

And then the service was over.

People around him gradually began to lower their arms and slowly make their way out of the temple. Endric waited until the group around him had thinned and started toward the dais at the front, hoping to catch the priest before he disappeared.

As he approached, he noted the priest lighting incense along an altar set behind him. The smoke trailed up and up, drifting in a thickening cloud as it rose toward the ceiling and away, vented in some hidden way.

A few people near the front of the temple eyed him strangely before turning away. Endric had made a point of wearing his robe and keeping his sword covered. In the temple—a place designed to celebrate and worship in peace—his sword would not be welcome.

Endric stood off to the side, waiting for the priest to finish lighting the incense. The smell became nauseating, nearly overwhelming him with its pungency. How did the priests manage to tolerate it as long as they did? Maybe it was like anything else, something he could grow accustomed to, but he couldn't imagine ever getting to the point where he welcomed the scent.

The priest glanced over, and Endric recognized him.

There had been a dozen or so priests he had interacted with when he had come with Tresten, all of whom had been influenced by the negatively charged teralin. Surprisingly—and coincidentally—this man had been one of them.

Any thoughts that the priest's recognition would encourage him to come over and engage in conversation faded as the man quickly turned away and hurried toward a hidden door near the back of the temple.

Endric blinked. Had the priest just *avoided* him?

It seemed that way, though why would the priest have avoided him? Was he embarrassed about the fact that he had been influenced by the negatively charged teralin? There had been plenty of others who had been similarly influenced, so there should be no reason for him to be embarrassed by the fact that he had succumbed to it.

Unless there was another reason.

Did the priest know something?

He glanced behind him and noted the temple was nearly empty. A few worshipers remained, though not nearly as many as there had been even a moment before. Those few who did remain stood transfixed, their gaze focused on the altar. Each of them breathed slowly, inhaling the stench of the incense as if it would help them reach the gods.

Would any notice if he went through the door reserved for the priests?

Did it matter?

If he were caught, the worst that would happen would be that he would be thrown from the temple. Even then, he could claim the need to speak to the high priest and could defend his decision.

What choice did he have?

The entire reason that he had come to Thealon was to find Tresten. Now was not the time to let something as simple as a door stop him.

Endric darted through the door and found himself in a narrow passageway. A single lantern lit the hall, the design created by Urik when he had still been in the temple. It glowed with a soft orange light and a hint of smoke trailed up from it. The hall stretched away from him, with the light of the lantern barely pushing away the edge of darkness.

The priest had disappeared.

Endric glanced over his shoulder. There would be no way out once he started down the hall. He could turn back and leave through the temple, and even attempt to gain access to the grounds where he and Tresten had first found the High Priest. That might be the safest plan.

Endric hurried along the hall. He assumed he would find other doorways, but he did not. He quickened his step, moving away from the lantern and the light and heading into darkness. It soon swallowed him. Another lantern glowed in the distance, and he headed toward it.

He thought of what he knew of the shape of the temple, and this hall didn't fit with what he expected—unless it ran underground. That was possible, especially considering the main hall of worship had been set below ground, requiring him to take steps down in order to enter it.

When he reached the other lantern, he found a doorway. It was locked. The hall continued onward, eventually disappearing into darkness much as it had the last time. Had the priest disappeared here? He could have gone through this doorway, or he could have continued along the corridor.

Endric crouched in front of the door, pulling one of his knives from his boots, and jammed it into the lock, popping it open.

The room on the other side was little more than a storeroom. Dozens of barrels were stacked near one corner. The shelf with boxes set into it was on the wall. A layer of dust coated everything. It reminded him of storerooms within the barracks in Vasha. The air smelled stale and had traces of the incense odor to it. This must be where they stored the spice they burned.

He surveyed the room, looking for another access point, but there was no other door.

He stepped back into the hall and pulled the door closed behind him, unconcerned about whether it locked. He hurried down the hall again, disappearing into the darkness before another lantern became visible.

When he reached that lantern, there was another door. Much like the door before it, this one was locked. Endric pried it open with his knife and pushed it open, expecting another storeroom. Instead, he found another hall.

He glanced back behind him and considered continuing along the path he had initially taken. The lantern light faded into darkness, but now that he had seen it happen a few times, he expected another lantern to appear, and likely another doorway.

What would he find along this path?

It was better lit than the other. A pair of lanterns hung on the wall, both shaped like those Urik had made. He could wander through these corridors indefinitely, at least until he came across one of the priests, much as he once had wandered through the teralin mines beneath Vasha. At least with these hallways he had a sense that he could find his way back out.

Endric decided to follow this path. More lighting made it more likely that this would take him someplace where he could find answers. In the unlit halls, he was less likely to find anyone who could help him.

The lanterns along this corridor were spaced evenly, and he found a few doors lining the walls. He checked the first few and found storage rooms behind them that reminded him of the one he'd seen in the other passageway.

After walking for a while, the hall ended in a doorway.

This door appeared different than most of the others he had seen. There was a patterning to the wood, carvings that were set into it that reminded him of paintings he'd seen in Vasha depicting the gods. The carving was skillfully done, and the door itself was stained a deep auburn. This door was locked as well.

Endric tried prying open the lock, but found no success. He

jammed his knife into the doorframe, hoping to pop open the door, but that wasn't successful either.

He stood back, considering the door. He could throw himself against it, attempt to break it down, but if he did that, he would be unlikely to get any help from the priests if they caught him.

The hall was empty. There was nothing along it other than more storage. There was no way to reach the priests and no alternative way out of the temple.

He backtracked, reaching the first door that had led him in, and glanced along the corridor, debating whether to continue along it or return to the temple.

He'd come this far and decided to try a little farther.

At the next lantern, and the next door, he found another storeroom.

He went farther, and each one was similar.

He found another corridor off this one, and it was much like the last, with storerooms lining the length of it and an impassable door at the end.

With frustration, he turned back and hurried toward the temple. Just because he hadn't seen anyone here yet didn't mean that no one would be coming this way. There wasn't a way out, not without having the key to one of those doors, which forced him to go back through the temple.

He had failed.

All he wanted was to find Tresten, and he had failed.

He had thought there would be something in Thealon for him to find, but he had learned nothing. Attempts to find the priests had failed him. How long could he remain here, searching? How long did he risk staying in Thealon when he needed to return to Vasha?

Maybe it was time to abandon his search. Tresten might *not* be dead—Endric couldn't be certain either way—but he *was* gone.

And he needed to acknowledge that he couldn't find him.

When he entered the temple, he found it empty. He glanced at the altar, noting the thick haze of smoke coming from the burning incense. Endric made a point of avoiding taking a deep breath, not wanting to inhale it. Frustration settled through him as he left the temple and reached the outside once more. He took a deep breath, clearing the stink of the incense from his nostrils, and made his way back toward the tavern.

When he entered the room, he froze.

Urik sat untied on the bed, but that wasn't what drew his attention.

Rather it was the man—the Mage—sitting next to him that did.

"Tresten?"

The elderly Mage turned to him and offered a tight smile. "Endric. It's good that you have finally come for me."

23

Endric stared at Tresten, barely able to believe the Mage was here in front of him. After everything he'd been through, how was it that Tresten now sat in front of him with Urik?

Endric slowly pulled the door closed and stepped into the room. He trembled, trying to gather his thoughts but finding it difficult to do so. "Where have you been?" he asked.

Tresten tipped his head to the side. He had a long face and eyes that seemed knowing, as if anything Endric might tell him, the Mage already knew. "You always knew where to find me, Endric. Why is it surprising that you would find me in Thealon?"

Endric pulled a chair out of the corner and took a seat. He let his gaze linger on Urik. The man was no longer bound, but he made no effort to move, as if simply having Tresten here with them was enough to suppress any desire he might have to escape. Urik pointedly ignored him and Endric resisted the urge to grab him and replace the ropes securing his wrists and ankles. At least Urik hadn't said anything—so far.

"Reports out of Thealon were that you were dead."

Tresten smiled. "Is that true?"

"That's what I had heard."

Tresten tipped his head. "I think you misunderstood. None of the reports said that I was dead. All of them claimed that I was lost."

"Why did you want people to think you were gone?"

"There is a certain value in the unexpected. You can understand that, can't you?" Tresten was looking at Urik, watching the man with a bright intensity.

Urik coughed and looked away from Tresten. "You were dead."

"It was a necessary deception for my protection."

"Yours?" Endric asked. "Who would want to harm you?"

"Do you remember the summons?" Tresten asked.

Endric nodded.

"I had begun to hear rumors that troubled me."

"What kind of rumors?" Urik asked.

Tresten studied him a moment. "The kind that made me think I could trust only Endric. There is something only you—and your father—can help with. Where is Dendril?"

"I don't know. He left Vasha—"

"Left? He should not have left. I warned him not to go."

"Why?"

Tresten tipped his head and his eyes closed. When they opened, he shook his head. "Troubling. We must move quickly now and begin."

"Begin what?" Endric asked.

"Begin to bring about the end."

Endric shook his head. Nothing that Tresten was saying made sense. "I need to return to Vasha. I've been gone long enough. My father—"

"Your father will be accepting of you taking this journey."

"My father would prefer I stay in Vasha and continue to work on gaining the necessary leadership skills to lead the Denraen. Besides, with him gone—"

Urik sneered at him. "With him gone, you prefer to spar with other soldiers, and your poor, drunk friend has no longer the same reputation he once did. And now your presence in the city has created a challenge for Senda." He laughed darkly, and Endric wanted nothing more than to reach across the distance between them and strike him in the face. "Poor Endric. He's run off to the Antrilii, and now that he returned, he can't resume his place in the Denraen."

Tresten watched Endric while Urik was speaking. There was a certain weight to his gaze and his eyes flashed, almost a knowing look behind them. "What is this? What happened while you were with the Antrilii that makes your return to the Denraen difficult?"

Endric leaned back and scrubbed a hand through his hair. "Nothing."

Urik laughed again, his laughter rising almost hysterically. "Nothing? I managed to gain enough influence with the Denraen during the time that Tresten was missing. Endric is no longer en'raen and can no longer serve in the way that he thought that he was going to."

Tresten frowned. "You have no need to mock Endric, Urik. Your place here is quite firmly established."

Urik met Tresten's gaze for a moment before he looked down.

It was the most that Endric had seen Urik conceding to anyone. Even with his father, there had been a defiance and an arrogance that still remained in spite of Urik claiming that he was restored from the influence of the negatively charged teralin. He took that arrogance out on Endric in ways that he never did with Dendril, but it was present with Dendril.

With Tresten, all hint of the arrogance faded.

Was it only that Tresten was one of the Magi?

Tresten glanced over. "You and I will discuss what you saw

while in the Antrilii lands later. The reports that I hear tell that you were witness to something that has never been seen before."

Endric nodded carefully. How was it that Tresten heard word of that? Did it come from his father, or did it come from the Antrilii?

"Why reveal yourself now?" Endric asked.

"Because you came for me. When I left the note, I thought you would come sooner, but it seems that you took your time. I fear that we are already too late."

"I couldn't read the letter."

"After your time with the Antrilii, you still didn't manage to learn enough of the ancient language?"

"I know some, but Senda took the letter and kept it from me. Only because of Urik…"

Tresten eyed him. "Yes. I'm not surprised that Urik would come for me."

Endric looked from Tresten to Urik. "How did you know I came for you? The priest?"

When the priest had disappeared, Endric thought that he was running from him so that he wouldn't have to answer questions about what happened to Tresten, but perhaps that wasn't the case at all. Perhaps he had scurried off to get word to Tresten.

"Since we restored them from teralin, the priests have served quite well." He cast a pointed look at Urik.

"What were you waiting for?"

"You."

"Me? Why would you be waiting for me?"

"Because you are needed to serve as my escort."

Tresten stood and motioned to Urik. The other man shook his head, keeping his eyes down and ignoring Tresten as he loomed over him.

"Stand, Urik. Do not make me carry you."

The idea seemed ridiculous. A Mage carrying a soldier? But

Tresten was not like any other Mage, and though he might be elderly, he was still powerful, exuding strength simply standing in the room. Even Urik must feel it, which, as Endric thought about it, was possibly the reason that Urik was more conciliatory. It was not a great leap of imagination to think of Tresten lifting Urik and carrying him from the room. Tresten might not even draw the same attention that Endric would.

For that matter, what would those in the tavern have thought of one of the Magi coming to a place like this?

Endric stood and looked over at Tresten. "How did you find me?"

"You are not so difficult to find, Endric, especially as you make no effort to hide yourself." He surveyed the room, noting the restraints above the bed without making any sort of indication that he knew why they were there. "I must admit that you have chosen a particularly interesting place to stay."

Endric shrugged. "It was the only place I could find that would not draw too much attention to Urik, bound and gagged."

"I suppose it wouldn't. A place like this is accustomed to having men bound and gagged."

Endric started to smile. "I've paid the king's rate, if you were feeling the need..."

Tresten pressed his lips together. "I am far too old for such proclivities."

Urik reluctantly stood. He clasped his hands together in front of him and while he glared at Endric, he barely looked up to meet Urik's gaze.

Maybe it was only that it was Tresten. Endric understood the reaction. Tresten was different than most of the Magi and carried himself with not only an air of authority similar to the other Magi, but there was a sense of knowledge and understanding that came with him as well. He was a Mage that Endric had no difficulty following.

With Urik now standing, Tresten pulled the door open and stood in the hallway.

"Where are we going?" Endric asked, moving next to the Mage. He glanced over his shoulder and noted Urik standing behind him. He made no effort to run, even though he was no longer bound or gagged. For that matter, he made no effort to scream and raise attention to the fact that he was still confined here.

"I believe you have a horse?" Tresten asked.

Endric nodded. "Two."

"Then we are going to the stables."

Tresten led them down the stairs and through the tavern. It seemed as if the crowd moved out of the way, almost as if they recognized that a Mage moved through, but they said nothing as they created space. As they went, Endric continued to watch behind him, concerned that Urik might try something, but the man never did, following contritely.

It made him uncomfortable to have Urik behind him, so he waited until Urik passed him and took up the rear position. Once out of the tavern, Tresten quickly went to the stables, where the young boy who had greeted Endric when he'd first come to the tavern sat in a pile of hay, chewing on a strand while tossing marbles across the stones.

When Tresten approached, the boy looked up and spit out the strand of hay. "Yes?"

The Mage nodded. "We seek this man's horses."

"So?"

"I believe as the stable boy, your position would be to gather and settle the horses," Tresten said. There was a hint of amusement in his voice. Had Endric not known the Mage before, he doubted that he would have recognized it. It was unlikely the boy recognized Tresten as a Mage because if he did, he would be unlikely to be quite so cavalier about how he spoke to Tresten.

"Two coppers," the boy said.

Endric stepped forward but Tresten raised a hand, stopping him. "Two coppers? Is that what your time is worth?"

The boy shrugged and gathered the marbles that had spilled out in front of him. "I don't know what my time is worth. Two coppers is what I'm charging."

Tresten leaned down so that he was close to the boy's face. "As you grow, one question you must ask yourself: What is your time worth? Once you answer that, you will be farther ahead than most."

The boy stared at him, unblinking for a long moment, before he shrugged again. "My father doesn't give me a choice. He tells me to collect coins, which is what I'm doing."

Tresten smiled. "All men have a choice. As you grow, that is another lesson you'll learn. Find the value of your time and decide whether you're willing to take what you're offered. If not, there is always another way, and there's always another path."

"What are you, a priest?"

Tresten sniffed. "No priest. Merely someone who has lived a long time and knows the value of many things." He pulled a coin purse from his pocket and fished the handful of coins from it, setting them in the boy's palm. "I believe this should be enough to gather our horses?"

The boy stared at the coins in his hand for a moment, his eyes going wide. There had to be nearly ten coppers that Tresten had pulled out, including at least one silver. Far more than what the boy had asked for, and far more than what such a menial task would have required. It was more than Endric would have given.

The boy lurched to his feet and scurried off, disappearing into the stable. "You're only going to encourage him to ask for more," Endric said.

"Or I might encourage him to begin to question whether he should ask different questions."

"What kind of questions?"

Tresten looked over. "The kind that matter."

The boy led the horses out and watched Tresten with a gaze that could only be described as awe. Had the boy realized that Tresten was one of the Magi? If he had, that would explain the expression in his eyes, though maybe it was only about how many coins Tresten had paid him, and nothing else.

The boy handed the reins of the horse to Tresten, who handed them over to Endric, smiling to himself. Endric took them and led them out of the stable, waiting for Tresten. The Mage leaned toward the young man and spoke to him quietly.

"What do you think he's telling him?" Endric asked.

Urik snorted. "Probably some Mage secrets that he thinks will convert the boy to the Urmahne."

"That offends you?" Endric asked.

"Not the conversion. I believe all must find the gods."

Before he had a chance to elaborate, Tresten rejoined them, leading a third horse.

Endric glanced over his shoulder at the young boy and noted that he held Tresten's coin purse. Endric shook his head, laughing. "I suspect you overpaid for this as well," he said.

Tresten merely smiled. "Did I?"

Endric eyed the horse. It was a stout animal, one that would not be the fastest ride, but would be unlikely to grow tired. Such a creature would have not an insignificant cost. Perhaps Tresten had not done nearly as poorly as Endric first thought.

"Where to?" Endric asked.

Tresten guided them through the city and toward the main road. Once they were on it, Endric noted the Tower rising above, casting a shadow that stretched along the road. A crowd filled the street, one that he now understood, considering this was the time of the Ascension, and many reminded him of the miners he had followed through the city.

Tresten glanced over, looking at Endric before his gaze

lingered on Urik. "Now we will head where Urik has long wanted to go. The reason that he thought to capture you and bring you to find me."

"Where is that?" Endric asked.

Urik watched Tresten, his eyes unreadable.

"He has wanted to know about the Conclave. Now he will. Both of you will."

Tresten started forward without hazarding another glance back and led them from the city, away from the crowd, and away from the Tower, leaving Endric only with questions. Urik stared at Tresten's back, saying nothing. The heat in his gaze said everything and left Endric with even more questions.

24

They reached the southern shores on the third day of riding. Urik had spoken little during the journey, deferring to Tresten. For his part, Mage Tresten had spoken very little as well. Endric still had not discovered why Tresten had disappeared or why he had made others believe he was dead and had begun to question whether he would.

They sat on a rocky overlook, the sea crashing far below them, sending occasional salty spray up toward them. Thick blankets of clouds swirled through the sky, the darkness within them hinting at rain that never came. So far, their journey had been uneventful and unmarred by weather. Occasional peals of thunder rumbled, shaking Endric, as if the gods chased them, sending them on their mission with Tresten. Even Urik seemed unsettled by the heavy thunder.

Endric helped establish camp quickly, digging out a small pit and getting a low fire crackling. If it did rain, Endric wanted to have some source of warmth, a way of keeping them dry. They were out in the open for the most part, with only a few trees for cover, nothing else that might provide any sort of protection if storms did come.

Tresten wandered along the shore, alone. He stared at the sea, something he had done often in the days since Endric and Urik had joined him.

"What do you think he's staring at?" Endric asked Urik.

Urik had been quiet, and Endric hadn't decided whether it was out of his anger at being captured or whether he was quiet because of Tresten's presence. Either would explain it.

When Endric had the fire going, he started toward Tresten.

"Leave him," Urik said.

Endric looked over. Urik's gaze seemed fixed on the flame, as if he found some answer in the crackling of the fire and the twisting of the flames.

"Why should I leave him?" Endric asked.

"Because it's Tresten," Urik said.

Endric grunted. "With your willingness to attack Vasha, I never would have expected you to have such devotion to the Magi."

Urik pulled his gaze away from the fire and looked up at Endric. The flames danced in his eyes, the firelight reflected there. "It has nothing to do with the Magi."

"Tresten, then?" Endric asked. He glanced over at the Mage, who remained motionless, his hands clasped behind his back, his body stiff and fixed as he stared into the distance. Was he watching the thick clouds that rolled across the sky? Maybe he feared a coming storm and worried about their safety. Or maybe there was something else, some other answer that Endric had not yet discovered.

"Tresten is… Tresten."

Urik had turned his focus back to the fire and he leaned forward, hands clasped over his lap. He seemed haunted, a shell of the man who had been so arrogant during their journey from

Vasha. The only thing that had changed had been his captivity by Endric—and the appearance of Tresten.

Endric took a seat across from him and forced him to meet his gaze. "You've been quiet since Tresten appeared," he said.

"What would you have me say?"

Endric grabbed one of the slender sticks they had gathered in their journey, one that had been meant for kindling, and began tracing it in the dirt absently. He made a point of not drawing the same pattern that had offended Urik before. "You wanted to know what happened to him, didn't you?"

Urik remained silent, but he watched the way that Endric traced the stick through the dirt, almost as if there would be an answer found in it.

"What is Tresten to you?" Endric asked.

Urik snorted. "I spent all this time thinking that you knew, and you didn't."

He took a deep breath and grabbed one of the other sticks of kindling and tapped it across his knees. Endric watched him, concerned that Urik might decide to attack him with it, but he doubted that the man would. There was something about Tresten's presence that had calmed Urik and had changed him from the angry and aggressive man he had been. It was almost as if Tresten's presence had quenched his remaining darkness.

"You traveled with Tresten, you've spoken to him countless times, but you know nothing about him, do you?"

Endric stared at him. "What's there to know other than that he is a high-ranking Mage? That seems to be all we need to know, at least, all I need to know as one of the Denraen."

Urik snorted again. "You need to know far more than that to understand Tresten."

Urik fell silent, still tapping the stick across his legs, and after a while he turned away from the fire and stared out at the sea.

Endric hadn't learned anything in time since Tresten had

joined them, other than that Tresten had been hiding in Thealon, among other places. With his willingness to travel, Tresten was more like the Magi of old, those Mages who had once spent considerable time attempting to influence the workings of the world, using their knowledge to guide.

Why did Tresten stare out at the sea?

He had done it each night, and Endric wondered what answers Tresten sought by staring off into the distance the way that he did. What could he think to see? Endric had no understanding of the Magi abilities but didn't think there was anything to them that would allow him answers in such a way.

Unless he was speaking to the gods.

Tresten had proven the Magi no longer needed teralin to communicate with the gods. Was that because *he* still possessed an ability to speak to them?

It would be ironic for Endric to have such doubt about the gods and about how he could serve, only to have spent time with Tresten, a Mage with the ability to reach them.

"What does he do when he stands there?" Endric asked.

"I don't know," Urik answered softly.

Endric glanced over. It was difficult for Urik to admit ignorance. He was a man who had pride in the knowledge he had acquired and pride in things that he knew that others did not. Urik had used that knowledge and had twisted it, forcing something that was forbidden to almost all others into his own service.

"Do you think he speaks to the gods?"

Urik eyed him strangely. "Why would he need to do that?"

Endric frowned. "Why would you need to speak to the gods?" he repeated. "Why *wouldn't* he? If he could reach the gods, he could get guidance as to what he was to do. There would be great value in it."

Urik grunted again. "You really are ignorant, Endric."

He stood and started away from the fire, in the opposite direction from Tresten. Endric scrambled to his feet, putting himself in front of Urik, using the length of kindling to jab at Urik's chest.

"You're not going anywhere," he said.

Urik looked down at the wood poking into the fabric of his shirt. Endric hadn't poked him hard, not wanting to annoy the man any more than necessary. "You're right. I'm not going anywhere." Urik looked up and met Endric's eyes. "Haven't you noticed how little I have attempted to escape since Tresten came?"

"I have. I don't know what you're planning, but I know you have something in mind."

Urik sighed and shook his head. "I did. I don't any longer."

"What changed?"

Urik looked over toward the shore, where Tresten stood. "He did."

Endric relaxed, stepping back and lowering the length of wood. He didn't need to make it quite so antagonistic with Urik. The man *hadn't* attempted to escape since Tresten had appeared, and Endric wondered whether he even would try to. It was possible that whatever he wanted was timed to Tresten's appearance. Likely even.

Whatever Urik had been after had been in Thealon. Urik claimed he wanted answers and that he no longer sought anything now that Tresten had appeared, but Endric didn't entirely believe that. Urik had proven that he had plans—and often, plans within plans. Whatever he was after required diligence on Endric's part to ensure that neither he nor Tresten were harmed.

Yet Tresten didn't see the need to keep Urik bound and captive. He seemed to believe that Urik was of no danger, and Tresten had proven himself more than capable and that he could often see things that Endric could not.

He would have to trust that Tresten was right in this as well.

And he had to find a way of working with Urik.

Endric still wanted to know the importance of the symbol. He couldn't recall where he had seen it before and whether it *was* from the Deshmahne he'd faced or whether he had seen it elsewhere. Symbols like that were not common, but he had seen strange markings in his travels. Could it have been on the groeliin when he'd hunted in the Antrilii land? There had been plenty of strange markings found there, brood marks that had significance that even the Antrilii didn't completely understand. Maybe there was something about those markings that Urik had discovered.

If that were the case, Endric needed to work with them. He needed to help understand because it would help the Antrilii. Endric wanted to help the Antrilii—as long as it didn't impact other his tasks.

"Why were you so insistent on finding Tresten?" Urik asked.

Endric shook the thought away and realized that Urik had been watching him. What had he seen? Urik had a keen mind and the things that the man might have seen, and what he might have uncovered, bothered Endric. Likely they were things Endric wanted to keep hidden, secrets that he wanted to keep to himself.

"Because he asked me to," Endric said.

Urik grinned. It was a wolfish expression, one that changed his entire face, that reminded Endric of how dangerous he could be. "He asked you to?"

Endric nodded. "When we were chasing your Ravers, he remained in Thealon and asked me to remain."

He hadn't done so directly, but had intuited that he would have been open and willing to have Endric remain. What would Endric have seen *had* he remained with Tresten? There had been almost a sense of hope on Tresten's behalf, a desire for something, though Endric wasn't certain what that was. At the time, he hadn't thought Tresten had any need of him. If anything, Endric needed Tresten more than the Mage needed Endric. It was the reason he had wanted to head to the north, to see what he could learn of the Antrilii and to see what he could understand about himself.

"And then when I began my return from the Antrilii lands, he sent word again, asking me to find him."

Urik's eyes narrowed. "He sent word to you?"

Endric nodded.

"Did your father know?"

Endric frowned. Had he revealed to his father that Tresten had sent a message to him, asking Endric to join him? He didn't know. It hadn't mattered, because the message had directed Endric to reach him in Vasha, where Endric was heading anyway. "I don't know. Probably."

"Probably. If you *had* told him, your father would never have left Vasha."

"What does that mean?"

Urik chuckled. It was a dark sound, one that carried out to the sea before being overshadowed by the sounds of the waves crashing along the shore. "You are so ignorant, Endric."

Endric tensed, squeezing his hands. "You keep reminding me of that fact."

"Then change it," Urik said.

Endric studied his breathing. "Change it? How am I to change it when I'm trying to do everything I can to keep alive?"

"Do you think the world will be any easier if you remain ignorant, or do you think that you will have a better time—an easier time—of knowing what you should do if you understand the workings of the world?"

"What do you think I've been doing? Why do you think I went to the Antrilii lands?"

"You went for selfish reasons."

Endric clenched his jaw. It was the same argument he'd had with Urik before, and the same argument that others of the Denraen had made, including Pendin. He hadn't thought that he'd gone to the Antrilii lands selfishly, but had he? Had it been more about personal need than about the needs of the Denraen?

No. He needed to understand who he was if he were to serve the Denraen in the way they needed. It might have been selfish, but it was selfishness that served the greater good of the Denraen.

"And what do you think I should have been doing?"

Urik considered him for a long moment. Even here, firelight seemed to reflect in his eyes, dancing brightly. His face had a severe quality to it, and the shadows made it even more so. Gone were the days when Endric found his face plain and unassuming.

"You should have been doing the very same things that I have been doing. You should have been searching for understanding, and you should have been looking for ways to learn, understanding the secrets of the world." He nodded toward the sword strapped to Endric's waist. "You've learned about teralin. How could you learn about something like that and not question that there is something more to the world, something that you would need to understand in order to be a part of it? How could you see the Deshmahne, face them and nearly be defeated by them, and not question your role in all of it?"

"I did question. That's why I went north."

"Do you really think the Antrilii have answers? They're warriors, but they've chosen to remain separate from the world."

That comment more than anything else told Endric all he needed to know about Urik's understanding. "I'm not the only one who's ignorant. I might not know everything that I need, but I'm willing to consider sources that don't fit into my preconceived ideas. The Antrilii that you disparage? If you would pay attention, if you would have any interest in them, you would know that they serve a purpose that might be greater than the Denraen."

Urik watched him, biting his lip as he studied him. "You *saw* them."

Endric blinked. Could it be that Urik knew? Was he only testing Endric?

Spending time with Urik made him question everything. It

forced him to think about all of the possible permutations of what he said and the way that Urik might take it and twist it. It forced him to think of possibilities in ways that Urik might have planned that Endric had not yet accounted for.

"I saw what?"

Urik grinned. "You saw *them*. You wouldn't make the claim of the Antrilii need had you not."

Endric flicked his gaze past Urik and noted that Tresten still stood along the shore. Should he reveal to Urik what he had seen? Did it matter if Urik knew about the groeliin? "I saw them," he said. "How is it that you know of them?"

Urik smiled, and this time there was no predatory quality to it. "What were they like? Can you describe them?"

Endric stared at him, incredulous. Could Urik really want him to describe the groeliin? His asking reminded Endric of Novan and the way the historian probed and took notes. It was the first time that he had ever seen the historian side of Urik.

"What's there to describe? They are creatures, horrible creatures. They attack in swarms and destroy everything in their path if that's possible."

Urik shook his head. "Not swarms, hordes."

Endric grunted. "Yes. Hordes. The Antrilii refer to them as broods."

"The guild has not been able to learn much about these creatures. We know they exist and suspect they have existed for a thousand years or more. There is a reason for the destruction we find evidence of. But we find no sign of these creatures, other than rumors and stories that drift out of the north, stories that always seem to have something to do with the Antrilii."

"I can tell you that these are more than stories."

Urik sighed. "I would have loved to have seen them."

"I doubt that you would have loved it. Likely as not, you wouldn't have survived."

Urik tipped his head, studying Endric. "You're a skilled swordsman, Endric, but you're not so far above me that I would have fallen as easily as that."

Endric just nodded. It wasn't for him to reveal that there was something to the Antrilii bloodline that allowed him to see the groeliin. Let that remain a secret, one that he would not reveal and that he would not share with the historian guild.

"Had you not twisted teralin the way you did, perhaps you could have seen them," Endric said.

Urik squeezed his eyes shut and breathed out heavily. "I have made many mistakes, but I've always served the same ideals." He opened his eyes and met Endric's. "Can you say the same?"

"All of us make mistakes. It's what we do when we make them that defines us," Endric said.

Urik smiled again. "Who said that one to you? Was that your father, or your brother, or was that something of Listain?"

There was derision in his tone, a reminder that though Urik might surprise him at times, the man still had a hint of darkness within him, and maybe more than a hint. It may not be that all of him remained dark, that only his heart might remain dark.

"That was me."

He stepped back and noted the way that Urik tapped the kindling on the ground. An idea came to him. He hadn't reached Urik so far, though he had tried. All he wanted was to try to get through to him, to find answers from the man and see what he had known and why he had felt the need to force Endric out of Vasha. In addition, he wanted to get Urik to open up about the strange pattern that had elicited such a strong emotion. There wasn't a good way to do it, but maybe he'd been going about it the wrong way. Maybe it wasn't that he needed to force Urik to share and instead needed to try to work with him to gain his trust and alliance.

"Would you like to spar?" he asked.

Urik looked up, confusion twisting his gaze. "Spar?"

Endric tapped his stick on the ground. "Spar. Like we do in the Denraen? I imagine it's been quite a while since you've had an opportunity to spar, and I just thought..."

Urik frowned. "Is this your way of wanting to harm me?"

Endric shook his head. "This is my way of offering to spar. Consider it a selfish request. You're a skilled swordsman and I suspect there are things I can learn from you by practicing with you."

As he said it, Endric realized that was truer than he had anticipated. There *would* be things he could learn from Urik, likely catahs that he would not have learned from his father, patterns that Dendril wouldn't even know. Endric wanted to learn all that he could and master as many of the catahs as he could discover so that he could integrate them into his fighting style.

"You realize that practicing with me also helps me gain skill," Urik said.

Endric shrugged. "I realize that. If you don't want to, we don't have to. I just thought..."

Urik watched him for a few more moments. He tapped the kindling stick on the ground and his brow furrowed. He chewed on the inside of his lip, his mouth working as if trying to solve some difficult problem. Endric imagined Urik's mind was racing, struggling to decide what ulterior motive Endric had in offering to spar. Likely Urik would be surprised to realize that Endric really *had* no ulterior motive. All he wanted was a chance to practice and he thought Urik would offer a challenge.

Finally, Urik nodded. "I would like that."

25

They continued their path along the sea. Tresten led them, now walking the horses rather than riding them. He spoke little, though when he did, he often referred to an urgency to what they were doing. Wherever they were heading, there was a time-frame that was important to him.

Urik had been different since the night Endric first sparred with him. He had been less withdrawn, and while he did not share anything more than he had before, when he spoke to Endric, there was less rage bubbling underneath the surface. They had sparred each night since and fell into a pattern that reminded Endric of Denraen patrols.

It had been nearly a week since they left Thealon and were deep into Gom Aaldia but had not seen any sign of soldiers. Endric was relieved. Oftentimes the men of Gom Aaldia could be difficult, even to the Denraen. They were pleased when they were chosen, though most men chosen from Gom Aaldia came from Saeline or from Gomald itself. Few from the outlying kingdoms were ever chosen. Endric didn't know if that created a sense of resentment or if they were thankful for the fact that they were rarely selected.

They stopped along the shores of a river, letting the horses drink. The water tumbled over the rocks with a violent energy before eventually spilling out into the sea.

"He still hasn't told us where we are headed," Endric said. *Something* had happened that prompted Tresten to send word to Endric, but what was it? When would he share?

Urik glanced over. "I don't think Tresten will tell us."

"But you suspect." Endric had begun to realize that Urik knew more about where they were traveling than he let on. Did it have something to do with the Conclave? Tresten had claimed they would learn about the Conclave but the Mage had so far said nothing else about it, keeping Endric in the dark.

"I've known about the Conclave since I was a part of the historian guild. They try to keep it secretive, but there are rumors of another guild of scholars, and..."

"You wanted to know about it," Endric said.

Urik nodded, standing and running his damp hands through his hair. "If there was another sect of scholars, I wanted to know. It was the only way that I would find what I wanted."

"What did you discover?"

Urik grunted. "Nothing. I knew of the Conclave's existence, but that was it. I was unable to determine who even sat upon the Conclave, other than a suspicion that historians were among them."

"And now?"

Urik looked over with a hint of a smile. "Now? Now I know of several members, but it brings me no closer to understanding their purpose."

"And you think their purpose is knowledge."

"What other purpose would there be? They seek to obtain long forgotten knowledge and prevent access to the rest of the world. They protect it."

That hadn't been Endric's experience with the Conclave, though admittedly, he wasn't a part of it. He had traveled with Brohmin and had spent time with Novan and Tresten, but knew very little about what the Conclave did and what intent they had. It seemed that Tresten intended to change that, though Endric wasn't sure that he was ready to learn more about the Conclave. He wasn't certain he was the right person, especially if there was some higher purpose to it.

"It's been my experience that the Conclave is about more than simply knowledge."

"You think the Conclave takes action?"

Endric shrugged. Hadn't they? They had taken action when Urik had brought the Deshmahne to Vasha, acting so that they prevented an attack on the city. Novan had been involved in the Ravers, as had both Brohmin and Tresten. It seemed the Conclave *did* act.

Whatever else they were, they took action when it was necessary. That seemed different than the historian guild to him.

"I've been a part of the historian guild, and I know how little scholars take action. They sit back, observe, and record, and yet let the world press on them if it means they can record it."

That wasn't Endric's understanding of what he'd seen from Novan. Novan had been involved, guiding him through the mountains to reach Vasha. Novan had helped fight off the Ravers.

"Maybe you don't know enough about the Conclave."

"I know enough. Scholars are the same the world over. They seek knowledge but never an application of it."

Endric could only smile. What would happen if Urik saw how much Novan had been involved? What would he do if he knew anything about Brohmin?

"Was that what you were after by seeking Tresten? Did you want to know what you could find of the Conclave?"

Urik looked away and Endric realized that he had gotten to the heart of it.

"You could have asked my father."

Urik's breath caught. He didn't look over at Endric, but Endric could sense the tension in his back. "Dendril is a part of the Conclave?"

"He is."

"How many others do you know?"

Endric shook his head. "Not so many that I can reveal all the Conclave secrets, if that's what you're thinking. I know my father, Novan, and Tresten. A few others." Endric was convinced that Elizabeth was a part of the Conclave, though she had not said anything about it.

"If you know as much as you do, I'm surprised they haven't asked you to join."

"There hasn't been the opportunity, Urik."

Urik looked up. Tresten stood off to the side, watching them. An amused expression lingered on his face. His hands were clasped behind his back and his posture was rigid, the way that it had been in the days since they departed Thealon. Lines around the corners of his eyes were deeper than when Endric had last seen him and his brow was more heavily wrinkled. He was aged, and it had seemed as if it accelerated. In spite of that, there was a power that hung around him, an aura that surrounded him, that gave him a sense of authority.

"I'm sorry if I spoke out of turn," Urik said.

Endric almost started to smile, but he realized that Urik was being honest. He *was* apologetic. What was there between Urik and Tresten that prompted Urik to be so compliant and practically subservient? What did Urik know about Tresten? It had to be something more than the fact that Tresten was a Mage, but Endric didn't know what it was.

"Not out of turn, Urik. Endric has gained a greater understanding of the workings of the Conclave—at least, a *part* of the Conclave—than many others. He has not been asked to join, but in my mind, that is an oversight more than anything else."

Tresten glanced at Endric but said nothing.

If asked, would Endric serve the Conclave?

Would it pull him even more from the Denraen?

Maybe that would be better. How could he return with what he knew? His father might serve the Conclave, but Endric had the sense that he did not do so nearly as well as the Conclave would prefer. Perhaps having Endric out of the Denraen would allow him to serve better.

"Is that what this is about?" Endric asked.

"I told you from the beginning where we were headed," Tresten said.

"The Conclave?"

Tresten nodded. "You who have seen more than I think your father expected have been needed once more to help the Conclave. You were summoned."

"Summoned for what?" Endric asked. But then he already knew. Tresten was the reason he had returned to Vasha. That summons was *why* he had left the Antrilii when he had.

"Summoned because events that are happening are accelerating. You have seen only the beginning of it, but it is a signal of something greater. The Deshmahne attack on Vasha is but a part of it. As is the uncertainty that was spread across the north. And now I suspect there is division within the Conclave."

"Division? How can the Conclave be divided?"

"There are some who would act and others who would not. The Conclave has existed for hundreds of years for a singular purpose, but we have not always agreed on how to achieve that purpose. I intend to reunite them in that purpose."

"Then why summon me? Why draw me to Thealon rather than telling me that you needed me there?"

"I tried, but it was not safe."

"Not safe? For who?"

"For me."

Endric blinked. "How could it not be safe for you?"

"You—and your father, were he to have answered the summons —were to be my escort. Dendril did not come. I am thankful that you did."

"Why do you need an escort? The Deshmahne aren't a threat here any longer. The Denraen have gained control of the north," Endric said.

"Have they? From what I see, there remains a level of uncertainty that even the Denraen are unable to settle. It might be more than can be accomplished without a greater intervention, which is why the Conclave must be united."

"What kind of intervention?"

"The kind of intervention that has been too long from the world," Tresten said. He glanced from Urik to Endric and then nodded. "Now, it's time for us to wade across the stream and wait for the help that I suspect we'll find." He turned away, leaving Endric and Urik watching him.

Urik stared after Tresten, a hint of eagerness in his eyes. Was it from his desire to know the Conclave or was there something else to it?

And why was Tresten in danger?

They continued to walk rather than ride the horses. At first, Endric thought Tresten wanted to save them for a need, preparing them for the possibility that they would need to ride hard, but he decided that wasn't likely. Whatever they might encounter could be countered by riding hard and avoiding the threat Tresten expected to find.

There was some other reason for them to be walking.

He watched Tresten, thinking that he might find an answer, but none came. It wasn't that Tresten made any effort to track as they went, not as Endric did, watching the ground for other prints and signs of soldiers or others who might have come through here. And Endric didn't sense that Tresten used his Mage abilities either. There was no sense of him demonstrating his talents, though Endric wasn't sure that he would have known if he had.

He and Urik followed from a distance, giving him space. It allowed them to notice when Tresten slowed, preparing for the possibility that he might stop suddenly and stare off at the sea, which happened more often than Endric would like.

"You won't figure out what he's doing," Urik said.

Endric glanced over. A sheen of sweat coated Urik's face and he licked his lips, the corners of his mouth twitching.

"What makes you think I'm trying to figure out what he's doing?"

Urik grunted. "Because it's the same thing I'm trying to do. He's up to something, but what? And how does it have to do with the Conclave?" Urik cast a side-eyed glance at Endric. "Those are the questions you have to be asking, if you aren't already. You have to think through what you've seen and try to determine what you might not be understanding."

"What makes you think I'm not understanding anything?"

Urik grinned. "I see the way you're watching him. There's a way you watch a man that gives away your thinking."

"You're telling me I'm not good at masking my emotions?"

Urik shrugged. "There aren't many men who are. It's a skill, the same as any other."

Endric looked away. He had never thought that he showed his emotion that plainly, but maybe he did. Before Andril had died, he had less control of himself, but he'd thought his time with the Antrilii had changed it.

"How would you propose I mask them?" Endric asked.

He glanced over at Urik, uncertain whether he would share anything. What would the point sharing be? Urik had abducted Endric. Why would he offer any help now?

"Practice, the same as you do when working with your sword. There's value in preventing others from knowing your thoughts. If they see you having the same emotion regardless of joy or fear, you can gain the upper hand."

"I don't recall you having such control when I faced you outside of Thealon."

Urik shook his head. "Teralin has many effects, not the least of which is how it prevents rational thought. I don't know if the positively charged teralin has the same characteristics"—he glanced at Endric, waiting for some response that Endric never offered—"but when you hold the dark teralin, there's something quite persuasive about it. It demands a price."

"A price?"

Urik nodded. "There's a price to power, Endric. It's the same with all things. The question you must ask is whether you're willing to pay it."

Endric grinned, unable to help himself. "Now you're the one playing the philosopher."

"I suppose that I am."

"What price does teralin require?"

Urik stared ahead for long moments before he answered. "Your mind."

They fell into a silence as they guided the horses, saying nothing as they went. What more was there to say? Urik suggested that he practice maintaining control of his emotions, but he wasn't sure how.

"What's the key to it for you?" he asked Urik.

"The key?"

"To concealing yourself. How you feel. What you're thinking. What's the key for you?"

Urik looked over at him. "I find that I have to focus on a memory at all times. I use that memory and let it guide how I'm feeling rather than what I'm reacting to."

"What kind of memory?"

"Whatever works for you. It needs to be one where you have some strong reaction to it so it can override the others, but you get to decide what you use."

"And you? What memory do you use to conceal how you're thinking?"

Urik shook his head. "That's not something I share."

"Why?"

He sniffed. "Knowing what memory I use would allow you to know how to control how I'm feeling."

"I doubt that."

"Trust me. The memory has to be something only you know, and it can't be anything that you share with anyone else. Keep it to yourself. Keep everything to yourself."

Endric wondered what he might use that would help him control his reactions better. He could see the value in concealing how he felt so that others didn't know whether they were getting to him. Even when facing Urik, it would be valuable to prevent him from knowing whether there was anything that he said that troubled him.

What memory would he choose?

If it had to be a powerful memory, he thought of learning that Andril had died. That had been a particularly painful moment, and it was a recollection that would overpower almost any other.

There were others—such as realizing that he wouldn't defeat his father when he'd challenged him—but it was the memory of Andril that stung the most.

Was that what Urik had done? Did he cling to the memory of his children and their loss as his way of maintaining his neutrality?

That would be an awful way to live if true.

He couldn't hold onto the thought and memory of losing Andril constantly. If he did, it would numb him and might leave him resenting his brother rather than cherishing the memory.

Maybe he could use a different kind of memory, one where he could cling to it… and be happy that he had.

What memory would that be?

While he had many happy memories, none of them were so strong that they would elicit enough of a powerful response to overwhelm all other sentiments.

It was possible that Urik's way of keeping himself even-keeled was not something Endric could replicate. And that was fine with him.

That didn't mean he couldn't serve as a soldier. It might mean he couldn't lead, at least not effectively, but then he had begun to question whether leading was what he wanted. It might be what his father intended for him, and it might have been something that he would have been able to do had he remained in Vasha following the Raver attack, but Endric wasn't certain what he wanted. He wanted to help the Denraen, but he wanted to be able to help the Antrilii if it came to it, as well. His father hadn't managed to do both, though Endric thought that he would like to.

Tresten raised his hand, calling them to a stop. They were near a sharp rise in the landscape that looked over the sea. Waves crashed over jagged rocks far beneath them. Spray splashed up at them, enough that the taste of salt filled Endric's mouth.

"We will stop here and wait."

"For what?" Urik asked.

"For the next part of our journey."

"How will we know what that is?" Endric asked.

Tresten turned his attention to the sea, staring into the distance. He clasped his hands behind his back and his posture was rigid. His eyes took on the faraway expression that they had so often as he stared. "We will know soon enough."

26

Endric wiped the sweat off his brow as he held the long stick of kindling. His breathing was ragged, a stitch in his side forced him to favor it, and his arm ached where he'd been smacked with a stick similar to his. All in all, it had been a good spar, one of the better ones that he'd had in quite a while.

Urik leaned forward, resting his head on his arms. Sweat dripped off his forehead as well, and there was a smile on his face as he looked over at Endric. "I nearly got you there."

"You struck me twice. I'd say you *did* get me."

It was more than anyone else had done lately. Endric hadn't sparred with Dendril following his return to Vasha. There was a part of him that feared doing so. If he did—and if he won—there would be expectations. It didn't have to be a formal challenge for those expectations to be placed upon him but the moment he managed to defeat his father, there would be others in the Denraen who would expect him to offer the challenge.

"The last few nights, I hadn't managed even to get close." Urik stood and ran his arm across his forehead, smearing his sweat. "I warned you that practicing with you would allow me to see what you know."

Endric nodded. That was a consequence of sparring. Both sides would improve. And Urik had definitely improved. Endric wasn't surprised by that. Urik had a sharp mind and had picked up on the catahs Endric used very quickly, noting the attacks Endric preferred and identifying the defense. It had forced Endric to be creative, mixing catahs together, often pulling from different patterns—some that were meant for the staff and some that had been from his father—in order to keep Urik off-balance. Even that had almost not been enough.

Urik was surprisingly creative. It was a useful skill for a swordsman, but outside of sparring, creativity could be deadly. If used at the wrong time, it could be used against the swordsman. Any off-balance attack might be enough to create an opening that he could exploit. With Urik, there hadn't been any real off-balance attacks, not enough that allowed Endric to defeat him easily.

The creativity challenged Endric in ways that his father did not.

Dendril was technically skilled, one of the most technically sound swordsmen Endric knew. He knew more catahs than any man alive—save for Brohmin. Brohmin might know even more, but Endric suspected there was something else about Brohmin that he didn't fully understand. The Hunter… he was skilled in ways that only the Deshmahne were skilled. Endric had managed to threaten Brohmin the last time they'd sparred, but he doubted he would beat him.

Urik, on the other hand, had a level of creativity that created movements that forced Endric to react. That was a different kind of challenge, the kind that he needed if he were to get better. And the purpose of sparring was for him to get better as well.

"I've learned about you at the same time."

Urik tipped his head. "Have you? What have you learned?"

It was an interesting question. What *had* he learned? "You're a gifted swordsman. You know the patterns, and even those you don't know, you manage to see a way to counter when confronted by them. You think in a different way than any other man I've faced. You're not afraid to take risks"—that had surprised Endric, though it should not have. Urik had taken many risks with the Denraen, so why would he be surprised that he'd take them while working with the sword?—"and you think as you fight, not simply reacting. You plan ahead. It might not always work out, but you try it."

Urik rubbed his neck. Endric's makeshift practice stave had connected on the back of his neck at least once, sending him tumbling forward. "Yes. They don't always work out would be an understatement." He watched Endric for a long moment. "You gather quite a lot from a man when sparring with him."

"You can't hide when you're holding a sword. You're exposed. That's one of the benefits of sparring."

Urik grinned. "And you have changed your approach. When I first knew you, and when you challenged your father, you had an eagerness to your approach. You would lunge forward, knowing that you were faster than almost any other man. It served you well, for the most part."

"Until I faced my father."

"There aren't many men who can face Dendril and do well," Urik said. "But since then, you've gained a measure of something I would call calculating. Your skill has improved, but that was a given considering how much time you have spent sparring with your father. He told me that you'd taken to working with him daily. That alone would make you more skilled. But it's more than that. You have a way about you that Dendril does not. That's how you were able to beat me."

"I beat you because I risked myself with the teralin."

Urik shrugged. "And that. I wonder, though, whether you

would have beaten me regardless. Would you have managed to overpower me even with the teralin sword?"

Endric didn't think so. He remembered the helpless feeling that he'd had while facing Urik. There had been the knowledge that Urik was better than him. He shouldn't have been—and now that they had sparred as often as they did, Endric knew that Urik *wasn't* better than him—but with the teralin sword and the dark powers that it allowed, he was.

"Maybe not then," Endric said. Now was a different matter. He'd gained even more skill working with the Antrilii. His technique was better and he knew catahs that he had not before. Most of that was from training with the Antrilii, but some came from necessity and facing the groeliin.

"Hmm. Maybe not then, but I suspect you would now." Urik stood and tapped the ground with the kindling stave. "Maybe I shouldn't work with you. It's making you all too aware of the fact that you can defeat me."

Urik turned away, leaving Endric standing alone by the fire they'd set for the night. Smoke billowed from it and it crackled softly.

A strange thought came to Endric. He'd been thinking that Urik had been challenging him as best as he could, but what if he wasn't? What if Urik intentionally held back, not wanting to expose the extent of his talent?

It would be the kind of thing Endric would expect of him. Urik *would* do something like that, and likely would refrain from displaying the full extent of his abilities, especially if he thought that Endric might face him again. That way he could spring an unexpected attack on him.

But Endric didn't think he'd done that. Urik was clever, but he'd demonstrated creativity as a way to defeat Endric, a way also to try and test him. Could he have held back while doing that?

He had to admit that it was possible.

What did he really know about Urik? He knew the man had a willingness to do whatever he thought necessary to achieve his objectives.

Endric would have to be more careful, especially if they continued to spar.

And he *wanted* to continue sparring with Urik. He did challenge him, and made it so that Endric had to push himself. That was the kind of thing that would make him better… if he could manage to stay ahead of Urik.

He smiled to himself. Working with Urik forced him to try and think like the other man, much as Elizabeth had warned him that he needed to, telling him that it was the only way that he would be able to defeat the man. Strange that Urik himself would be the one to teach him those lessons.

A mournful howl split the night and Endric looked up.

"It's only a wolf," Urik said.

He had heard plenty of wolves during his travels, but that sounded more like one of the merahl than any wolf he'd ever heard. When he'd traveled through the north, making his way beyond the edge of the mountains until he reached the Antrilii flatlands, he had heard the merahl howl often enough that he recognized the sound. This was close enough that it seemed as if it *had* to be merahl.

He said nothing. Had Tresten been there with him, he would have asked the Mage. He had a sense that Tresten would have known what he'd heard, or would have known whether it was a merahl. If it *was* one of the merahl, there would have to be some reason for it to be here, something that would explain why they had ventured so far south. Would any of the Antrilii have come with it? If they had, that might mean there had been a groeliin attack. There shouldn't be. The Antrilii kept them confined within the mountains. Another escape would mean that the groeliin moved in numbers again.

Endric remained on edge, listening to the night, but the sound didn't come again.

He settled in near the fire, resting his head on the ground, and stared up at the sky. Clouds blocked most of the stars, though there were a few that twinkled through. Not enough for him to count, not as he had on the other nights and certainly not enough to make it seem as if the gods watched over him. What shone down now were only a few, as if the hundreds of gods had been reduced to something less, so that only a few of the gods looked down on them, watching from above.

He awoke to a hand on his shoulder.

Endric jumped up, unsheathing in a single motion, and spun to face whoever had grabbed him. Tresten stood in front of him and his eyes locked onto Endric's.

"Good. You will need that. Be ready."

"For what?" Endric asked.

The fire had burned down and left very little light for him to see. Strangely, even in the darkness, he managed to see well enough and could make out gradations of shadows, enough that he could tell where to find Tresten and that Urik remained motionless, sleeping soundly.

How could he sleep through an attack?

Could Endric allow him to sleep, or did he have an obligation to wake him and get his help? If there was an attack, Urik might be needed. Tresten certainly wouldn't fight. Though he carried a staff much like Novan did, it was more decorative and would be good for nothing more than pushing back any attackers, not disabling them. Sometimes, they would need a firmer hand. It might require others to die. Tresten likely wouldn't be ready for that.

A low howl came again, this time close enough that Endric

could tell that it was a merahl. He turned to the sound, the hair on the back of his neck standing on end, and listened.

"That's a merahl," he said to Tresten.

"Most likely," the Mage said.

"That means groeliin."

Tresten shook his head. "That means they hunt. They do not only hunt groeliin."

That was the first Endric had heard of that. The merahl were creatures of the north, massive cats with incredible intelligence that were particularly suited to stopping the groeliin. If there were no groeliin, there would be no reason for them to have made it here.

"What are you expecting, Tresten?" he asked. "Is this why you needed me?"

"Not expecting. Worried that I might find might be a better way of framing it."

"You worried that you might find groeliin here? We're nearly to Gomald. If they reached this far south, they would have destroyed half the countryside getting here."

"That's a possibility."

Endric looked over at the Mage. He stood with his hand resting casually on his staff, his posture rigid as it had been during their entire journey. He had always stood stiffly, but this was even more than usual for him.

Something troubled Tresten.

Was it the merahl? If they were here—and if it *didn't* mean the groeliin were here—Endric would need to find them and see why they had come. There might be something that he could do—some way of communicating with the merahl, even though he was not fully Antrilii and he'd not mastered that part of speaking to them when he had been in their lands.

The sound came again, but it had veered to the south.

"I'm going to check on what they're hunting. Will you be safe with Urik?"

He expected Tresten to argue with him or tell him that he needed to remain near them, but the Mage didn't. Tresten nodded. "Be careful, Endric. I don't know what you will encounter."

"You don't know?"

Tresten looked at him, his eyes carrying a haunted expression. Shadows stretched over his face, leaving his features almost harrowed. "I have searched for answers, but I don't have them. Something moves through here. Whatever it is possesses power. It is why I needed an escort. It is why I thought to have you here."

His breath caught. "Deshmahne?"

"This is not Deshmahne. They have remained in the south. And this is not their priest. That man would not risk confronting us so directly."

"The Deshmahne priest?"

Tresten nodded. "He's a man we know all too well. He would not confront us openly, though he would do so in the shadows. Still, I don't think this is him."

"How do you know it's power?"

Tresten stared into the darkness, his face taking on that faraway look that it had when he'd been staring out at the sea. He was quiet for a moment. "I can feel it. The sense of it fills the air. Can't you detect it?"

Endric listened, focusing on the sounds around him, but heard only the crashing of the sea. Moisture dampened the air and there was a distant sound of thunder, that of the storm that had seemed to chase them since they left Thealon, though they had so far managed to stay ahead of it. Was there anything else to it that he could pick up on?

Endric didn't think so. If there was, he wasn't attuned to what it might be.

"I can't detect anything."

The merahl howled again, now to the west. It was moving quickly now, enough that they wouldn't run into it if they stayed where they were.

Was that what they needed to do? Should he remain, or should he chase after whatever was out there and find what the merahl hunted?

It wasn't really even a question. If there were merahl—and if it meant that Antrilii had come—he needed to find out why, even if it meant that there were no groeliin.

Perhaps especially then.

"You'll be fine with Urik?"

Tresten smiled. Surprisingly, there was a hint of menace in the smile, an expression that Endric would never have expected to see from one of the Magi. "Should I fear what he's been learning from you?"

Endric shook his head. "Not fear, but I don't want you to be in any danger because I left you alone with a man who has betrayed so much."

"There is no danger to me. I think Urik has questions of me, but he cannot harm me any more than you could harm me."

It seemed a strange way of phrasing it. Endric suspected that were he to attack Tresten—something he couldn't imagine doing—he would have little trouble subduing him.

The merahl howled again, now farther away and faint.

"You should go or you will miss your opportunity."

27

The night surrounded Endric, an oppressive sense. There was no sound other than his feet across the ground and the steady sound of his breathing as he jogged. He'd run rather than taking the horse, preferring to be on foot. It was better to sneak this way, though he might not be fast enough to catch the merahl. If he was not, they could track them in the daylight.

Too much time had been spent talking to Tresten, debating what he would do about the merahl. Their howl occasionally split the night, but it was less frequent than before. Had he missed his opportunity? He didn't think so, but he would need to hurry to catch them.

Thunder continued to rumble, and now it had an urgency to it, one that matched his pounding heart. The air was thick with moisture and damp enough that he didn't have to sweat for his face to be sopping wet. Dew stained his boots as well.

Endric lost track of how long he'd been running. Hours. Long enough that his legs burned with the effort. Even when he did catch up to the merahl, he wouldn't be of any use. They continued west and the howls grew louder, subtly so, to the point that he was nearly upon them by the time he realized he had neared them.

Reflection off eyes in the darkness caught his attention.

Endric froze.

Would the merahl be any that he recognized?

When he'd been in the Antrilii lands, he had met a dozen or so, but there were many others that he hadn't met. Would the merahl recognize that he was connected to the Antrilii?

The creature stalked forward.

Like all of the merahl, this one was enormous, larger than any wolf. It had striped fur and a long snout. Pointed ears swiveled, likely allowing the creature to hear everything around it.

As it approached, it sniffed Endric.

He tipped his head forward. "I'm Endric Verilan, son of Dendril, descendant of the Antrilii."

It no longer felt strange speaking to the merahl as if it could understand him. Endric knew they could. He might not be able to know what this one was telling him—but he hoped the creature would have some way of sharing what it wanted of him.

The merahl snarled and lunged at him.

Endric remained motionless. If this creature were like the others in the north, it wouldn't want to attack. They had partnered with the Antrilii; they never attacked them.

The merahl circled around him. As it did, another merahl howled.

This one was close.

The hackles on the merahl circling him raised and the creature snarled.

There was something off about this merahl.

When he'd been around them before, he had experienced the ferocity with which they attacked, and had known the keen intelligence they displayed. A single merahl could handle many groeliin, enough that Endric had hunted with them and had felt confident in the ability to take on an entire brood. This creature watched him with a predatory intent, one that none of the merahl had ever focused on him directly.

It made his heart race.

Tresten had mentioned another power. Could this other power have coopted the merahl somehow? Could they have trained them and turned them, much like teralin had turned the Deshmahne—and the Ravers?

Was there some connection to teralin?

That would be the hardest to imagine. The merahl wouldn't be able to use negatively charged teralin, but there definitely was something off about the creature that he couldn't quite put words to.

The nearby howl came again.

The merahl across from him snarled. Its ears swiveled, listening into the night.

Endric shivered.

Slowly—moving carefully so that he didn't draw the merahl's attention too quickly—he reached for his sword.

The merahl lunged.

Endric had been watching the creature, needing to anticipate what it might do no differently than when he'd faced groeliin. It was only because he had that he noticed the twitch of muscle beneath the creature's fur alerting him to the attack.

He rolled to the side, unsheathing his sword.

Conflicted emotions rolled through him. When he faced the groeliin, he wanted only to stop them, and doing so required that he use all the force and technique that he could summon. With the merahl, he didn't want to hurt the creature. They were allies. Whatever had happened to it needed to be reversed.

If only he could discover what it might have been.

Could it be teralin?

The metal certainly could influence others, which meant that it *could* be responsible for what he had encountered, but he didn't think that was likely. There was no teralin here.

Was there another way to influence the merahl?

There were many powers in the world that he didn't understand, so he could easily imagine that there *were* some powers that might be responsible, but what would they be? What could turn an intelligent creature that was an ally to the Antrilii into one that would attack him?

He had no answers.

The merahl lunged at him again.

Endric rolled, ducking off to the side, trying to keep from getting injured. Somehow, he would have to engage the merahl and stop its attack, but he didn't know how. What could he do to stop it?

The merahl snapped at him, and on instinct, Endric swung his sword toward it.

Fear lurched through him. The blade seemed to glow, likely reflecting the faint light of the moon, though it was positively charged teralin so it was possible there was another explanation.

The merahl cowered away from his sword.

Endric's gaze flicked from the sword to the merahl.

Was it afraid of the teralin blade?

When he'd been with the Antrilii, the merahl had never feared his sword. Most seemed drawn to it, likely having something to do with the way they mated near positively charged teralin.

Why would the merahl shrink back from it?

He would have to use it to keep himself safe.

Another merahl howled. In the faint light, Endric saw it appear at the edge of his vision. He danced back, keeping a distance between himself and the other creature, enough space so that he could watch both as they approached.

The second merahl snarled at him, snapping, until he swung his sword in its direction.

Like the first merahl, it jumped back, dancing away from the blade.

How would he stop not only one merahl, but *two*, and do so without harming them? He needed to find some way of trapping them so that they could study and find out what had happened. He would need to send word to Nahrsin and see if his cousin could help, but first he had to survive.

Creativity.

Could he borrow from what he'd learned from Urik and apply it to this situation?

He might need to harm the merahl, but could he do it in a way that only incapacitated them and didn't leave them lame?

Both merahl lunged at the same time.

Endric dropped, swinging his sword around, and grazed the first merahl.

There was a strange pressure against him, much like when he'd changed the polarity of the teralin, and the merahl howled.

Endric rolled back, getting onto his feet.

The injured merahl snarled at him and snapped, but Endric brought his sword around, blocking the merahl from getting too close.

The other attempted to circle around, but Endric shifted his feet, keeping it from reaching him as well.

"I don't want to hurt you. There's something wrong. Let me help you."

The first merahl snarled.

Endric feigned moving to his left before cutting back the other way. The merahl followed his first movement and he sliced at it, catching it along the flank. Much like the first time, there came a heaviness and the same sense as when he altered polarity. The merahl let out a pained cry and withdrew.

It left him facing the other merahl.

The creature watched his sword, keeping focused on it.

Endric darted right, then shifted. The merahl anticipated the move.

He had to jump out of the way of one of its massive paws, barely avoiding getting raked by it.

Endric swung around, hoping he wasn't too aggressive with the move, and slashed at the merahl. He caught it more deeply than he'd intended, piercing the flank.

The howl from the merahl split the night.

The merahl snarled and crawled away from him, joining the other.

Both merahl watched him, the light reflecting off their eyes.

Endric stepped into a ready position, holding his sword in front of him.

The merahl stared at the blade. Endric had a sense that they were far more concerned about the sword than about the man wielding it. They howled in unison and darted away, disappearing into the night.

Endric stood in place, trembling. He might have stopped the merahl, but why had he needed to? What had happened to them? And how could he keep it from happening again?

No answer came. Instead, he had only the occasional sound of the merahl.

Sighing, he sheathed his sword. He had come this way seeking answers. He still didn't have them.

He turned toward the darkness, back in the direction he'd been tracking the merahl. Whatever had happened to them was still there.

Now wasn't the time to race into the darkness.

Endric turned away, making his way back to Tresten. He could track for answers in the daylight.

With each howl of the merahl, his heart fluttered and he wondered if he'd missed an opportunity to help them or whether leaving them alive would come back to haunt him.

28

Daylight began to spread by the time he returned to Tresten and Urik. Endric found the Mage awake and staring out at the sea, standing rigidly as he had so often over the last few days. A faint sheen of moisture coated his face, likely mist rather than sweat. His face had a weathered appearance, and the muscles in his cheeks were slack, leaving him more heavily wrinkled than Endric had seen before.

Whatever was happening with Tresten was aging him, and rapidly.

Urik remained asleep as Endric arrived. The man slept fitfully, every so often kicking at the air. What dreams assaulted him in the night to cause him so much difficulty?

Endric took a seat along the shore. From here, he could look down and see the rocky coastline far below. Occasional waves crashed, sending spray up toward him, but the sea was calmer today than it had been in some time. There was a peaceful quality to sitting here and listening to the sound of the ocean, one that he never would have expected. Endric had never spent much time near the coast, though had heard others who'd spent time near the sea describe their love for it in ways that reminded him of his feelings about working with the sword. For him, there was a peace in holding his sword, in flowing through the various catahs, and in the emptiness he forced his mind into so that he could focus on the task at hand.

"What do you see when you look out?"

Endric hadn't heard Tresten appear and now the Mage sat next to him, his legs bent beneath him and his eyes locked onto something in the distance. What would he see? Magi eyesight was better than that of others, and he likely saw something out in the distance that Endric could not.

"I'm only looking at the waves," Endric said. "The sound of them… the rhythm… it's relaxing."

Tresten started to smile but it faded. "There is power in the sea. Much power." He took a deep breath and blinked. As he did, the emptiness to his face changed, the muscles in his cheeks tightening and the lines along his eyes fading, if only slightly. He turned his attention to Endric. "What happened?"

"There's something wrong with the merahl," Endric answered. He hadn't come up with any answers during his walk back to Tresten and Urik. Endric wasn't certain whether there would be any. Likely he would have only more questions. When Tresten nodded, Endric frowned. "You knew there would be."

"I suspected. There have been sightings. It is why I needed an escort."

Endric thought about the times he had thought he'd seen the merahl but hadn't been certain. How could he when it seemed so unlikely that they'd have come out of the northern mountains?

"Why not ask the Antrilii?"

"I fear this isn't something the Antrilii can solve."

"Why me? Why my father?"

"You have already seen why."

"That's why you wanted me to go."

Tresten patted his arm. "If you saw them, then you know what it was that I feared."

Endric sighed and looked back out over the water. "I saw the merahl, and I saw the way they seemed to have been… twisted." He shook his head. "I don't know of any other way to put it than that. I thought it might be teralin, but…"

"You don't think it could be?"

"How would the merahl be influenced by teralin?" He turned to Tresten, looking up at him. "There's something I saw when I was in the north. The merahl are tied to teralin the same as the groeliin." Could *that* be why Tresten wanted him to come?

He watched a massive wave roll in until it crashed along the shore. Power. That was what Tresten had said. Power like that would destroy over time and wash away everything, but the rocks remained standing in spite of it.

"You have learned something that many never do, Endric. The metal is not good or bad. It simply *is*. Those who have studied it once believed that it was the power of the gods, but perhaps a better way to describe it is a remnant of creation. There is something quite primal about it. The metal stores power, and power can change it, make it into something else, which then has the power to change other things."

The idea made Endric's head spin. "I don't have any power."

"Don't you?" Tresten pulled Endric's sword from his sheath faster than he could react. Endric reached for it, but Tresten only held it out, studying the blade. "You have taken what had been charged a certain way and changed it so that it was charged in another. I would argue that is quite a bit of power."

"That's the Antrilii part of me."

"Is that what you believe?"

Endric shrugged. "What else should I believe?"

Tresten handed his sword back over. "You spent months with

the Antrilii and you have returned believing that your only connection is to the teralin?"

"And the groeliin. There's something about the Antrilii that allows them to see the groeliin."

"The same reason the Magi can see them, Endric."

Endric tipped his head. "What reason? The Antrilii have been gifted by the gods?"

Tresten sniffed. "The Antrilii and the Magi share a connection. How else do you think they have been able to stop the groeliin?"

"The Antrilii or the Magi?"

"Does it need to be one or the other?"

"The Magi don't face the groeliin."

Tresten clasped his hands in his lap and turned to stare out over the water. "Not anymore. You were raised in Vasha, so you know the stories of the Founding of the city. The Magi do not hide the fact that they claim ancestors who once were soldiers. What do you think they fought in the time before the Founding?"

"Groeliin?"

Tresten studied him as he nodded.

As he fell silent, Endric stared at the sea with him, breathing in the salt air. The sky began to lighten and thick clouds remained in the distance, but so far, there had been no thunder that rumbled. There was nothing but the sound of the sea and that of Endric's heart pounding steadily in his chest. He breathed deeply, savoring the peace he found here.

He thought through what Tresten had said but still didn't come up with any answers. There seemed no reason for the merahl to have been changed the way they had seemed to have been, unless it did have to do with teralin. The groeliin had been tied to the negatively charged teralin as well. Was there anything to that connection that would help explain the strangeness of the merahl and their attack?

"You said 'they.'" Tresten glanced over, arching a brow at

Endric. "When you were describing the Magi and the Founding of Vasha. Not 'we.'"

Tresten stared, saying nothing. Eventually, he stood. "It is daylight. It's time for us to begin our journey again."

Endric watched him, wondering what he might be missing. The Mage had often been odd, but this was strange even for him. Since finding him in Thealon, Tresten had not said much, not nearly as he had in the past when Endric had spoken with him. *Had* something happened to him? Maybe there was more to the rumors than Endric understood. There had been the claim that Tresten had died, which had to have come from somewhere. He didn't like to think of the Mage having such difficulty, but there was no doubting that he seemed more aged than he had before.

Plenty of men struggled at the end of their lives, especially if they lived long enough. There had been a few soldiers of the Denraen who had similarly struggled. Their minds would begin to slip and they would often more easily remember things that happened decades ago than they would recall what was happening around them, leading them to reminisce.

Was that what was happening to Tresten? Was he seeing the signs of a Mage fading?

If he was, should Endric follow him?

They were troubled thoughts, and ones that he didn't have any easy answers for. Maybe he shouldn't be following Tresten. When he'd been abducted from Vasha and gotten free, should he have returned rather than continuing on toward Thealon? Endric had wanted to know what motivated Urik, thinking that he might find answers to Tresten's disappearance, and had not expected to find the Mage still alive.

Yet, if Tresten's mind *was* slipping, could he abandon him? Shouldn't he stay with him and see if Tresten needed him? Wasn't that part of what the Denraen were called upon to do?

Endric returned to the campsite and helped break it down,

burying the fire and readying for departure. He glanced over at Tresten from time to time but came up with no answers. When Urik woke, he studied Endric and the glint of his eye made it seem as if he noticed something was off, but said nothing. Endric didn't share and they departed, heading west in silence.

They picked up the trail not far from the edge of the trees. Endric noted shallow prints that looked as if they could have been made by a wolf, but he knew better. These were merahl prints, and frequent enough that the creatures had been nearby. That troubled him. Their proximity meant that they were willing to approach much closer than Endric had expected, and that they had been close enough to attack.

Urik seem to notice the prints as well, though he said nothing. He had claimed the howling they had heard had been wolves, and Endric wondered whether he still felt that way or whether seeing these markings in the soft ground had changed anything for him.

There were other prints as well. Most looked as if they were from horses, which left him wondering who led the merahl. The Antrilii would travel by horseback, though this was incredibly far south for them to have traveled, especially without any word of their presence getting out.

Unless that was the reason Dendril had departed Vasha.

When his father had left, he had done so without leaving any indication as to why, or where he was going. Endric had only been back in the city for a short time and hadn't the opportunity to regain his father's trust, and certainly wasn't part of his inner circle, not as Senda now was. Endric tried not to think of the irony that Senda was the one who prevented him from knowing details of his father's plans, much like Listain once had done.

Tresten made no sign that he noticed the markings, but he

followed them just the same. They moved swiftly, trailing after the prints marking the passing of the merahl, and they found themselves continuing to make their way west. Eventually, this would take them to the city of Gomald. If the merahl had traveled all the way to Gomald, would the people of the city be in any danger?

When Endric had been in the Antrilii lands, such an idea would have been ridiculous. He never would have imagined the merahl harming anyone other than the groeliin, but after what he'd seen, and after Tresten's vague comments, he no longer knew whether they would be safe from the merahl. He'd faced two of them and managed to prevent them from killing him, but what would happen to someone without his training?

What would happen to someone who wasn't willing to merely incapacitate them and was more willing to slaughter them? Would it draw attention to them? Would it bring hunters into the northern mountains, seeking prizes? The merahl had been left alone, had been unknown, before now. If they were hunted—and killed—one of the greatest allies to the Antrilii would be lost. Without the merahl, the Antrilii would eventually fail in their mission.

That troubled him as much as anything else. Did Tresten think about that? Was that part of the reason that he was so motivated to bring them after these creatures? He was more enlightened than most of the Magi Endric had met and was a part of the Conclave, and so would know about the groeliin and the role the Antrilii played, but would they intervene?

If it came to it, Endric would have to. He couldn't risk the merahl drawing attention to their presence and couldn't risk something happening to the creatures. They were too valuable in the fight against the groeliin, a fight that would not be over anytime soon.

The longer they went, the more the markings in the damp soil from the merahl began to fade, spacing out more and more before they disappeared completely. Endric couldn't tell if the merahl had gone elsewhere or whether the earth was now too dry for him to follow. He didn't have much tracking skill but was relieved that Urik didn't seem to notice the tracks either. Tresten didn't alter his course, so if they were present, and if that were the reason he made his way through here, he had another way of following.

Evidence of horses coming through here increased. It was more than the way the ground was trampled, and more than the occasional broken branch. He saw evidence of horse dung that had hastily been cleaned up. What would the riders have done with it? Endric imagined men scooping it and throwing it into the sea as they thought to obscure their passing, but that seemed extreme for soldiers. Even the Denraen wouldn't have gone quite that far.

As they traveled, Endric watched Tresten. He kept his eyes on the Mage when they stopped, waiting to see what he would do. At times, Tresten would make his way to the ledge looking out over the sea and would simply stand and stare with his hands clasped behind his back, his face going slack as it did in the evenings. Other times, he would remain motionless, particularly when they paused at the streams with water spilling out into a waterfall that cascaded down the ocean.

Urik seem to pick up on it as well. He didn't say anything, but he watched Tresten and occasionally he would glance over at Endric as if waiting for Endric to reveal his concern, but Endric never did. It wasn't his place to share what he feared with Urik. He could be wrong. There could be nothing at all that troubled Tresten. It could simply be that the Mage worked through thoughts that bothered him, though his general silence left a sense of unease hanging between them.

When they stopped for the night, making camp, Tresten disappeared as he had each of the other nights. Endric and Urik prepared the fire and Endric sat near it, leaning forward. He was exhausted from the day and from a sleepless night and had fought against his exhaustion. If they encountered the soldiers they tracked, or even the merahl, Endric wouldn't be of much use. With as tired as he was, he would likely make a mistake. He needed sleep.

They ate dried jerky that Tresten supplied, as well as a few of the berries they had gathered along the journey. "What I wouldn't give for a hot meal," Endric muttered.

"Just a hot meal?" Urik asked.

Endric glanced over. "What else would I want?"

Urik shrugged. "You used to be the kind of man who preferred a mug full of ale than a belly full of food." He laughed, and it did nothing to pierce the strange anxiety that remained between them. "There were a few times when we had to get you from the stockade. As much as he tried to hide it, your brother had a soft spot for you. He was never willing to let you remain in the cell for too long."

Endric squeezed his eyes shut, thinking back to those last days that he'd had with Andril. His brother had been frustrated with him, and whatever soft spot he might have once had was long gone by the time that he departed, heading south to confront the Deshmahne—and die.

The smile on Urik's face faded. "I'm… I'm sorry about Andril. I never wanted him to die."

"What did you expect to happen?"

"I thought…" Urik looked down at his hands, holding a stick of jerky. He shrugged. "I thought that if nothing else, Andril would see the threat of the Deshmahne. He would convince your father when no one else had been able to do so. I had not expected the Deshmahne to have come in such numbers as they did."

Endric didn't like talking about this, and didn't like talking about what had happened to his brother, or losing his brother. Those thoughts were still raw and the memories still too painful, even though his brother had now been gone for nearly two years.

That was time Endric hadn't had his brother's guidance and hadn't had his brother's buffer between himself and their father.

Maybe Urik hadn't intended for Andril to die. The anger Endric felt at Urik was justified, but perhaps unnecessary. Urik couldn't change anything now, and Endric might dishonor his brother's memory by holding onto rage that Andril would not have wanted of him.

"You miscalculated with my father," Endric said. "Dendril can't be prodded into action." Urik arched a brow and Endric grunted. "He can't usually be prodded into action. I think he was willing to face you on the battlefield because he thought it would end whatever violence that you had brought. I doubt he expected you to pose any real threat to him."

Urik grunted. "Thanks."

Endric snorted. "It's not arrogance when he's been the best swordsman in the world for as long as he had been." Endric said nothing of Brohmin, not needing for Urik to know of how skilled the Hunter was with the sword. He didn't know what to make of him anyway. How would he explain the level of skill that Brohmin possessed?

"Perhaps not. Yet, were it not for you and what you can do with teralin, things might be quite a bit different."

Endric stared at the crackling fire. His father likely had the same ability, which made Endric wonder why he hadn't been the one to change the polarity of the sword Urik used. It seemed unlikely for Endric to be the only one of his family to have such an ability, especially as they had a shared connection to the Antrilii.

"You needed to be stopped. Had you taken command of the Denraen, using your connection to the negatively charged teralin, you would've forced the Denraen into war."

"I still think that the Denraen need to confront the Deshmahne." Urik took a bite and chewed slowly. When he finished, he let out a long breath. "It's not even about my selfish desires anymore. Once, I claimed that. Perhaps I still do. I lose track of things these days," Urik said. He attempted a smile. "My desire for vengeance and the need to destroy the Deshmahne aren't incompatible. They can coexist, much as the Magi and the Denraen coexist."

It was an odd comparison, but perhaps apt. The Magi valued peace, while the Denraen were soldiers, trained in fighting and in war.

"I don't disagree the Deshmahne will need to be stopped," Endric said.

"If they do nothing more than maintain their position in the south, the Denraen will not act."

"Why would the Denraen need to act?"

Could he actually be arguing on behalf of the Denraen to leave the Deshmahne alone? There had been a time when Endric wanted nothing more than to destroy them and get his revenge. And perhaps he still did. Perhaps that still motivated him, but now he was aware of it. He hated that he was driven by such desires for vengeance, and for revenge. There had to be another way—a better way.

"You never saw what I did. Be thankful that you didn't. There is a darkness within them."

"Much like the darkness that consumed you when you held onto the teralin."

Urik's eyes narrowed. As they did, shadows danced within them and left Endric with the same question that he often confronted when he watched Urik. It was these quiet moments when he wondered whether Urik had been freed of the influence of the negatively charged teralin. It was times like these when he could no longer tell. Supposedly he had been treated, and it had been done by Tresten himself, which would make it seem as if he should be free of it. Especially as they traveled together. If anyone would be able to recognize the ongoing influence of teralin, wouldn't it be Tresten?

But if something was happening to the Mage, if his mind were slipping, maybe he wouldn't recognize it.

"It is much the same. The intent... The intent was different."

Urik fell into silence and Endric let it grow between them. He wouldn't argue with Urik on this. There was no point.

As they sat there, they heard a howl in the night.

Endric sat up. The sound was distinct and clearly one of the merahl.

Urik seemed not to have heard.

When it came again, this time closer, Endric got to his feet.

"I didn't think you are in the mood to spar," Urik said.

Endric shook his head. "Not spar. This is something else."

The sound came again, much closer this time. As he listened, there were multiple voices to the merahl, enough that he recognized that they called to each other, an entire pack of merahl.

And they were coming toward the camp.

29

Endric peered into the darkness, looking for movement. Where they had camped was near a line of trees and he saw nothing through their thick, round leaves. There was no sound in the night other than that of the waves crashing along the shore and that of his own breathing, a sound that had quickened since he'd heard the merahl's howl. Those cries continued, picking up intensity and focus.

With each howl, Endric's heart hammered. If there were this many, he would be forced to do something other than incapacitate.

Endric didn't care for the idea of harming the merahl. If they were somehow tainted, there had to be a way to save them.

But was there? Was it only his connection to the Antrilii that made him feel that way, or was it the right thing to do, regardless? Would attempting to save the merahl sacrifice something else?

He needed help.

Endric looked back. Urik still sat by the fire, but his posture was rigid. He tipped his head, listening, as if only now hearing the cries from the merahl. Was there something about them that masked their presence from others without the Antrilii connection? Endric had never asked that question before, but considering how only those with Antrilii bloodlines—and perhaps the Magi—had an ability to see the groeliin, maybe the merahl were included in that as well.

"Tresten?" he called into the night

Urik appeared next to him, standing at Endric's shoulder and following the direction of his gaze. "What is it?"

"Do you hear it?"

"I hear the sound of wolves braying, but nothing more than that."

Endric frowned. "Those aren't wolves."

"What are they?"

Tresten appeared out of the darkness before Endric had a chance to answer. "It is time for us to depart," Tresten said.

"Depart? We just camped for the night," Urik said.

Tresten held tightly to his staff and tapped it on the ground. Endric noted that he seemed to do it each time there came a call from the merahl. There was a rhythm to it that he hadn't noticed before, but Tresten must have. "We have only just camped, but that doesn't change the fact that we must get moving. Things are escalating now and it is time for us to prepare for what is to come."

"What's escalating?" Endric asked.

Tresten breathed out. "The ending." He moved past and grabbed the reins of his horse, climbing into the saddle.

They had been walking over the last few days, and it surprised Endric that Tresten would choose to mount now, especially in the darkness, when the horse could easily catch a hoof and become lame. The path they'd been traveling was not the easiest. There was some underbrush, and the weeds and grasses that grew near the rocky ledge overlooking the ocean were thick here. Many had brambles that caught on their boots and pants and that buried in the horses' hair. They brushed them each night, removing as much of the brambles as they could, but it seemed cruel to send them through the darkness, riding at night when even the horses' footing would not be that steady.

Tresten glanced back. "Now is not the time to question my sanity, Endric."

Endric shook his head. Had Tresten known what he was thinking? Had he recognized the fact that Endric struggled with following him, and the way that he had continued to stare out into the darkness? He must have.

Urik obeyed more quickly than Endric did and climbed onto his saddle and started off after Tresten. Endric hastily put out the fire, quenching the flames, and when he was finished, he looked up to see that both Urik and Tresten had disappeared into the darkness.

He had started toward his horse when a flash of fur caught his attention.

Endric dropped.

The movement might have saved his life.

A dark-furred merahl leaped over him and went tumbling at Endric's sudden disappearance.

Endric jumped to his feet, reaching for his sword, and noted that another merahl waited near the tree line.

Two of them.

Could he handle two merahl again?

How many more would be coming? From the sound of them, from the steady howls that he heard in the night, there were more than only two of the creatures, but would they be after Tresten?

With any other animal, Endric wouldn't attribute such intelligence, but the merahl were different. They studied him, almost knowingly. They would be able to work together, and he suspected they had some way of speaking to each other, whether it came from their howls or from some other way that he did not fully understand.

If that were the case, it was entirely possible the merahl intended to split them up. It would make them easier to take down one at a time, especially if they separated him from the much more powerful Mage.

With his sword unsheathed, he prepared to attack.

He didn't like the idea of harming the merahl. And the thought of killing one of the creatures bothered him in ways that he couldn't fully explain.

Somehow, he would have to find a way to stop them.

Unless there were more than two.

Endric placed his back to the ocean, using the ridge overlooking the sea as a line of protection. He could use it as a barrier and make it so that he only had to fend them off from a single direction. They could still outnumber him, but using the ridge, he could prevent them from overpowering him.

Surveying the trees, he noted there were only the two merahl.

Two might still be too many.

They stalked toward him, moving in unison. As they did, one of them snapped at his sword. Endric darted back. When he did, the other merahl snapped, forcing him to take a step away, toward the rocks.

They were smart. If he continued to back up, he would throw himself into the ocean. He would not have any way of surviving a fall like that, especially considering how sharp the rock edges were down below. He had spent enough time staring at them, trying to understand what it was that Tresten saw, that he realized he wouldn't have any chance of survival if it came to that.

He would have to stand his ground.

Facing the merahl working together would be more difficult than facing two the night before. If these were the same two, they would have learned—and they would have likely strategized a way to defeat him.

Somehow, it would have to come down to him using his sword and whatever influence the teralin had on them.

One of the merahl lunged, and this time Endric didn't turn away.

Instead, he darted forward, bringing the hilt of his sword down on top of the merahl's head.

The huge cat cried out, snarling at him and snapping at his hand, but Endric withdrew, spinning and kicking out with his foot, catching the other merahl in the side and sending him spinning.

He breathed heavily. The night was cool and the spray coming off the ocean dampened his skin, but sweat still streamed down his brow.

Where was Tresten?

He needed the Mage to realize that he hadn't joined them and to return. Endric suspected Tresten had some way of slowing the merahl, though what?

Both of the large cats stalked him, circling around.

They had the advantage. They could wait, and all they needed was for him to make a single mistake. When he did, one—or both—could lunge in and tear him apart. He'd seen what they did to groeliin and knew he would pose no more of a threat. All he had was his sword keeping him alive. They respected the sharpness of the blade.

One of them darted forward.

Endric dropped, bringing his fist up, and punched.

A jaw grabbed his ankle. He was thrown, sent flying toward the campsite. When he landed, his breath was kicked out of him and he gasped for air. He kept a grip on his sword, fearing releasing it, fearing what might happen if he were to lose that connection. He needed the sword more than anything else.

Endric got to his feet, shaking. The leg the merahl had grabbed throbbed, but thankfully did not appear to be broken. He could bear weight on it and doubted he would have managed if it were significantly injured.

"You don't want to do this," he said to the merahl. "I have worked with the Antrilii. I have hunted groeliin."

One of the merahl howled. The sound was piercing and the hairs on the back of Endric's neck stood on end. It was a pained sound, one that he could not ignore.

The other merahl raced toward him, snapping at his sword.

Endric twisted the blade, keeping it from the merahl's biting jaw, and brought his fist around, hoping to catch the merahl on the snout.

He missed.

The creature barreled into him and knocked him down.

His sword was caught off to his side, and one of the merahl's massive paws forced his arm down, trapping it beneath him.

Endric brought his foot up, kicking at the merahl, and managed to catch his back leg. The merahl buckled and Endric shoved him off. The creature was heavy, and he grunted as he moved him.

It was enough to get his arm free and Endric brought his sword around, placing it between himself and the merahl.

Where was the other creature?

Endric had lost track of the fight. The moment the merahl had clamped onto his leg, all thought had gone. Any planning and calculated movement that he might otherwise have had disappeared. He was too far away from the ledge, so that provided him no advantage. They could circle him now.

Could he reach the trees?

If he could, he could climb them, but he didn't have any faith the merahl couldn't climb after him. He'd seen how they scaled steep rock walls in the northern mountains as they faced groeliin, so what would a simple tree be to them? Likely they would be able to climb that just as easily.

He would have to fight, and he would have to stop them. Somehow.

One of the merahl reached him. Blood stained its jaw. Endric fell as much as he moved to the side. As he did, he reached toward the merahl, grabbing around the creature's neck.

The merahl thrashed, trying to free him, but Endric wouldn't let go. At least this way, the other merahl couldn't reach him and couldn't attack with the same ferocity.

One hand still gripped his sword. Endric feared letting it go, feared what might happen if he did, but he couldn't cling to the merahl's back with only one arm.

He let go of the sword.

He gripped the merahl's fur, hanging on as the creature tried to throw him free. Each jump nearly tossed him off its back, but Endric gripped tightly, knowing his life depended on it.

Where was the other one?

It was possible they still could work together and that the other merahl could grab him and try to tear him free, but he hoped that by holding on to the first merahl, he would be able to stay safe. At least for now.

Eventually, he would have to let go. Eventually his grip would give out and he would fall. When it did, he would be in danger once more.

Could he choke the merahl out?

He squeezed around the creature's neck, careful not to completely crush its windpipe. He didn't want to kill the merahl, though the longer this went on, the more that might be necessary. He hoped it was not.

The merahl wheezed and the thrashing began to intensify.

Endric clung tightly.

The thrashing slowed and finally stopped. The merahl fell to the ground.

Endric held on another moment before finally releasing his grip. He sat up and saw a flash of eyes.

He dropped.

The other merahl jumped and started to sail over him. Endric reached, grabbing a handhold of fur, squeezing tightly. He managed to hold on to enough that he could shift his hands around, getting a better grip.

He was beneath the merahl, and it snapped at him. He kept his head down, preventing it from getting any vital organs. Endric wrapped his arms around the merahl's neck, squeezing as he had to the other one. The creature wheezed quickly so Endric squeezed more tightly, fear forcing him to abandon any thought of not harming the creature.

One of the merahl's claws raked at him and he screamed, but he hung on.

The merahl dropped to the ground, trying to roll. If it succeeded, Endric might be thrown free, but he held tightly, not letting the creature toss him off.

The wheezing continued and then stopped.

Endric squeezed again, holding until movement ceased.

The merahl didn't move.

Endric let go, looking over at the other. He lay near the ledge, overlooking the sea. Had they rolled any farther, he would have been thrown into the water, down onto the rocks.

That would've been the merahl's intent. It was willing to sacrifice itself to kill Endric.

What was this about?

What happened to these creatures? What had changed them, twisting them so that they attacked him in the way that they had?

He tried to stand but pain coursed through him, starting along his back and racing down his leg. He was injured, but he didn't know how badly.

He needed to work quickly to tie up the merahl before they awoke and attacked again. Endric reached the campsite and tore strips of cloth from his cloak. He quickly bound the merahl, tying their legs together and then wrapping a strip around their jaws as well. He didn't know how well it would hold, but it would have to do for now.

He scooted toward the tree line, putting the bark of one of the trees up to his back, and leaned against it. He intended to rest a moment. After the attack, and after the pain he now felt, he needed a moment of rest. He fought sleep as it tried to claim him, but the last few days caught up to him and he was no longer able to keep his eyes open.

30

If Endric dreamt, he didn't remember it.

He awoke to pain still surging through him. His leg throbbed with a pulsing sort of pain, one that mixed with a throbbing that filled his head as well. Had he hit his head? He didn't remember. He'd been tossed around while trying to hold onto the merahl so much that he couldn't keep track of what he'd injured.

Light filtered through his lids and he opened them to see an overcast day.

How long had he been out?

As he came back around, his mind starting to jump back into focus, other questions raced back into the forefront of his mind.

Where was Tresten?

The Mage had ridden off with Urik. Wouldn't he have returned when he realized that Endric wasn't with him? Wouldn't he have wondered what happened to Endric rather than continuing into the night?

Unless the merahl had managed to get to them and overwhelm them.

Urik would have been useful at fending them off, but would he have been *too* violent? Gods, but Endric hoped that hadn't been the case. What other answer was there?

What of the merahl he'd stopped?

He looked around and found them still lying where he'd bound them. They were still tied, and still breathing. They were breathing.

More than that, both had their eyes open.

One of the merahl whined softly, but the other made no sound.

Endric tried to stand and found he couldn't bear weight on one of his legs. He'd thought it not broken, but maybe that had been a mistake. Had he only been able to stand on it out of fear for his life?

He crawled forward. Pain coursed through him as he did. Each movement sent a fresh wave of pain streaming through, shooting along his back and up into his head, mixing with the steady throbbing of his leg.

"Shh," he said as he approached the merahl. In the daylight, he could better make out the stripes along their fur. Both were a deep auburn, striped with either silver or black. They turned their attention to him, eyeing him with intelligent eyes that seemed to take in much more than they should. "I didn't want to hurt you. There's something wrong and I want to try and help."

The nearest merahl started whining, his voice—and now that it was daylight, Endric could tell there was a male and a female—rising painfully loud in the early morning. He had the silver stripes and was slightly larger than the female, though in the darkness, they had both appeared enormous.

Endric reclaimed his sword from its resting place between them, slipping it into its sheath. His leg screamed with pain as he did, but he steeled himself, forcing himself to ignore the agony.

What was he to do with them?

He couldn't leave them here. If he did, they would eventually starve. He'd risked himself enough to keep from killing them that he wasn't willing to do that. He didn't dare release them, not without knowing what had happened to them to lead to their change in behavior.

What then?

Was there any way he could reverse the effects of what happened to them?

If Tresten were here, he would ask the Mage, but without him, Endric would have to determine the answer on his own. He didn't know what the answer would be, and didn't know how he could reverse the effects of a change to the merahl without knowing what it was that had happened to them.

He would have to examine them to see if he could figure out what had happened.

It was dangerous and would force him to get close enough that they could harm him if they managed to get free... but what choice did he have? Leaving them like this wasn't an option.

He approached the merahl slowly, keeping his hands raised as he did, holding them out to placate the merahl. If they lunged, he would be ready. If they somehow managed to get free, he would also need to be ready.

The pain in his leg made it difficult for him to move and he approached carefully.

The merahl whined.

The more he heard it, the more it seemed a mournful sound. There was something else to it, a message that Endric could almost make out, but wasn't sure whether he really heard it or if it was his imagination.

"Shh," he said again, trying to soothe them.

It probably didn't matter. The creatures would ignore him either way. Endric wanted only to get close enough that he could try to calm them.

As he reached for the merahl, it tried to kick at him and caught him on his injured leg, knocking him over. Endric glared at it. The merahl had managed to hit the one part of him that was most susceptible to injury.

He sprawled out next to the merahl. It attempted to claw at him, raking toward his arm. Endric grabbed the forelegs and twisted them, pushing them out of the way. The merahl whined again, but he ignored it.

The other merahl watched him silently. There was a violent patience in the way she eyed him that nearly forced him to look away, but that was what she wanted. If he pulled his attention off them, they would be more likely to harm him.

"What happened to you?" he asked. "The merahl I've hunted with wouldn't do this. They wouldn't attempt to attack anything other than groeliin." Endric didn't know whether that was true or not. The merahl were intelligent creatures, but they were still animals. It was possible that they *would* attempt to harm him, though it didn't seem quite right.

The female watched him as he moved the legs of the male. Endric had thought the male merahl the one leading the two of them, but that didn't seem to be the case. The female seemed in charge.

Endric dragged himself forward. There was nothing off about them. He hadn't expected there to have been, though a part of him hoped that he would find some sort of teralin that would explain what had happened. He ran his hands along the thick fur, looking for other signs of injury or anything that would explain what had happened to them, but there was nothing.

He sat back, staring at the merahl.

There had to be *something* that would explain what had happened here. The merahl would not have attacked. He believed that more than he believed anything else. But why had they?

Was there another explanation?

He got to his knees and started running his hands through the merahl's fur once more, not looking for a new injury and not looking for teralin. If they were there, he hadn't discovered them. There might be something else he *could* find.

The merahl whined as he worked his hands through the fur, parting it as he went, searching for signs of scarring—or of markings. That was what he expected to find. Would there be anything like what he'd discovered on the groeliin? That seemed to tie those creatures to the teralin, much like what he suspected the Deshmahne used to tie themselves to the metal. If that were the case, there might not be anything that he could do.

He found nothing.

Endric leaned back, studying the merahl. Would the female have anything?

He crawled over to her and restrained her legs before she attempted to catch him the same way the male had. After searching through her fur, he found nothing. There was no sign of injury to her either.

Maybe there *was* nothing wrong with either of them.

If that were the case, what choice would he have but to destroy them both?

The idea sickened him. What would Nahrsin think of him needing to kill two of the merahl? Endric would *have* to tell him, but the Antrilii would need to know what happened, and would need to be able to try and prevent future merahl from turning like this, if they could.

What had happened to these merahl?

If it wasn't an injury, and he found no sign of teralin, what had twisted them? It seemed impossible that there had been nothing, but without any evidence otherwise, Endric was left believing that the attack came from an innate desire of the merahl to harm him.

He breathed out a sigh and tried to stand, but his leg didn't bear his weight.

As he looked around the campsite, he noted that his horse had run off, likely long ago. He had his sword and the two merahl that he'd somehow managed to capture, but there was nothing else here.

How was he to catch Tresten and Urik?

He would not. He would be stuck here, remaining where he was until his injuries either healed enough to allow him to continue onward or he perished.

Perhaps his fate was no different than the merahl.

As he sat there, the female worked at the binding that held her muzzle. She managed to get her tongue free and worked at the length of fabric wrapped around her jaw.

Endric scooted back, staying away from her jaw, not wanting to give her any chance to snap at him again. Now that the excitement of battle no longer surged through him, he wasn't certain he would be able to defend himself well enough to keep her from hurting him.

She managed to get the wrapping off her snout and snarled at him.

Endric watched her but couldn't muster the energy he needed to feel fear. He should. Considering how dangerous the merahl could be—especially if she managed to chew through the strip of cloth that was the only barrier between her attacking him and keeping her legs confined—he *should* feel fear. As tired as he was, it was difficult for him to generate the necessary energy.

The merahl snarled at him again and Endric shook his head. "Make all the sound that you want. None of us are going anywhere."

She showed a flash of teeth. Rather than being concerned by the fact that she attempted to intimidate him, Endric frowned.

There had been a marking along her gums.

Endric started forward, moving carefully.

The merahl snarled at him again, showing him a flash of sharp fangs. Endric was ready for it and held his sword out, preventing the merahl from snapping at him. She watched the sword, more concerned about that than anything else that Endric could do. What was it that worried her about the sword? There had to be something, though wasn't it only the sharpness of the blade, or was it the fact that it was made of teralin?

The female merahl attempted to snap at him but Endric lunged, wrapping his arms around her neck and pinning her head to the ground. She thrashed, but without the use of her legs, there was little that she could do.

"Quiet," Endric said.

She huffed, breathing heavily through her nostrils. He held her down with one arm and used the hand still holding the hilt of his sword to peel back her lip, doing so carefully so that she could not bite him.

He leaned in, smelling a faintly bitter odor to her breath as he studied the marking he found on her gum line.

It reminded him of markings that he'd seen on the groeliin.

Why should that be? Who would have placed those markings on the merahl?

It was branded into her skin and he traced a finger across it, ignoring the way she trembled beneath him, trying to get her head free. She shook, but though she was strong, Endric outweighed her and was able to keep her pinned down.

"Who did this to you?"

The merahl started growling. It was a deep sound, one that seemed to come from her chest as much as from the back of her throat, and her body practically shook with it.

"Whoever did this to you intended to claim you. This is not who you are."

Why was he talking to the merahl in this way? There might not be anything he could do. With the branding, if it truly changed her, if it was responsible for tainting her, there might not be anything that he could have done to have helped her.

Possibilities worked through him. Could he cut the marking off her lip? If he did, would that even matter?

Was there another possibility? Could he somehow alter the marking, changing it so that the pattern no longer tainted her?

There was something very familiar about the marking, though Endric wasn't quite certain what it was. Was it only that it reminded him of the groeliin marks, or was there more to it?

It wasn't the one that Urik was so intent to know more about. If it were, Endric would need to find out who placed it, and what intent it had. It was similar enough that he wondered if the same person had placed the marking on the groeliin and had been the owner of the marking Urik seemed so intent to learn about.

Somehow, he had to find a way to help these merahl.

He wrapped the strip of cloth back around her snout, keeping her bound once more.

He crawled toward the other merahl. The male watched him with a dark intensity to his eyes. Endric pinned his head much the same way he had done with the female, holding him down, and then peeled back the strip of cloth wrapping around his snout until he was able to lift the merahl's lips and study the merahl's gums.

As he suspected, there was another marking here.

Was there anything he could even do that would help them?

When he had faced them the first time, he had felt the way the sword had influenced them. Could it do that now?

He didn't want to harm the merahl, but… if he could use his sword, and the teralin influence, maybe he would be able to help them.

It was the only thing he could think of.

Endric kept his weight on the merahl's neck and brought the tip of his sword around and pressed it against the marking. The merahl growled and the female snarled, scratching at the ground.

Endric ignored her.

He made the slightest cut into the merahl's gumline, slicing through the marking. He pressed, using the same energy as he had when attempting to change the polarity of teralin.

It felt right, though he couldn't explain why.

There was a steady buildup of pressure that came from him and surged through his sword. Light flared along the length of the blade and flashed onto the merahl's gum line.

Endric withdrew. The marking had been blurred and appeared charred, as if he had burned it free. The merahl whined but Endric didn't release his weight. He shifted the creature's jaw, looking at the other side, and noted a second marking there. With a sigh, he did the same thing as he had on the first side.

When he was finished, he rewrapped the merahl's snout and scooted back.

He turned his attention to the female and crawled over to her. She thrashed, attempting to scratch at him as she had before, but he threw himself on top of her, pinning her down. With his weight on top of her, there was no way for her to move. He pulled back her lips and set his sword against the branding, slicing through it and pushing as if he were changing teralin's polarity. He did the same thing on the other side, much as he had with the male.

The female attempted to bite at him and Endric started back, releasing pressure on her neck as he realized that there was another marking on the top of her mouth.

Gods. Who had done this to the merahl?

This one would be more difficult to reach.

He shifted, throwing himself back on top of her once more, and used both hands to spread her jaws apart. He forced her mouth toward the tip of his sword. It was difficult. The merahl was strong and resisted, but slowly—almost too slowly—he managed to bring her mouth around to the end of the sword and so he could slice through the marking, pushing against it as he did. As with the others, there came a flash of light and a surge, and the marking disappeared.

Endric rewrapped her muzzle and crawled over to the male, needing to check if he were similarly marked. As he pried open the male's mouth, he realized that he was not. It had only been the female marked in such a way.

Endric crawled away, leaving the merahl lying on the ground. He made his way back toward the tree, putting his back against the bark and keeping the two creatures in sight. It might not even matter, but he would see whether they would respond to what he had done.

His sword rested across his legs and he watched them.

31

Endric must have slept.

That hadn't been his intent, but he awoke to darkness. The sound of the ocean crashed beneath him, slamming on the rocks along the shore. The air was heavy and damp, the humidity of a coming rain. Thunder rumbled more urgently than it had in days. It sounded close. If he didn't find cover, he would be drenched.

His body ached, but less than it had before. His leg still throbbed and his head pulsed as it had, but there was less of it than he expected. The pain that had been in his arms and back had eased.

How long had he been asleep?

He sat up with a start and looked over at the merahl. He noted with relief that they were still lying bound as they had been before. Both seemed to be resting, neither snarling as they had been before, and neither of them whining.

A cool wind gusted off the ledge, swirling around him in tight eddies. Endric reached for his cloak and found it tattered, but wrapped what he could around himself, clinging to the warmth that it brought.

Where were Tresten and Urik?

He had expected Tresten to have turned back, searching for him, but it had now been at least a day—possibly longer—and neither man had returned. Had something happened to them? Had Urik betrayed Tresten and attacked him? Urik had seemed compliant and had made no effort to harm Tresten in the time that they had traveled together, but he wondered whether something had changed. Had Urik decided to use Endric's absence as an opportunity? Did he think to take advantage of that and harm the elderly Mage? Or had Endric been right—had Tresten's mind been slipping?

If that were the case, maybe they wouldn't come for him.

Endric crept forward, wanting to check on the merahl. As he approached, the female lifted her head and looked at him, staring with that bright-eyed intelligence that was a feature of their kind. The male merahl remained resting, not looking up as Endric approached.

"Are you any better?" he asked. His voice came out as a croak, his mouth dry. How long had it been since he had anything to drink? They hadn't camped near a stream, so there was no supply of water other than what had been in his saddlebags, and those were now missing, gone with the horse that had run off.

The merahl's ears perked and swiveled toward him. She watched, making no sound.

That troubled him.

Had he harmed her so badly that she couldn't make any sound? That had not been his intent. He hadn't wanted to hurt the merahl. He wanted only to save her, to rescue her from whatever darkness consumed her, but had he cut into her mouth and gums too deeply?

He continued to scoot toward her.

A particularly loud peal of thunder crashed and Endric jerked his head around with a start. It seemed to come from across the sea, rolling in with it, moving on the waves as they crashed against the rocks. Lightning streaked across the sky, a bright burst of light that seemed nearly as vibrant as daylight. When it passed, when the lightning finally faded and the echoes of thunder eased back to nothingness, Endric looked over at the merahl.

They still watched him. Her ears swiveled, an alertness to them that hadn't been there before. Was there less hatred and violence in her eyes than there had been?

It was too much to hope for. He couldn't believe that she had been cured of whatever had tainted her simply because he'd sliced through the markings with his sword and pushed on them as if they were teralin whose polarity had needed to be reversed.

No, this was likely a ploy by the merahl, another way of convincing him to release them. Endric wanted to. In spite of himself, despite of knowing that he should not, he wanted to release the merahl from the strips of cloth wrapped around their legs and mouth. It pained him seeing the creatures confined in such a way.

"Why did you have to attack?" He sat up on his knees, leaning forward. It caused pain to shoot down his leg, but less than he expected. Maybe it wasn't fractured as he had feared. "What happened to you? Where are the Antrilii?" The merahl made no sound, only watching him with her intense stare. "You are supposed to hunt the groeliin."

At the mention of the groeliin, the merahl started growling.

"Groeliin?"

The merahl growled again, this time a deep, rumbling sound that seemed as if she intended to compete with the thunder rolling from the distance.

"That's the response I expected. Merahl hunt the groeliin. The Antrilii hunt the groeliin. And I am descended from the Antrilii."

He scooted forward, watching the merahl's response, but there didn't seem to be any. She watched him, her ears twisting as they had since she'd awoken, but she made no other sound. "Do you remember attacking me?"

The merahl snorted. Was that a shake of her head, or was that his imagination?

"You attacked and forced me to subdue you. I couldn't kill you. I probably should have, considering you were trying so hard to kill me, but… you are merahl. I've hunted alongside your kind."

Endric moved forward, staying on his knees. One hand remained close to his sword, ready to swing it around if necessary, but the merahl didn't attempt to claw him as she had before. She did nothing other than watch him.

Could he have restored her?

That seemed too much to hope for, but whatever had happened no longer seemed to be influencing her in quite the same way. Maybe she *had* been healed. The only way to know with certainty would be to remove the wrappings from her mouth and legs, but doing that exposed him to the potential of attack. Was he ready to do that?

Could he do anything otherwise?

If he left her this way, he would be forced to find a way to feed her and get her water or he would need to simply bring an end to her. He couldn't keep her confined indefinitely. Doing that was cruel, and Endric had no interest in cruelty.

"I'm going to remove the wrapping around your mouth so that I can look at the marks inside it."

The merahl made no sound. Endric crawled closer and reached her head. He was ready for her to spin and snap at him, but she did not. He leaned on her neck the same way he had before and carefully began unwrapping the binding around her snout. When that was done, he lifted her lip.

The marking had healed.

There remained a hint of a scar, little more than raised flesh, and it was discolored, but it was not the same marking that had been there before.

He twisted her jaw, looking at the other side. It was the same. When he spread her mouth open, he found that the lining of her mouth was discolored and slightly raised with a scar, but there was no evidence of the marking that had been there.

Endric left the wrapping off her mouth and scooted back, watching her.

She eyed him the way that she had before and ran her tongue along her lips, but made no other sound. She made no effort to try chewing at the bindings on her legs, though if he left her like this for much longer, he suspected she would. She would be too smart to not think of it. It was a matter of time before she attempted to escape in that way.

Endric stopped at the male merahl and examined his mouth. The markings had healed equally well on him. The male remained asleep and barely stirred as Endric lifted his lips, looking first at one side, and then at the other.

He left the wrapping off his mouth as well.

Endric sat back, watching the two merahl. The female did nothing at first, and then, gradually, she started sliding toward the male. When she neared him, she started licking his fur and then moved around to lick at his mouth. Slowly, the male stirred and began licking at the female's mouth.

Thunder rumbled in the distance. A flash of lightning followed, leaving a sizzling energy in the air.

Endric suspected he imagined it more than anything else, but the merahl moved closer, and that energy seemed to build.

Rain no longer threatened and began drizzling down on him.

Endric slid back toward the tree, getting near the cover of the overhanging branches, and watched as the merahl continued running their tongues along each other. After a while, they reached the wrappings along their legs. The female looked up and caught Endric's eyes, and in a flurry of sharp fangs, she tore the wrappings off the male, and he did the same to her.

Endric sat ready, watching to see what would happen.

The female got to her feet and made a slow circle of the clearing. She sniffed at the air and then nuzzled at the male until he got up.

If it came to a fight, Endric would fail.

He stood, ready to climb the tree, doubting that he would have much protection. He hoped the destruction of the markings on the merahl had been enough and that they no longer were tainted in the way that they had been.

Was that even possible?

The merahl turned and crouched, turning their attention to him so that they could watch him. The female made a strange sound and there seemed to be a message buried within it, but Endric didn't know what it would be. The male seemed to understand and repeated it, making a similar sound.

They didn't attack.

Endric considered that progress.

"You don't have to stay with me," he said. "It might be better if you didn't. I don't know if you're healed, so I don't know if it's safe for me to stay this close to you." He set his sword across his legs and watched the merahl.

Neither of them moved.

Thunder rumbled again. The rain began to pelt down, slicing through his cloak, and he shivered. The cloak had been damaged in the fight with the merahl, leaving it in tatters. There was only so much protection it could offer now, and a chill began to run through him.

His stomach rumbled and he tipped his head back, catching some of the rain in his mouth, moistening his dry lips and throat.

When he looked back, the merahl had crawled closer to him.

All he wanted was to find Urik and Tresten and see what the Mage had planned. Tresten had been chasing something, unless it had all been a part of a growing confusion on his part. Endric didn't want to think that was the case. He wanted to believe that Tresten still had his full faculties and that he had not begun to slip, but after everything he'd seen—and the fact that he hadn't come back for Endric—he wondered if that were the case.

The rain began to sleet down.

After days spent with the thunder chasing them, the steady rumbling a constant threat, it wasn't surprising that it finally came. It was unfortunate that Endric was so unprepared for it, and unfortunate that his cloak had been shredded. Even more unfortunate was that he had no fire to provide warmth and nothing for shelter from the rain.

The merahl crawled closer.

They were near enough that they could attack. One single lunge—one quick snap—and they could reach him.

Had they been healed?

All he had done was damage markings that had been placed inside their mouths. It made no sense that that alone would be enough to taint them, that that alone would be enough to twist them so that they would attack him rather than continue their hunt for the groeliin.

Teralin required intent. It was likely that whatever had happened to the merahl had an intent, but whose intent? Who was responsible for this?

Could the groeliin have been responsible?

He'd seen the way they had placed similar markings, so that certainly was possible. Could it have been the Deshmahne? They used markings that had a similar quality, but those were dark and inky, nothing like what had been placed on the merahl.

Thunder rumbled again and the rain sheeted down.

The merahl pressed against him. Neither made any noise, and

neither made any attempt to harm him. They pressed their bodies against him, warmth radiating off them, pushing away the chill.

"Thank you," Endric said.

The female merahl made a soft sound, something like a whistle mixed with a howl.

Endric almost understood that. It was an acknowledgment, a recognition that they could help him, and could there have been an apology buried within it?

He suspected that was only his imagination.

Endric brought his arms around and rested them on top of the merahl. His hands entwined in the thick fur and he sat like that, staring out at the night, listening to the sound of the storm and the waves crashing, thankful that he was still alive, and thankful that the merahl seemed to have been restored.

32

The storm lasted most of the night, during which the merahl remained next to him, providing their warmth and a sense of comfort. Endric wondered how much of their presence was for his comfort and how much of it was for theirs. It was possible that both of them got something out of it.

As dawn broke, Endric stood. His body was stiff and he still had a pain in his leg that matched the throbbing in his head. He didn't recall hitting his head, but didn't recall many of the injuries he'd sustained while trying to subdue the merahl.

With the passing of the storm, the humidity in the air lessened, leaving it cool, practically cold with the wind that whipped off the sea. There was an earthy scent to the air, and it mixed with something almost floral, a pleasant aroma.

He'd left his sword unsheathed, and now that he stood, he slipped it back into its sheath and started toward the ledge looking out over the ocean. The merahl shook themselves and joined him.

As he stared out across the sea, Endric contemplated what he needed to do next.

Finding Tresten, discovering what had happened to him, had to be a part of it. In addition, he needed to ensure that Urik hadn't attacked the Mage. And then there was discovering what happened with the merahl and seeing why they had been tainted.

He risked himself standing this close to the ledge with the merahl that had attempted to kill him only a day before. If they attacked, lunging at him, they could toss him over the edge, down onto the sharp rocks below where the sea would claim him quickly.

Endric looked over his shoulder. The merahl watched him. The female in particular sat back on her haunches, her eyes blazing brightly. The male sat behind her, no less intensity in his gaze.

"I can't walk, not well."

The female stood and rubbed up against his side.

Endric grunted. "I need to find Mage Tresten. He's left me here."

Why was he sharing with the merahl in this way? It was unlikely that they would understand what he was saying or what he needed, but for some reason, he felt compelled to speak.

The female nudged him again. She pushed him away from the ledge and toward the trees.

"My leg," Endric said, looking down at his shredded boot. He wasn't angry about what had happened, especially if the merahl had not been in control. What good would it do for him to be angry with them, especially when he had seen others who had been similarly affected?

The female nudged him again.

"I can't walk any significant distances." His leg had begun feeling better, but it still throbbed. Even walking to the trees left his leg aching.

The female dropped her head and pushed on him.

What was she trying to do? Where was she trying to get him to go? He wouldn't be able to get very far, not injured as he was, and if that was going to anger the merahl, it would be better for them to head out on their own.

"You can return to hunt the groeliin," he said. "You don't need to remain here with me."

The female nudged him again, this time with enough force that he was lifted and tossed onto her back. He started to slide off, but she shifted, forcing him back atop her. She started running, streaking into the trees with Endric atop her. The male raced alongside.

Endric gripped her fur, fearing another injury were he to let go.

Was this her intent? He'd never heard of any of the Antrilii riding atop the merahl, but then, how many of the Antrilii had been injured by them? Endric wanted Nahrsin to answer questions. After what he'd been through, he had dozens of questions about the merahl and about the Antrilii that he hadn't thought to ask when he had been in the Antrilii lands before.

The merahl ran quickly, their strides fluid and not jarring as Endric would have expected. Had he been sitting atop his horse, each step would have sent pain shooting through him. With the merahl, there was barely any pressure when her steps touched the ground before she leaped off again. Each step carried them quickly into the trees, racing away from the shore that he'd been following for the last week while traveling with Tresten.

Was this even the right direction?

"I need to find Mage Tresten," Endric said.

Wind from the speed of their running tore the words from him, and he wasn't even certain whether the merahl heard—or understood. They continued racing through the forest, running long enough that Endric began to lose track of time. The trees blocked out the sunlight but also blocked out most of the wind, other than that which whistled past him from the speed of their travels.

They emerged from the trees and appeared on a massive

rolling plain. Grasses stretched in front of them. They had to be too far south for this to be Saeline, though it had much of the same appearance. The merahl turned, heading westerly. Every so often, the female would slow and sniff the air before she streaked off, moving quickly again.

Once free of the forest, they veered slightly south.

Where was she taking him? She smelled something, though whether it was a Mage or whether it was something else, he did not know.

By late in the day, they began to slow.

The landscape had changed, leaving it hillier, less of the flat lands they had been crossing. The tall grasses of the open plains had shifted, becoming drier. The merahl no longer raced as they had before. It surprised Endric that they would slow here, rather than through the trees. They had moved more swiftly through the forest than they did along the grasslands. Could they be tired? Certainly, the female would be. She'd carried Endric on her back, his fists gripping her fur so that he wasn't thrown off, but he had a sense that they slowed for a reason not related to fatigue.

A tall hill rose in front of him.

As they reached the summit, the female stopped. She lowered her head and let Endric climb off. He patted her side and whispered a soft thanks.

When he was free of her, she lowered herself, crawling toward the peak of the hill, where she remained low to the ground. The male followed her and Endric decided to see what it was that they detected.

He shimmied along the ground until he reached the space between the two merahl. His leg didn't throb as badly as it had when they first started. His head no longer pounded. Strangely, he felt refreshed. Only his forearms throbbed, and that was from maintaining his grip as long as he had while riding in this direction.

When he poked his head up, his breath caught.

Far below, he counted a half dozen other merahl.

They sat in a circle, their attention focused toward a dozen men in the middle. Tresten and Urik were among them, but who were the others? From the distance, it was difficult to tell.

"This is what you wanted me to see?" Endric asked.

The merahl whimpered softly.

"What is it you expect me to be able to do? There are too many of them."

The female flashed her teeth at him. No—not her teeth, but the injured part of her mouth.

"You want me to heal them."

She nuzzled up against him.

Endric knew how to help the merahl now, but in order to do so, he would need to separate them. Six merahl were too many for him to attempt to contain at one time. Even two had been almost more than he could handle.

"Can you draw them off?"

The female rubbed up against him.

"I can't take them on in a group like that. I don't want the others to harm them, so we'll have to find a way to draw at least one or two of them off so that I have a chance to do the same as what I did with you."

The female swiveled her head and fixed him with her intense stare.

"I intend to help. You don't have to worry that I will abandon the merahl."

She licked his hand.

Endric turned his attention back toward the grouping. As he did, the female stood, making herself visible, and let out a strange, angry howl. It made the hairs on the back of his neck stand on edge. She repeated it and then bounded away, running down the hillside.

When she was a dozen steps from him, she turned and crawled back up the hill.

Her calculating nature impressed Endric. She used strategy to attempt to draw off one or more of the other merahl. Endric didn't know if it would work, but suspected that their distinct call might draw off the others more easily than if he were to have attempted something.

He looked down into the valley and noted that only five merahl remained.

Where had the other gone?

The merahl moved quickly, but it couldn't have been so quickly that it would have disappeared. The two merahl with him would have been able to follow it.

The male suddenly twisted, jumping to his feet and snarling.

Endric rolled, barely in time.

The missing merahl landed where he had been lying.

The female lunged, knocking the newcomer, sending him tumbling down the hill. The two merahl jumped after it, quickly pinning it to the ground.

The female whined softly and Endric hurried down the hill.

His heart hammered. He unsheathed his sword as he approached and threw himself on top of the merahl, covering its neck. This was a massive creature, even larger than the two that he'd been traveling with. Without them to help hold this one down, Endric doubted he would have been able to restrain it.

He peeled back the creature's lip and found a marking much as had been on the other two. Endric barely hesitated, using his sword to slice through the marking, and then *pushed,* sending a sense as if he were changing the polarity of teralin. With a flash, a charring changed the marking, obscuring it. He did the same with one on the other side of the merahl's mouth.

Before relaxing, Endric pried the creature's mouth open and looked at the roof of his mouth. There was no marking there.

Why were there only two for the males but three for the females?

Or maybe that had nothing to do with it.

Endric quickly ran his hands through the merahl's fur, looking for any other markings that he might have missed, but he found none. This merahl had darker fur, brown so deep that it was almost black, and stripes that blended in, making them almost invisible, although the stripes were smoother than the rest of the fur. He released his grip and crawled back.

The female began licking the mouth of the trapped merahl and a sizzling energy filled the air that reminded Endric of what he'd felt after lightning struck.

The female released her grip, and the male did the same.

Endric held tightly onto his sword, prepared to attack if necessary.

The massive merahl snarled once, then ran his tongue across his mouth and shivered, a trembling that worked through him. When he stood, he sniffed the air and whined softly.

It would be difficult to trust that this merahl was not still influenced, but Endric would trust the other two merahl for now. If they believed that he had somehow healed this one that quickly, he would have to believe that it had been done.

"We have to get the others," Endric said.

The female let out a soft cry, and the newcomer responded in kind.

Endric could almost make out what they were saying to each other, though as before, he wondered if that were only his imagination.

The large male bounded off, disappearing around the side of the hill, letting off a sharp howl. Another answered.

Endric understood this one. He needed to be ready.

When the next merahl appeared, he was ready for it. The two that he'd traveled with from the coast trapped it between them and landed on top of the newcomer, but not before he managed to let out a ferocious snarl that echoed across the hills.

They would be discovered.

Endric worked quickly, jumping onto the merahl's back and slicing through the marks. This was a female, and much like the other female, he found one on the roof of her mouth. He searched her fur but there were no others. He released her and the two merahl licked her mouth, leaving energy hanging in the air.

He might start the healing process, but something the merahl did completed it.

If this worked, the numbers would be even.

Four merahl remained.

Endric crept up the side of the hill until he could once more look out and over it. From his vantage, he made out the four remaining merahl. They stood, two of them sniffing the air. One prowled in a circle. The forth—a massive merahl much larger than any of the others—remained near the captives.

The merahl knew something was off. Endric needed to work carefully—and quickly.

He looked over at the female. She crouched next to him, her nose barely poking above the side of the hill and her head tipped so that one eye could peer more easily. Unlike in the mountains when hunting, her fur stood out among the green grasses.

"They know we're here," Endric whispered.

The merahl sniffed. It was the only reaction she made.

"Can you take on the others?"

The numbers made it even, but they needed to capture—and heal—the remaining merahl, not harm them, and certainly not destroy them.

She didn't make any sound.

Endric didn't know whether he should take that as agreement or whether there was concern from the merahl.

"We can try drawing another of them off," Endric suggested.

The merahl whined softly.

This time, he was certain he knew what she wanted: Agreement.

How would he draw off the merahl?

They were smart, which meant he would have to outsmart them. They were fast, but he now had four other merahl who would help him and would protect him if they managed to move past him.

They'd already used the merahl to try and draw the others off. That meant there needed to be a different approach.

It would have to be Endric.

He stood.

When he did, the merahl in the valley turned to him immediately. They howled softly, enough that it echoed, the sound bouncing off the hillsides. Were they in the mountains, he imagined it would be an impressive sound.

None started toward him.

He had hoped that he would be able to pull at least one of the merahl off, but they remained near the captives.

Endric started down the side of the hill. He kept his sword unsheathed and his body tense. Pain still throbbed through his ankle where it had been injured, though it was much better than it had been. At least he could walk. If it came to a battle—if he had to use his sword to fight off whoever twisted the merahl—he wasn't certain that he would be able to do so. All he had to do was undo what tainted them. Then they would have enough support.

The closer he got to the merahl, the more impressed with the massive creature he was. She—and there was no question the merahl was female—was almost half again as large as the female Endric had restored near the sea. The remaining others were equally impressive but didn't draw his attention in the same way.

Endric paused to consider who had been captured. There were Urik and Tresten, but he realized with shock that his father and a dozen or so Denraen with him had been captured as well. Only Tresten stood. The rest were sitting.

That surprised him. The Denraen would not sit, especially his father. Not when they were trapped and standing might give them an opportunity to escape. Had they given up?

Endric pushed the thought away.

There was another figure in the middle of the circle, one he should not have been surprised to see.

Novan.

All members of the Conclave.

The betrayal *must* have been real.

Could that be why the merahl attacked?

Endric glanced behind him. None of the merahl he'd restored crested the hillside.

Was it a trap meant for him?

Had he *not* restored the other merahl?

His heart hammered. Dendril shook his head. A long gash ran along one side of his face—likely made by a merahl claw. Novan sat in the middle of the circle, no sign of his staff.

Tresten watched Endric. All traces of the fatigue and the weakness that Endric had seen in his eyes were gone. He was the same powerful Mage Endric had known before.

One of the merahl howled.

It was a harsh and painful sound, and it made the hair on the back of his neck stand.

Other merahl responded, but none who stood in the clearing.

And they weren't behind him.

There were more.

There might be four remaining twisted merahl, but that wasn't the end of them.

If he didn't act quickly, he would be outnumbered again.

And now they knew he was coming.

33

Endric glanced behind him, expecting the other merahl to appear, but they did not.

He turned his attention back to these. He had to stop them—and had to repair whatever had been done to them. He didn't believe he'd been forced into a trap, and he didn't believe the merahl he'd helped intended to attack him.

But that didn't mean they could help.

The others in the clearing would need to help.

Endric started down the side of the hill once more. With each step, he felt a growing unease. Whatever happened would need to be quick. The distant howls were growing closer. He figured he had a few minutes, but not much longer. After that, he would be overwhelmed by attacking merahl.

He needed help. The merahl he'd restored needed to assist him, but he wasn't sure whether they could.

What choice did he have?

As he neared, Tresten spoke. His voice was soft but managed to carry to Endric, as if drifting on the wind. "I don't know what you've done with the others, but you cannot destroy them. There's something wrong with them."

Before he had a chance to answer, one of the merahl lunged toward him.

Endric held his sword out and pushed through it, preparing to use it to undo the damage to the merahl.

Light glowed along the blade.

That was the first time he'd seen it do that. Was it because the teralin prepared for what he intended or was there another answer? Did *he* somehow access a strange power? For him to change the polarity of teralin, he would have to have some connection to power, as strange as that might be to admit.

Did the answer even matter?

The merahl leaped and he ducked.

Within the clearing, someone gasped, though Endric ignored it.

He rolled, holding onto his sword, and grabbed a handful of fur.

A single thought reverberated in his head: He had to act quickly.

Endric threw his arm around the merahl's neck, pinning it.

He threw himself on top of the merahl, holding its face to the ground, avoiding the attempt at clawing him free. Vaguely, he saw movement out of the corner of his eye and risked looking up.

The other restored merahl had arrived.

Two merahl pinned the others to the ground—all but the largest of them.

Endric worked quickly, lifting the lip of the merahl and slicing his sword through the marking. The merahl managed to nip at his hand, drawing blood, but he ignored it.

Switching sides, he pulled the lip on the other side, doing the same.

He checked the inside of the mouth, but there wasn't a third. A male, then.

Endric released him.

When he rolled to his feet, he saw the massive merahl stalking toward Tresten.

With a glance, Endric realized the other two merahl were contained. He had time—at least until the others appeared. Tresten might not.

Endric ran toward the massive merahl, but not before she lunged.

"No!" he cried.

Endric threw himself at the merahl, landing atop her back.

Tresten caught the merahl's front legs and pushed her back. The merahl had to outweigh Tresten by a significant amount but he managed to hold her, keeping her off him.

"Work quickly, Endric," Tresten said.

Endric shifted his grip, sliding up the merahl's fur, and reached for her neck.

With a furious shake, she threw him off.

Endric went sprawling.

He landed near his father.

This close, Endric could see the injury to his father. It was more than only a massive gash along his face. His arm was mangled and his leg looked as if it had been broken. The other Denraen were similarly injured. They didn't sit because they'd given up but because they couldn't stand.

What of Novan? Had the historian been hurt as well?

Endric rolled, looking for the historian, but couldn't see him.

When he jumped to his feet, he understood why.

Novan helped Tresten, and together they pushed the merahl away.

Surprisingly, Urik helped as well.

Endric limped toward the merahl. She was snapping at Novan but he managed to move out of the way, keeping her from getting too close. She strained to get free, but Novan and Tresten gripped her front legs, holding her. Urik had wrapped himself around her back legs.

"Force her to the ground," Endric said.

"It is more difficult than you suggest," Tresten said. He didn't sound stressed but Endric couldn't imagine he was anything but strained by the effort of holding the merahl in place. "She is quite powerful."

Endric glanced over his shoulder. The merahl he'd restored when he first came to the clearing lay on his side. Had he been too aggressive with him? Endric didn't think so. Maybe it was the fact that he needed the merahl to use whatever ability they had to help complete the restoration.

He would need to finish this first.

The merahl stood on her back legs, shaking her body back and forth as she struggled to get free. Novan and Tresten managed to hold tightly, anchoring her.

Endric climbed onto her back.

He gripped her fur, pulling himself along, wrapping his legs around her body. She attempted to throw him again, but he was better prepared than the last time, and he managed to hold onto his grip and resist getting thrown.

"What are you doing?" Novan didn't mask the tension in his voice nearly as well as Tresten had. It trembled slightly, much like the way his arms trembled. How much longer would he be able to hold on before he lost his grip on the merahl? When he did, Endric doubted Tresten would be able to hold her for much longer.

"Attempting to end this."

"You can't destroy this creature," Tresten said.

Endric gritted his teeth. "I didn't destroy any of the others."

He reached the merahl's head. Holding onto her back like this, it would be difficult for him to confine her enough to burn off the marks. Could he wrap himself around her throat and drop her?

That was how he'd managed to stop the other merahl. She was almost too large for him to get his arms around.

There was another concern.

Doing so would require that he drop his sword.

If he did, he risked not having it if he had to do something more aggressive to slow the merahl. If he didn't, he might not be able to stop her from harming them.

Endric released his grip on the sword. It dropped near the merahl's rear legs.

He grabbed her around the throat and squeezed.

She thrashed, but now that he'd dropped his sword, he had a better grip than he had before and he managed to hang on. Endric continued to squeeze, but the thrashing continued.

Novan lost his grip and went sprawling.

Endric squeezed tighter.

"You need to hurry," Tresten said. He no longer spoke as calmly as before.

Endric squeezed. There was a balance between squeezing hard enough to drop the merahl and so hard that he crushed her throat. He didn't want to do that.

Her rear legs managed to get free.

She thrashed, jumping into the air, carrying Tresten and Endric with her.

Endric started to slip but squeezed even more, bracing himself for their landing.

Where was Tresten?

Had she crushed him?

Endric clung to the merahl's back. She was incredibly powerful. This merahl needed to live and hunt groeliin. It would be devastating if she could not.

Howls filled the air.

Endric tried not to think about how close they were. They continued to reverberate, filling the air, but he needed to hold onto this merahl and finish it. If he could, the others could be restored and they would have the numbers needed to help the arriving merahl.

Finally, the thrashing eased.

Endric held on until she stopped moving.

He looked up. Urik stood above him with his sword. Endric's heart hammered. What would Urik do? Would he attempt to attack Endric now that the merahl had incapacitated him—and Dendril?

Urik flipped the sword around and handed it to Endric, hilt first. That was Endric's hilt, Endric's sword. Urik was actually helping and Endric gave silent thanks as he took it and pulled back.

Endric took it and quickly pulled back the merahl's lip, slicing through the markings there. He did the same on the other side of her jaw, as well as the roof of her mouth. When he was done, he leaned against her a moment, catching his breath.

Where was Tresten?

Endric stood. His legs shook; the effort required to hold him on the merahl's back had left him weakened. He staggered toward the other two merahl, both trapped by those he'd already restored.

"Endric?"

It was Novan's voice. Endric ignored the historian as he made his way to the nearest of the merahl. It snarled at him, but the others held it down.

Endric quickly destroyed the markings in his mouth and went to the other merahl.

Energy sizzled in the air, and he knew the merahl had completed the healing. Would they go to the large female as well? They would need her as much as any of the merahl, especially if they were attacked by more of them.

When he finished, he sank to the ground.

His legs no longer held him up. Pain throbbed through him and the injuries to his ankle seemed to flare once more. He looked around the clearing, trying to take stock.

The restored merahl worked on the others, licking their mouths. The sizzle of energy—like lightning in a thunderstorm—hung in the air, mixed with a scent much like a fresh rain. The Denraen didn't move, lying where they had been when he'd first appeared.

Novan hobbled over to him. He was injured, but not as badly as Endric would have expected. A gash in his arm bled, bite marks evident.

"How did you know what to do?" he asked.

Endric attempted to stand but couldn't, and fell back to the ground.

"Don't," Novan said and sank next to Endric. Urik stood behind him, watching both Novan and Endric. Behind him, Tresten sat next to Dendril. At least he still lived.

"Luck. I discovered it by chance."

Novan chuckled. "There's no chance, not with what I saw you do. That took thought and understanding."

Endric attempted to smile, but it was difficult. "You didn't think I had it in me?"

Novan shook his head. "That's not what I would say at all. I knew that you did."

"I couldn't kill the merahl, if that's what you were asking. After what I've seen..."

Novan sighed. "Of course. Your time with the Antrilii would have shown that you cannot destroy them. Sometimes I forget just how much you have seen and how much you have experienced. You have proven yourself more valuable than you will ever realize."

"Valuable how?"

"That's a conversation for later. For now—"

The howls of the merahl intensified, cutting Novan off as they drew closer.

Endric perked up. He was exhausted, but it seemed the work wasn't complete. Not yet. The female merahl came over and rubbed her head against him.

Endric ruffled the fur behind her ears and nodded.

"I'll need your help," he whispered to her.

She licked him. When she did, he felt a flash and a sizzle of energy.

When he climbed onto her back, he looked at Novan. "I'll return when I can."

34

Exhaustion washed over Endric, but it was not quite the same as he had expected. He ached, but less than he should. The task was completed. The merahl—nearly a dozen more—had been restored. Thankfully none had been the cub he had rescued, but if one of them had been, would he have attacked Endric or would their connection have protected him?

The hunt had gone quickly. The massive female had made quick work of it, wrangling the other merahl, forcing them toward the other waiting merahl so Endric was able to use his sword to restore them.

Almost twenty merahl in all.

How had they been twisted as they had been? Who had placed the markings on them? And for what purpose?

Those were the questions he needed to answer.

The female stopped near the same hill where the captured others had been. She lowered her head, letting Endric climb off her back. He managed to stand, the pain in his ankle fading. It seemed to do so more quickly when he rode atop her, though he knew he wouldn't be able to do so for long. The merahl would need to return to the northern mountains and would need to resume their hunt.

"Thank you," he said. He rested his hand on her head, feeling her strength and the warmth radiating from her. Without the merahl, he wouldn't have been able to rescue the others. He wouldn't even have known they needed rescuing.

She yowled softly. There was a message there, one that seemed just on the edge of Endric's understanding. They spoke to him though he wasn't prepared to understand what they said.

She licked his hand. As before, he felt the sizzle of energy in the air and was left with a surge of warmth and strength. It was momentary, long enough that he was able to take a deep breath and stand upright, bearing his weight more solidly on his injured side.

When she vocalized again, Endric knew what it meant.

She was leaving.

The other merahl echoed the call. They remained distant, though the massive female was near enough that Endric could see her. She led the pack.

As he stared at her, Endric realized the similarities between her fur markings and the first female he had restored. They were near enough that they could be siblings… or mother and daughter. Was that the connection?

Endric patted her head once more and she loped off, moving with increasing swiftness until she disappeared over another hillside. The pack leader watched him for another moment, intelligence burning in her eyes, before she followed the other, also disappearing.

He remained in place for a few moments before starting over the hilltop.

When he summited, he saw the grouping had changed. There

were more soldiers—dozens more than had been there before. All were Denraen, and they were led by Senda.

Endric's heart caught.

What would she think about the fact that he had disappeared from the city for a while? He had been abducted, but she didn't know that, and he had made a choice to continue toward Thealon when he'd managed to get free from Urik, choosing to find what had happened to the Mage rather than return. Would the fact that he had not returned for the Denraen upset her?

Did it matter?

Had he not, what would have become of the merahl? Had Endric returned, he wouldn't have been discovered by Tresten and he wouldn't have traveled with the Mage out of Thealon, and he wouldn't have discovered the merahl. That discovery seemed far more important than anything he could have done while in Vasha, especially as his time in Vasha had not been valuable.

With that being the case, what would he do now?

He *should* return to Vasha, but he needed to get word to the Antrilii about the merahl and about what had happened to them. First, he had to understand what had happened here. He knew so little about this, other than the fact that it seemed to involve the Conclave.

As he approached, he saw Tresten still sitting.

How badly had the Mage been injured by the merahl? Novan crouched next to him, Urik on his other side. Dendril remained with the Denraen.

Though he wanted to know what had happened to Senda, he veered toward Tresten.

"How bad is he?" Endric asked when he reached Novan.

The historian looked up. "He's… weakened. He was not well before all of this occurred, and this attack has taken much out of him. Had he not been needed, he would have remained in Thealon, where he would have been safest."

"In Thealon? Why not Vasha?"

Endric looked from Novan to Tresten for answers, but none came.

"You did well," Tresten said. His voice sounded thready and was much weaker than Endric remembered. His face was drawn and pale, and the lines that Endric had been seeing along the corners of his eyes were much more prominent.

"You left me," he said to Tresten.

"We were captured," Urik answered for Tresten, stepping forward. "We kept thinking you would come after us, and when you didn't, we thought the creatures killed you."

"They're merahl," Endric said. "Not creatures."

"How?" Urik asked. Novan moved off to the side, allowing Urik to get closer. "How did you stop them?"

"I've hunted with the merahl before. I couldn't destroy them, even if they were attacking me. I knew that whatever had happened with them was not right."

Urik looked over the hill, his eyes going distant as if he expected to see the merahl appear. "They're so… violent. They ripped through a dozen Denraen, tearing them down."

At least Endric knew what had happened to the rest of the men who had traveled with his father. He expected that there would have been more than the few who had been there, so for there to have only been a dozen remaining… the merahl would have killed them.

"I've seen them tear through a line of groeliin, so it's not surprising that they'd manage the same with the Denraen." Though Endric was surprised the merahl fared that well against armed men. He wouldn't have expected them to have done so. Most of the Denraen wouldn't have had his experience and wouldn't have been nearly as hesitant to harm the merahl. "What happened to them? Why were they after the Conclave?" He asked the question of Tresten.

"They were for me," the Mage said. "Not the Conclave. Your father left Vasha thinking he could protect me, but he wasn't enough."

"Why do you think they were after the Conclave?" Urik asked. There remained an eagerness to him, one that Endric suspected had to do with his interest in the Conclave more than anything else.

"Tresten. Novan. Dendril. They had many of the Conclave captured here."

"Not the Conclave," Tresten said again. He coughed, and Endric noted a bubble of blood rising to his lips. "It was for me. Novan and Dendril tried to help, but they were not enough. Only you," he said to Endric, a smile crossing his face before fading.

"Why were the merahl after you? Who leads them?" There had been no sign of anyone else, and Endric had a sense that there would not be.

Tresten attempted to smile. "There was once a man who sat among us who betrayed us. He still seeks power and will do everything he can to gain it. He uses all the knowledge he has acquired over the years to do it. He intends to destroy the Conclave. He fears us."

With the mention of a betrayal, Endric glanced at Urik.

"Ah, his betrayal is much worse than what you experienced," Tresten said. The Mage turned his attention to Urik and he smiled. "You have atoned for your mistakes."

"Atoned? He abducted me from Vasha."

The Mage snorted, and it turned into a cough. "When you didn't come, it was the only way I could ensure that he would do what I needed."

"You *wanted* me to find you?" Urik asked.

Tresten fixed him with a hard gaze. "You could have followed the instructions on the letter left in your quarters and it would not have been necessary."

Urik blinked and looked down at the ground. "I couldn't fully understand it."

Tresten watched him and turned to Endric.

"What did it say?" Endric asked.

"I wanted to send Dendril and you from the city."

"You needed the Denraen? As a Mage, you could have just asked!" Endric said.

"Not the Denraen. As I have told you, I had need of *you*."

Tresten motioned for Endric to come closer. When he did, the Mage took his hands, squeezing them with a grip that was much stronger than Endric would have expected after what he'd been through. "You have done more than most to serve the Conclave, Endric. I must ask that you do even more."

"What do you expect of me?"

Tresten sighed. "Expect? Perhaps nothing. You need to continue to serve the Denraen. You understand nearly as much as your father, and in time, you will be called on to replace him. You should be ready. Until then, you will work with the Conclave. Understand why we serve. Novan and others can guide you."

"What about you?"

"Me? My time is short. It's why I left Vasha in the first place. I stayed away because it wasn't safe, but I had wanted to return to the Conclave to ensure our purpose."

Endric glanced over at Urik. "Even with him?"

Tresten sighed. "The Conclave may welcome Urik if he will choose knowledge over power."

"The Conclave?" Urik asked. There was something other than eagerness in his tone this time. There was hope.

"They serve peace, as I believe you once did. You can serve it again if you would choose." Tresten coughed and blood burbled out of his mouth. "I wasn't certain, but I saw the way you worked with Endric. There is still good in you, though you would hide it behind your pain. I would ask that you feel your pain and that you move past it, as I would ask Endric to move past his. The Conclave must work together or we will all lose."

"Tresten—" Endric said.

The Mage squeezed his hands. As he did, there was a sense like what he'd detected from the merahl licking him, and Endric felt a surge of warmth... and strength.

Endric waited, expecting Tresten to say something more, but he didn't.

Novan gripped Endric's shoulder. "He's gone, Endric."

"Gone? How can he be gone? He just fought off a merahl!"

"It was his time. That attack used much of what strength he had remaining, and the rest... you will understand in time."

Endric held Tresten's hand a moment longer. When he released his grip, he noted Urik crying. It surprised him that Urik would feel so strongly for the Mage, especially after he had done all that he could to betray them.

Endric looked around and found Senda watching him. She stood near his father and her posture told him that she wanted to come closer, though seemed as if she hesitated. Dendril stared his way, a question in his eyes. Endric nodded and Dendril's jaw clenched.

"What does this mean for me?" he asked Novan.

The historian stood and let out a heavy sigh. "It means that you will continue to do as you have. If you're willing, you will continue to serve the Denraen."

"Tresten wanted me to work with the Conclave."

"He did. If you are to be a part of it, you will need to understand its purpose."

"And that is?"

Novan smiled sadly. "Serving something greater than yourself. Greater than even the Denraen. How does that sound to you?"

Endric looked at the Denraen, and then his father. Dendril had done both, and maybe that was the lesson Dendril had wanted him to learn all along. It was the lesson he'd learned going to Farsea and working with the Antrilii. He could be both. He could serve, and he could be more.

Wasn't that what he wanted?

If he remained with the Denraen, he could help Pendin. His friend still needed him. And he could find a way to bridge the distance between himself and Senda, if there was a way. He had to believe there could be, that she could see him as the man he was and not someone who had abandoned his vows for selfish reasons.

And didn't he want to be something *more* than an oathbreaker? That was why he had struggled when he had first returned to Vasha. He had *known* there was more for him to do, but he wasn't allowed. If he served the Conclave, he would have that. After what he had seen and experienced, he needed to do more than simply serve the Denraen.

"That sounds like what I've been searching for," Endric said.

Book 5 of The Teralin Sword: Soldier Scarred

The Conclave calls to Endric and threatens to pull him from the Denraen again.

While the merahl are restored, the price was high. The Conclave asks Endric to bring Tresten to his final resting place, leading him to the island of Salvat and the headquarters of the Conclave, but forcing him to bring an old enemy with him.

When the mission takes a dramatic turn, Endric wants only to save Senda, but doing so brings him into a conflict that his Denraen training has not prepared him for. Can he trust Urik while saving Senda and still discover the secrets of the Conclave, or will he be the reason that Salvat falls?

Check out an exciting new series: The Book of Maladies. Book 1, Wasting:

In the city of Verdholm, canals separate the highborns in the center sections of the city from the lowborns along the outer sections. The city is isolated, surrounded by a deadly swamp and steam fields which should protect the people of the city from the dangerous outside world. Until it doesn't.

For Sam, an orphaned thief who wants only to protect her brother, protection means stealing enough so she can one day buy her way into a better section. She's a skilled thief, and when she's offered a job that can change everything for her, what choice does she have but to take it?

Alec is an apothecary who longed to join the prestigious university and become a physicker, but they rarely accept students from the merchant class, and he's now too old to enroll. The surprising discovery of strange magic can change his fortunes, but only if he can fully understand it.

When the natural protection of the city fails and her brother is thrown into danger, Sam must become more than a thief to save him, but she can't do so by herself. Somehow, she and Alec are linked through an ancient magic and together they might be the only ones able to stop an attack that threatens to disrupt the balance within the city and bring the dangers of the outside world to them.

Have you read The Lost Prophecy yet? Catch up with what Endric is up to decades after The Teralin Sword series!

Book 1: The Threat of Madness

The arrival of the mysterious Magi, along with their near invincible guardians, signals a change. For Jakob, apprentice historian, and son of a priest longing for adventure, it begins an opportunity.

When his home is attacked, Jakob starts a journey that will take him far from home and everything he has ever known. Studying with a new swordmaster, he gains surprising skill, but also strange new abilities that make him fear the madness which has claimed so many has come to him. He must withstand it long enough to finish the dangerous task given to him, one that with his new abilities he may be the only person able to complete.

With a strange darkness rising in the north, and attackers moving in from the south, powers long thought lost begin to return. Some begin to suspect the key to survival is the answer to a lost prophecy, yet only a few remain with the ability to find it.

ALSO BY D.K. HOLMBERG

The Teralin Sword

Soldier Son

Soldier Sword

Soldier Sworn

Soldier Saved

Soldier Scarred

The Lost Prophecy

The Threat of Madness

The Warrior Mage

Tower of the Gods

Twist of the Fibers

The Lost City

The Last Conclave

The Gift of Madness

The Great Betrayal

The Cloud Warrior Saga

Chased by Fire

Bound by Fire

Changed by Fire

Fortress of Fire

Forged in Fire

Serpent of Fire

Servant of Fire

Born of Fire

Broken of Fire

Light of Fire

Cycle of Fire

The Endless War

Journey of Fire and Night

Darkness Rising

Endless Night

Summoner's Bond

Seal of Light

The Shadow Accords

Shadow Blessed

Shadow Cursed

Shadow Born

Shadow Lost

Shadow Cross

Shadow Found

The Dark Ability

The Dark Ability

The Heartstone Blade

The Tower of Venass

Blood of the Watcher

The Shadowsteel Forge

The Guild Secret

Rise of the Elder

The Sighted Assassin

The Binders Game

The Forgotten

Assassin's End

The Lost Garden

Keeper of the Forest

The Desolate Bond

Keeper of Light

The Painter Mage

Shifted Agony

Arcane Mark

Painter For Hire

Stolen Compass

Stone Dragon

Made in the USA
Lexington, KY
01 February 2018